after forever

by jasinda wilder

This is a work of fiction. Names, characters, places, and incidents are either the product of the author's imagination or are used fictitiously. Any resemblance to actual events, places, organizations, or persons, whether living or dead, is entirely coincidental.

AFTER FOREVER

ISBN: 978-1-941098-03-5
Copyright © 2013 by Jasinda Wilder

Cover art by Sarah Hansen of Okay Creations. Cover art © 2013 by Sarah Hansen.
Interior book design by Indie Author Services.

This book is for anyone who has spent those countless days, months, and years at loved one's bedside, waiting, hoping, and praying.

into the maw

Caden

Shock hit me so hard that I blacked out momentarily. *"What?"* I couldn't get my eyes to focus on Dr. Miller. "She what?"

"Your wife was pregnant, Mr. Monroe. Eight weeks, perhaps? Maybe less. She…she hemorrhaged. Lost—had a miscarriage. Before the EMS even arrived, she'd lost it. There was nothing to be done. I'm—I'm so sorry. I can't tell you how sorry." Dr. Miller was a tall, slim black woman with tightly curled hair and piercing brown eyes.

I was finally able to see straight, and the torture I saw on Dr. Miller's face…nothing short of profound. How many times had she delivered such news? How did she stand it?

"She was pregnant?" The words were nearly inaudible particles of sound falling from my cracked lips. "She—she had an IUD. Just—she just got a new one put in. She didn't…she never told me."

Dr. Miller closed her eyes briefly—the same as a sob from anyone less stoic. "Even IUDs can fail. Indeed, most pregnancies that occur in a patient with an IUD occur in the first few months after implantation." She sighed deeply and stood up. "As for not having told you? I think perhaps she did not know. It was very early, and she may not have noticed any symptoms to get tested."

A whimper escaped me. "God…Ever."

"If…if she wakes up, due to the nature of her injuries, not just to her head, which are the most severe, but to her abdomen, it is unlikely she will ever conceive again. I'm…I'm so sorry again, Mr. Monroe."

I heard her shoes scuff on the tile, and then stop abruptly. I opened my eyes to see Eden standing behind Dr. Miller. She'd clearly heard the conversation. She was shaking her head, tears falling in a torrent from her chin onto her hand, her mouth.

And suddenly, looking at Eden was impossible. I tried to look away, but all I could see were Ever's eyes, jade green, and her nose, her mouth, her lips.

Eden approached me.

"Caden...how did this happen?" Her voice broke.

Mine was worse. "I don't know. It was so sudden. It happened so fast."

Then their father was there, too, behind Eden. I couldn't meet his eyes. Had he heard, too? About the—the baby?

Dr. Miller came back in with a clipboard and a pen. "I need you to sign this." She extended the clipboard to me. "We need your permission to do some further testing."

Mr. Eliot took the clipboard, assuming she meant it for him. "What tests?"

Dr. Miller reached for the clipboard. "I'm sorry, Mr. Eliot, but...I was speaking to Mr. Monroe."

He let her take it. "Him? Why? I'm her father, her legal guardian."

The doctor looked at me, and she seemed to understand—that maybe he didn't know.

I swallowed hard. "Because she's my wife," I said. "We got married three months ago."

His face went red and mottled with fury, his voice low, hissing. "You—you *got married?* How—she— how did I not know this? Why didn't she tell me?"

"We eloped," I explained. "It was...how she wanted it."

"But—but—" Mr. Eliot stumbled backward, anger warring with shock and confusion.

Eden took him by the arm. "Come on, Daddy. Let's go get some coffee, okay?"

He let her take him, but then turned back to glare back at me, as if I'd stolen something from him.

When he'd left, Dr. Miller said gently, "No one but you, and your sister-in-law as well, it seems, knows that she was pregnant. Maybe that's important to you."

"Thanks," I said. Dr. Miller only nodded, and left.

Ever had been pregnant?

I would have been a father.

Never conceive again.

Probably won't wake up.

I'd lost her.

And if I thought that I'd been broken before, I wasn't. Ever had healed me, and now the accident had irreparably shattered what was left of my soul.

steps in the darkness

Eden

Daddy was a wreck. I mean, yeah, of course he was. How could he not be?

Maybe "wreck" was a poor choice of words.

He sat at the table in the cafe of William Beaumont Hospital in Royal Oak, staring into space. His coffee was untouched, and he'd refused food. I had to keep it together for him. It was fucking hard, though. My twin was in a coma. Ever…god, Ever. Cade hadn't seen her yet, and that was probably a good thing. He was physically still in bad shape. I don't think he realized how bad, honestly. His right arm had been mangled by a piece of metal during the accident, and he'd only made it worse by fighting to get to Ever, to try to free her from the car. His left leg was broken in several places, he had bruises all over, and the shattering glass had sliced him to bits. He'd cracked his skull—that's why they'd kept him under for the past week. He was lucky to be alive. Ever was lucky to be alive.

But Ever…she was only alive in the loosest sense of the word. Her heart was beating, her lungs were drawing breath—and even that much was with the help of machines. But the essence that was my sister, my best friend, my twin, half of me…that was gone. Maybe forever. Her skull had been caved in when the truck flipped and rolled over a dozen times. Her ribs were broken, her wrist smashed, her arm broken. The fingers of her right hand were intact, which meant that—if she ever woke up and retained function—she would still be able to paint. So there was that.

But the chances of her waking up? Nil. Maybe five percent. Less, the longer she was in a coma.

She'd been pregnant. She'd never have children… if she woke up.

That phrase…fuck. It had been a little over a week since the accident, and that phrase—*if she ever woke up*—was becoming a spear of horror stabbing my heart every time I said it, thought it, heard it. Six syllables. Five words. Fifteen letters. My future, contained, imprisoned. My heart, shredded.

It physically hurt to look at her. The bandages, the bruises, the cuts. Black and blue and red, so little unblemished skin.

They'd had to shave her head to patch the hole in her cranium.

I sat across from Daddy, just as lost as he was.

"Did you know?" He whispered the question to me, eyes suddenly blazing.

"Did I know?" I knew what he meant.

"About *them*. Eloping."

I stared at the table. "Yeah. I…I was their witness."

A sob wrenched itself from him and he tipped his head back, covering his face with both hands. "Why? Why was I kept out of it?"

"Because…it was how she wanted it. We…you were…" I scratched at the flaking blue nail polish on my left thumb. "Look, Dad. Nothing has changed. Between you and me, and you and Ever, and us. Her being in a coma, it doesn't change the fact that you fucking walked away from us—emotionally, and physically—with all the hours you worked. We didn't want your goddamned money after Mom died, we wanted *you*. We didn't have you, and when she fell in love with Cade and they decided to get married, you weren't a factor. You haven't been a factor in our lives in years, except as dollar signs, checks in the mail sent to Cranbrook."

"Not a factor?" He scrubbed his face, wiped the sleeve of his pale blue dress shirt across his eyes. "I just…I don't understand. I didn't even know she was seeing this guy. I saw you guys…god, yeah, it was just over six months ago, on your birthday. And she was still with that…what's his name, the rich kid. The horn player."

"Billy. Billy Harper. And it was the trumpet."

"Whatever. I thought she was with him?"

"Dad, it's a complicated story. I don't really know most of it. And does it really matter?"

"YES!" he shouted, startling everyone around us. He lowered his voice and leaned forward. "Yes, it matters. It matters a lot to me."

"Why?" I asked.

He didn't answer right away; he stared out the window at the falling snow. "She's my daughter. She got married without even telling me, much less invit-ing me to the wedding. Who else was there? How does she even know this Cade guy?"

I sighed. "Dad, I really—you should ask Cade about them. It's their story to tell, not mine. You don't deserve answers. I'm here with you, we're in this together, because we're family. But I'm still angry at you. I've been angry at you for seven years. So has Ever." I couldn't look at him. I pulled the lid off my coffee and sipped cautiously at the thick, burnt, bitter black liquid. "I'm your daughter, too, you know. Do you know anything about me? Do you know who I'm with? Who's broken my heart, who my friends are? What my grades are? *Anything?*"

He shifted uncomfortably. "Okay," he whispered. "I get it. I get it. What do you want me to do?"

He looked so confused, so hurt, I almost forgave him. Almost. "*Try*, Dad. Just…try. I can't promise I'll just…forgive and forget, or that we'll be happy-clappy after a couple of heart-to-hearts, but just…try. And, like it or not, Cade is your son-in-law, and he's a good man. He loves Ever. More than life, I think." I hoped my voice didn't reflect the jealousy I felt.

I wondered, though, if I should tell him about Ever's miscarriage. But I didn't. That wasn't my news to tell, and I didn't think he could handle it, anyway.

His phone chirped and he slid it out of his pocket, then stood up. "I've got to take this."

I sighed. "Which means you're going in to work."

"I have to at least go outside and call in. I don't get reception in here."

"Like I said, you're going in to work." I stood up, capped my coffee, and slung my purse over my shoulder. "Whatever. 'Bye, Dad."

He let me get out of the café before catching up with me.

"What do you want me to do? I can't just stop working."

"Your daughter stopped *living*, Dad! She's in a coma! Isn't that more important than work?"

He turned away, running his hand through his hair in frustration. He'd had some gray at his temples already when Mom died. Now he had more silver in his once-black hair. "Exactly! She's in a coma! She might never come out! What am I supposed to do?"

I gaped at him. "Sit with her. Talk to her. Spend time with her. Studies show—"

"I'm a senior vice president of one of the biggest corporations in the country, Eden. I have responsibilities. I can't just abandon all that to sit next to her twenty-four hours a day. I've been here for four hours already today. I *have* to work."

"Escape, you mean." Three little words have never sounded so bitter.

He'd pushed past me, started down the hallway. At my words he whirled and stormed back. "*YES!*" he hissed. "Okay? Yes. Escape. It's what I do, clearly. I can't handle this. It's too much. Too much. Too…too fucking much. First your mom, and now Ever? Yes, I need to escape. I'm weak, and I'm running away. I'm sorry I'm not—not strong enough. Not enough." His face contorted, and he turned away, trembling.

"Dad—" I began. I couldn't finish, though. He walked away, looking broken.

I was broken, too, but I couldn't leave Ever.

I took the elevator back to Ever's room, sat in the chair I'd dragged to her bedside. Machines beeped and whirred, pumped, performed their functions. I made myself look at her, examine her. I made myself see her features through the wounds. She didn't look like herself, like me, like anyone. She looked like a victim.

But she wasn't. She was my twin.

"Hey, Ev." I put my hand on top of hers. "So Dad's up to his same old antics again. You know how he is. Except this time, I got him to admit to it. You know what he said to me? He told me he's weak. That he knows he's escaping. He can't handle this. That's what he said. And you know what? I get it. I do. He lost Mom, and now…now you're here. But I lost Mom, too, and we—we lost Dad at the same time. What about us? What about me?"

I paused, watched her chest rise and fall. Listened to the machines. To the distorted echo of someone being paged over the hospital PA.

"I'll be here, though. Okay? Every day. I won't leave your side. You're my twin, and I'll be here. Even if he won't." I laughed through the tears that were stuck in my throat. "Except, I do have to go home to shower and change. I've been in these clothes for three days. I have to talk to school, too. About you, and our classes. But I'll be back, okay?" I kissed her cheek and left, choking back the tears. I couldn't cry. Not here, not in the hospital. Not in front of her.

I was in the lobby when I thought of Cade. Maybe I should see if he needed anything. He didn't have anyone, I didn't think. No one to visit him or bring him clothes. I stopped, considering. He needed *someone*, and it looked like I was it.

He was half-asleep when I entered his room, the TV in the corner tuned to some soap opera.

"Hey," I said. "I thought maybe I'd come and see you." That came out awkward. I tried again. "See if I could bring you anything from home or…or anything."

He blinked a few times, touched a button on the bed to raise his torso. "Th-thanks." His voice sounded hesitant. "I'm fine."

I took another step into the room, twisting the strap of my purse in my fingers. "Sure? Can you—are you able to eat? Normal food, I mean? I could bring you McDonald's, or something. A book?"

"McDonald's has books now?" he asked, a barely there note of teasing in his voice.

I rolled my eyes. "Don't be a smart-ass. You know what I meant."

He chuckled, but he sounded weak. "A book would be good, I guess. There's literally nothing on except *Days of Our Lives*, or whatever the hell this is."

"Food?"

"Nah. I can't eat much right now. Just…not hungry. Thanks, though. They do feed me, and the food's not bad."

I sensed that he was glossing over his lack of appetite. His eyes searched the room as he spoke, lighting on the TV, the hallway, the window. He looked everywhere but directly at me."

Standing in the middle of the room and talking to him felt strange and awkward, so I pulled a chair up next to the bed. "How are you, Cade? Really?" I wasn't sure I wanted to know, but I had to ask. Someone had to ask him. Someone had to care.

"Okay, I guess. I feel dizzy sometimes. The pain comes and goes." He tried to lift his right arm, failed. "What worries me is this arm. My hand. I guess I fucked it up pretty bad. I can barely move it. It's hard to even wiggle the fingers."

"That's your drawing hand?" I knew how important that was. If the fingers of my left hand—the ones I used to work the strings of my cello—got hurt, if I couldn't use them…I'd be a mess.

He nodded. "Yeah. I mean, I'm right-handed. I do nearly everything with my right hand."

"Well, you can move it a little, right?"

He stared at his right hand, and I could see him focusing, flexing, straining. The index finger and middle finger twitched. "That's it. And that was… it was a fucking effort." He wasn't kidding; he was sweating, shaking.

"Well, hopefully with some physical therapy you'll get use back."

"Yeah. Guess we'll see."

Silence.

I didn't know what else to say. I didn't know him, not really. We weren't much more than strangers, even though he was married to my twin. Was it imposing too much to ask how he was doing emotionally? I could see the answer to that, though. In his eyes. They were agonized, simultaneously dull and lifeless, yet rife with haunted horror. I tried not to stare at him, but despite the cuts on his face and the bandages around his head I could see why Ever had fallen for him. His eyes, even as conflicted as they were, shone amber, hypnotizing with the vivid clarity of their color. He had strong, sharp cheekbones, a square chin, several days' worth of stubble. He was handsome, in a rough and rugged way. Not beautiful, but ruggedly good-looking.

I tore my eyes away and stared at my feet, embarrassed. Had I just been...checking out Ever's husband? What was wrong with me?

I shot to my feet and turned away. "I should go—"

"I want to see her," he said at the same time.

I halted. "She's...she's not in good shape, Cade." I couldn't look at him.

"You think I care? I need—I *need* to see her."

I sighed. "I'll talk to the nurses." I found a nurse at the desk, conveyed Cade's request.

The nurse, a woman in her mid-thirties with curly black hair and a quick, efficient manner, followed me into Cade's room. "I'm not sure we should move you just yet, Mr. Monroe," she said.

"Just…please. I need to see her. Please." He sounded…pale. I wasn't sure how that worked, but it was true. It was as if his voice was a bloodless husk of what it should be.

The nurse took a deep breath and nodded. "I'll see what I can do."

Twenty minutes later, she unhooked various machines and wires, and hung them on the poles attached to his bed. She unlocked the wheels and pushed the bed out of the room, down the hallway, and to the bank of elevators. As the elevator took us to Ever's floor, I sneaked another glance at Cade. He was white as a sheet, trembling, leaning back against the sheets with his eyes shut tight, as if against a spinning world.

Ever hadn't moved, of course. She was on her back in the bed, trailing a maze of tubes. Eyes closed. Bruised and broken. It hurt to look at her, every single time. I watched Cade. His eyes were closed as the nurse moved his bed in next to Ever's, locked the wheels, and left us alone. He didn't open his eyes right away. I could see the war on his face, needing to see her but not wanting to look.

Finally, his eyes slid open, and his gaze landed on Ever. He shuddered, and his features twisted. "Oh, god," he choked. The fingers of his left hand curled into a fist, shaking violently as he white-knuckled the sheet.

I looked away from him, then; the vulnerability in his eyes was far too private for me to witness.

He reached for her with his left hand but fell short. His hand rested on the metal railing of Ever's bed, and he seemed to be straining, as if he needed simply to touch her hand. I leaned over him, far too close to him, smelling him, took Ever's hand and lifted it so he could brush her knuckles with his fingers. He sighed, a wretched, trembling sound, as he touched her. I held on, leaning over him, my eyes closed to avoid seeing him from so near. Their beds were too close together for me to fit between, no space at the head, too far away at the foot. I was conscious of my hair brushing his chest, an intimacy too great for the strangers that we were.

When I couldn't hold the position any longer, I laid Ever's hand down on the bed and moved away, brushing my hair back over my ears. I was shaking from the bizarre tension of the moment, holding her hand so he could touch her.

"Thank you." He whispered the words.

"You're welcome."

He just looked at her then. Watched her, his thoughts inscrutable. Unknowable, to me at least.

"Want some time alone with her?"

He turned his head to look at me. "Alone with her?"

I shrugged. "To…to talk to her." He blinked, as if not understanding the idea. "I talk to her. They say people in comas might be able to hear you. That it helps. Somehow. So I talk to her."

"Oh." He returned his gaze to Ever. "Yeah."

I left the room, but not before I heard him clear his throat and start to speak, his voice barely audible. "Hey, Ever. It's…it's me. Caden. I'm here." His voice trailed off, broke, and then he tried again. "I'm—I'm so—so sorry, baby. I should—I shouldn't have—" But his voice broke again, and now I heard the choking, gasping sound of his struggle to contain his guilt, his tears.

I closed the door behind me. He blamed himself. I couldn't listen to his grief.

Not without giving in to my own.

I fled to my car, sat in the frigid darkness and shook, felt tears trickle down, unable to stop them. I drove home in silence, through the thickly falling snow, with tears freezing on my cheeks, tears stuck in my chest, grief shut down and compressed and denied.

Caden

I heard Eden close the door. I was thankful she'd left, relieved. I couldn't stop myself from crying as I stared at Ever's broken body. My Ever. Barely breathing, so still. I willed her to move, to wake up. She had to wake up. She *had* to. She would wake up. Right? Tears slid down my face and I didn't care, didn't wipe them away, just watched her, willing her to wake up.

"Baby. Please." I heard my voice. "Wake up. Please. Wake up. I need you. Please."

She didn't move, didn't stir, didn't wake.

I sat there, wishing I knew what to say, until the nurse returned and wheeled me back to my room, pretending not to see the tears. I didn't know her name, but I was grateful for her silence.

Alone in my room once more, I sat with my eyes shut, the TV off, and tried to move my fingers, my right hand. Tried to ignore the way it hurt, the way my whole body hurt. My head throbbed. My leg ached. My arm was on fire.

My heart was shattered.

I fell asleep, and when I woke up, Gramps was in the visitor's chair, Grams beside him.

"Hey there, kiddo." His voice was deep and gruff. "How are you?" He stood up, moved to stand by my bed. He was the same as ever: tall, commanding, whip-cord lean, silver hair and weather-lined face.

I pushed the button to raise the upper part of the bed so I was sitting. I was so weak, I couldn't even sit up on my own. "Fine," I said.

"Bullshit," Gramps said.

"Connor!" Grams chided. Grams was much like Gramps, with silver hair and a slim, straight body, dark eyes.

"I'm your family, boy. Don't lie to me." His eyes reflected his love, even if his way of showing it was very much his own unique brand.

I sighed. "It hurts, Gramps." I looked away, out the window, where all I could see was snow and more windows. "So bad."

"You'll heal."

"Not what I meant."

"I know. Still the truth."

I met his eyes. "No, I won't. Not without her."

"You really love her, huh?"

I nodded. "More than I can say. God…I feel like I can't breathe. She's in that room, and she's not gonna wake up. But she has to. She—she has to. She can't leave me. She promised me."

Gramps could hear what I wasn't saying. He didn't speak, just stood at my side and nodded.

Grams came to stand next him. "Talk to her, Cade. Be there with her. That's the best thing you can do."

"It's not enough. And…it hurts. To see her. To talk to her and not hear her voice."

"I know," Grams said. "But you'll be there for her. And you'll be there when she wakes up." She seemed to be struggling, fighting some emotion I didn't understand. She'd always been just like Gramps, steady and solid. Now it seemed like she was near tears herself. "Excuse me." She turned abruptly and left the room.

I looked up at Gramps in confusion.

"She spent nearly every day for two years in a hospital room," Gramps said, his voice low. "Her ma. Got sick, real sick. Went into a coma, just like your Ever. Grams was real close with her ma, so it was… the hardest thing for your Grams."

"Did she get better? Great-grandma, I mean?"

Gramps wobbled his head to one side and the other. "For a while. Point is, bein' in a hospital is hard for her."

"Yeah," I said. "I know how that feels."

I'd spent hours, days, weeks in the hospital when Mom got sick. I hated hospitals. I hated being in one, and I knew each and every day, every moment would be torture. But I'd stay here with Ever, no matter what.

"I just want you to know, son, that we'll be here for you. We're here for you."

Gramps was restless, though. I could see it. He hated being inside, hated sitting in the chair, hated the close walls and the smell of sickness.

"You should go back to the ranch." I picked at the thin, scratchy white blanket, tugging on a loose thread.

"Gerry and Miguel can handle it."

"There's nothing for you to do here, Gramps. I'll be out of here before long, and then it'll…it'll just be me sitting in Ever's room." I was tired suddenly. Again. So tired. A broken heart was tiring. "For real, Gramps. I'll be fine."

"We'll stay a few days." He said this in a way that made it final. I nodded, and felt myself drifting.

solace in the strings

Eden

I pulled the bow across the strings, eyes closed. It was off, a raw note, and I brought the bow away. Sighed, drew a deep breath, and tried again, stilled the shaking in my hands and the ache in my chest.

Perfect.

I started slowly, playing one note, a second, a third, and then I was into the prelude to "Suite No. 1 in G Major, " as played by Yo-Yo Ma. His *Six Unaccompanied Cello Suites* was a masterpiece, and when I didn't know what else to play, what else to do, I would find myself playing that. Bach, yes, but Yo-Yo Ma's interpretation specifically. There was something about his tone, the way he emoted through his instrument, that spoke to the core of my soul.

I floated away, then sank into the rise and fall of the notes, the sweep of the bow and the voice of my Apollo, my cello. I let the music pull me under its spell, made it mine and let it take hold and erase all the thoughts within me, all the hurt and the confusion. It was my solace, this cello, the music, the sonorous voice singing to me, appealing to the notes of my blood, the eloquence in my hands. It could soothe me, shelter me, for a few moments, from the hurt and the darkness and horrors of being alive and so, so alone.

I moved and breathed in a lonely world, and Apollo alone knew my tears, felt them fall upon his shoulders. He scoured them from me, took them and allowed them to fall, and never judged me. When my heart broke, he comforted me.

"Suite No. 2 in D Minor" rippled from the strings, and I poured myself into it, let it flow like a river. Let the grief go with it, the pain.

I found myself playing the *allemande* to "Suite No. 6 in D Major" and I cried then. It was Ever's favorite piece to listen to me play. I'd auditioned to Cranbrook with it. I faltered near the end, my bow slipping on the strings as I sobbed. I played through it, played through the shivering, shuddering, wracking sobs, playing through it for Ever, because this was the only way I could grieve.

When the piece was done, I let the bow slip from my fingers and rested my face against Apollo's neck, struggling to breathe through the pressure of grief in my chest and the ten-ton weight of misery in my soul.

Ever was, truly, my only friend. I'd never made many friends in high school, and none here at Cranbrook Academy of Art. I was too wrapped up in my cello, in mastering each new piece, in my classes and homework. There'd been a few brief forays into friendship, usually with guys from the music department, and those always devolved into the *friendship-sex-Eden-gets-dumped* cycle. And every time, Ever was there to eat junk food with me and force me to work it off at the gym and listen to me bitch about men and how stupid I was to think anything would ever change.

More recently, I'd been consumed with my attempts to compose my own cello solo. It was a project that was quickly beginning to take over my entire life—getting each note right, each movement and section. I didn't dare work on the concerto now, though. It required absolute focus, complete internal composure. I lacked those things, lacked any sense of self. I could barely see through the tears, even as they slowed, as I forced them to slow.

I still couldn't seem to stop crying.

I kept playing. A different piece, something that struck my memory, something Mom used to play. The notes wavered in the air, hung, and were joined by the rest, all nine minutes of it rising from the depths of my heart.

When I opened my eyes, now mostly dry, Daddy was standing in the doorway of my studio space, which I'd left open in my desperation to get to my cello, to exorcize my demons. He was crying, fist at his mouth, watching me intently. It had been three days since I'd seen him at the hospital. He'd vanished again, back into the void of workaholic escapism.

"That—" He paused to clear his throat and take a deep breath. "That was your mother's favorite piece. She told me the name of it a thousand times, but I could never remember. She would listen to it while painting, and she'd play it over and over again."

"It's the 'Sonata For Solo Cello,'" I said. "Zoltán Kodály."

"Yeah." He blinked hard, and stepped into the room. "God, you play it just like her. You sound…the way you play, especially those vibratos…you sound *so* much like her."

I'd never heard that. I had a vivid memory of sitting on the floor of the formal living room where she used to practice, watching her long black hair shimmer and wave and sway as she moved with the arc of her bow. I remember being enraptured by the sound, by the way she seemed to get lost in the music, the way the essence that made her Mom, that made her *her*, would be swallowed whole and she would just be gone and in some other land. I wanted to be *just like her*. I would sit on a chair and pretend to sway the way she did. What I don't remember is the way she sounded, not with my adult ear.

"I do?" I choked on the two words. They hurt to expel.

He nodded. "It's…eerie. If I close my eyes and listen to you play, I hear—I hear her." He pointed at my cello. "And that…that instrument. She loved it. So much. It's a family heirloom, you know. It belonged to her grandfather, and now you're playing it. Seeing you with it, hearing you play it, sounding so much like her, it's…it's so bittersweet."

"She was good, wasn't she?" I asked.

He threw his head back and breathed deeply. "Yes. Very. She played for the DSO, you know. Before we had you and Ever. That's how we met. One of my friends from college had a crush on a bassoon player named Marnie, and he dragged me to a concert so he could ask her out. Turns out Marnie was one of your mother's friends, and I couldn't take my eyes off your mom from that moment on. I went to every concert I could, eventually got her to go out with me." He glanced around the room, found the extra chair and sat down in it. "She was this exotic thing, this incredible cellist with these strong, delicate hands. She took me to a showing of her art as our second date. She neglected to tell me it was her work that was on display, just that she wanted me to go with her as her date. I was…so ignorant. I was a business and finance major, and knew nothing about music or art. She was so *cultured*. Me? All I had going on was looking good in a three-piece suit. I still—still don't know why she fell in love with me. I never deserved her, but I was grateful for her, every single moment of our lives together."

It took me a moment to process that, to figure out how to respond. "Wow. I never knew any of that. I knew that you loved her, I mean, I saw that in the way you were together, but I've never heard you talk about her that way."

He shrugged, staring down and scratching at the knee of his suit slacks. He swiped at his eye with a thumb, discreet. "I haven't talked about her. Not since she died. Not like that."

"Maybe you should? I mean…maybe *we* should."

"Maybe." He gestured at my cello. "Play something else? Please?"

I settled the cello in place, adjusted my grip on the bow, closed my eyes and summoned the muse. "Song VI" by Philip Glass and Wendy Sutter.

With the last note quavering in the air between us, he seemed to be struggling against tears, against the welter of emotions I knew I was feeling, and god knows he had to be feeling more, other things. His wife and now his daughter, gone. I mean, yeah, maybe Ever would wake up and be fine. Maybe she wouldn't wake up. Maybe she would wake up in two months or two years or even twenty years, but she'd be about the same as a bunch of asparagus. There were a thousand maybes, a thousand possibilities, but right then, in that moment, all we knew was that she was gone from us.

"I don't know what to do, Eden." Dad's voice was thin, stretched. "I'm no good at this. At being *there* for you. I can run a company. I can make numbers make sense and make multimillion-dollar decisions, but… how do I fix this between us? I'm sorry, Eden. I'm so sorry. Forgive me."

I couldn't take the cracking strain in his voice, the grief and the guilt. "Just… *try*, Dad. This is a good start."

"I was in my office, but I just couldn't think of anything but Ever, and you. And even that poor boy. What's his name? I don't even know his name."

"Cade," I said. "His name is Cade."

"Cade what?"

"Monroe."

He nodded. "So Ever, she's Ever Monroe now?"

"Yep."

"What's he do?"

I glanced up at him as I put my cello back in his case. "Find out from him. He's your son-in-law now. And he's gonna need support. He doesn't have anyone."

"No one?" Dad asked.

I shook my head. "Just Ever and his grandparents, I guess. But they're old and live in Colorado or Wyoming or something. I think they're only here for a few days."

He hugged me, and it was awkward. I hadn't hugged my father in…years. The smell of him was a shock, a throwback to being a little girl sitting on his lap. His stubble scratched my cheek as he pulled away, and the scent of his cologne and his proximity, it all made me feel like a child all over again, reminded me how lonely and scared I was.

I had to fight it off, the heat behind my eyes, the thickness in my chest and the burning in my heart. I fought it off until he left, and then I sat on my chair and tried to rein in the onslaught of fresh tears.

I couldn't function without Ever. I just didn't know how. She was me, half of me. The thought of waking up and not being able to call her, talk to her, visit her, flip through her paintings while we talked, while she painted, it made me want to crawl into bed and never come out. I didn't talk to her every day, but just knowing I *could* was comforting. Now…I didn't have that. And I didn't know what to do.

So I went back to the hospital. And I had to focus on not crying the whole time. I wasn't sure why, but I brought my cello with me.

Caden

Gramps had brought me some things from our—from *my* condo. Our. *Our* condo. She might not have been awake, but it was still her home. He'd brought me books to read, sketchbooks and pencils, which I couldn't use yet, my phone charger and my earbuds. In one of those freak outcomes, my phone had survived the crash without a scratch. The truck was completely totaled, a mangled wreck. Ever was in a coma, my arm was shredded and my leg broken so badly I'd need physical therapy to use it again, and I'd suffered a cracked skull plate and a severe concussion. But my phone, plugged into the USB port so I could listen to my Pandora station, was untouched. Not even dinged.

They'd left yesterday, my grandparents. It had been a difficult goodbye, for reasons I couldn't fathom. As if I wasn't saying simply "see you later," but truly "goodbye." The entire time Grams and Gramps had been here with me, Eden had stayed away, stayed in Ever's room. When I got a nurse to wheel me down there, she'd leave me alone with Ever.

That was good. Her absence relieved me, although a part of me ached with the loneliness washing through me all over again. Ever had banished the loneliness for a short time, such a brief, blissful time. But now she was gone, and I was alone.

And Eden, she was...*there*. Even when she wasn't in the room, I could feel her presence. She was part of Ever, as much as I was, and I could see Ever in her face, in her eyes, and in the timbre of her voice, the soft music in her words.

Eden was her own woman, though. She kept her hair dyed honey blonde and, the few times I'd been around her, kept it styled, curled, braided, pinned, always something interesting and different, whereas Ever was given to simply leaving her hair down or in a basic ponytail. Eden was curvier than Ever, enough so that, hair color aside, you'd be able to tell them apart despite their identical features.

I tried not to see Ever in her. I tried not to see her at all. She was Ever's sister, that's all. And I couldn't let myself look at her. It wasn't right.

But when she came into my room, wearing skin-tight black yoga pants, I couldn't help myself. She had her cello with her, a huge thing, almost bigger than she was. She shucked her winter coat and left it on the visitor's chair, and I had to focus on my phone to avoid the fact that she was wearing a gray V-neck T-shirt that scooped entirely too low for my comfort.

"Hey." She gave me hesitant smile and a half-wave, a stunted crescent motion with her hand, leaning the cello against her front. "Have you been down to see Ever today?"

I shook my head. "I asked a few hours ago, but no one's been back since. They're saying I'm gonna be released soon, and they've been taking me down in a wheelchair." I pointed at the wheelchair folded in the corner.

"Going home soon, huh? Ready to be out of the hospital gown?"

I shrugged. "Yeah, they do kind of suck. My head seems to be healing fine, no damage to my brain. That's what they were holding me to observe, I guess. My leg's gonna need therapy, and so's my arm, but that'll be outpatient."

Eden rested her cello against the wall and brought the wheelchair around next to the bed. "Need help getting in?"

"Going to see Ever?" I avoided saying *we*. I wasn't sure why, but I instinctively did.

She nodded. "I'm gonna play some of Ever's favorite songs. She likes hearing me play. So I thought…I guess I thought maybe you'd like to sit with her. While I play." She seemed self-conscious, her eyes finding every part of the room near me except my eyes. "If you—if you wanted to, that is. You don't have to, I just thought…maybe you'd—"

"That sounds great," I said, before I could rethink the idea.

"Do you need help?" Eden asked.

I would need help. I knew it. I just...something in me, some part of me shied away from having her help me. "I should be able to make it." Macho bullshit, stupid macho bullshit.

Gramps had brought me an old pair of my loosest track pants, the kind that buttoned down the side, so at least I had real pants on, albeit with one side open from the hip down. I sat up, slowly, painfully, and swiveled so my legs hung off the bed. I was already panting and sweating, and that was the easy part. I focused on sliding forward, inch by inch, rather than on Eden, who was hovering a foot or two away, clearly wanting to help, yet not wanting to at the same time. I'd never tried this on my own, mainly because it was a stupid idea. I got my good leg planted, my foot firm. I had a good hold on the railing, leaning forward to reach for the wheelchair. This was where I needed help. I was off balance, about to tip forward, and I wasn't sure the wheelchair's wheels were locked, and even if they were, I couldn't really twist in midair on my own.

I tried to get my weight up on my good leg, but with only one arm, I simply couldn't. I slid forward, slid forward, shifted my weight, reaching for the armrest of the chair. I tipped myself forward, felt my leg catch my weight. I had it, I had it...then my knee wobbled, and I had to either sit back on the bed or topple forward and damage myself worse.

I sat back on the bed, and with my one good arm extended forward to reach for the chair, my balance shifted completely backward, forcing me to lie down across the bed.

I laughed, because it was either that or curse. "I guess maybe I do need help," I said, struggling back up to a sitting position.

Eden didn't say anything. She just wrapped her arm around my waist, helped me slide forward, stood up with me. My arm was around her shoulders, holding on, too tight. I hobbled on one foot, and we swiveled together so I was lined up with the wheelchair, facing away.

She smelled like citrus shampoo, fabric softener, and some kind of flowery lotion. Not like Ever. Ever always smelled like Bath and Bodyworks Warm Vanilla Sugar body lotion. I'd always smelled it on her, but it wasn't until we moved in together that I discovered the source of the smell, the joy of watching her sit naked on the edge of the bed, the bottle of lotion on the bed beside her, slathering it on her skin, rubbing it in, massaging her legs, her hips, her stomach and sides and arms, her boobs and her shoulders, and then she'd have me rub it onto her back, and usually that led to other things, even if those other things had been the reason for her having taken a shower in the first place.

Eden smelled more like…cherries. Flowery, delicate and feminine. I felt her pressed up against me, and I was never so aware of anything in all my life, never so uncomfortable with how I felt, how her body was soft against mine, familiar yet foreign all at once.

I gripped the armrest of the wheelchair, gritting my teeth as my leg protested the weight of my body. I lowered myself slowly, hanging on to Eden in lieu of using my right arm. She lowered me, kneeling with me, holding on to me. She was strong, very, very strong. I could feel the power in her body as she'd held up my weight.

So much ran through my mind in those brief seconds of physical contact. She was soft, curvy, and yet beneath the curves was a solid core of strength that Ever lacked. Ever didn't go to the gym very often, didn't seem to care. She'd go with Eden once in a while, but for the most part Ever never seemed to obsess much about exercising or dieting. She didn't indulge in unhealthy food all that often, but she didn't go on strict diets, either.

In Eden, I felt cords of muscle, and I remembered how many of Ever's letters had been about her sister's ongoing struggle with her shape, her weight, her sometimes fanatic dedication to working out, to diets and fitness. Lately, according to Ever, Eden had settled down a bit with the whole weight obsession, but I could still feel the difference in their bodies.

I hated myself for even noticing a difference.

I was in the chair then, sitting down a little too hard in an effort to get away from Eden. From my own awareness of her.

I was lonely, scared, and hurting. That was all. I missed my wife, and Eden was her twin sister. It was inevitable that I'd draw comparisons, that, if I was attracted to Ever, I'd be attracted to Eden as well. But I wasn't, was I? I wasn't *attracted* to her, not really. It was just *seeing*. She was beautiful, just like Ever. And that's all it was, noticing the similarities.

I shifted in the chair, breathing hard, grinding my teeth through the pain of my throbbing leg, having jarred it as I sat down. The pain was okay, though, because it was a distraction. Then she was behind me, out of sight, pushing the chair with my cast-framed leg extended out in front of me. Neither of us spoke until we got to the elevator.

"Shit," Eden said. "I forgot Apollo." She turned us around and started back to my room.

"Forgot who?"

"My cello. His name is Apollo. You know, the Greek god of music?"

"I thought Apollo was the god of light or the sun or something like that?"

"It's kind of complicated. He represents a lot of things at different times in Greek culture. But to me,

Apollo is primarily the god of music, and thus, my cello is named Apollo."

"Is your cello a—"

"No, it's not a Stradivarius." Eden laughed. "If I had a dollar for every time I was asked that, I could probably afford one, though. It's a Vuillame."

"How old is it?"

"It was made in 1832. It's worth…a lot. It's been in my family for four generations."

I was impressed, of course. "Isn't it…I don't know, nerve-wracking, playing something so old and expensive?" We reached my room and she grabbed the cello, then stopped, obviously debating how to push my chair and carry the huge instrument at the same time. "Here, just set it up on my good leg. I can hold it with that arm."

She hesitated. "I don't know. I don't think so. It's heavy, and if it shifted by accident, it could hurt you worse—"

"And damage your cello," I added.

She shrugged. "Yeah. That, too." She glanced out into the hallway, saw an orderly ambling toward us with his nose in a cell phone. "Hey, could you help us out? Can you push him for me?"

"Sure." The orderly was a middle-aged man with receding blond hair and a thick beard. He took the handles of my chair and pushed me toward the elevator. "Where are we going?"

"Room 319," I said. Ever had been moved to the general ICU a few days ago, until such a time as the doctors decided to move her to a long-term care facility.

I hated being immobile, being helpless. I still needed help getting into a wheelchair, much less anything else. I was dreading having to go home and being alone and unable to do anything. Grams and Gramps had wanted to stay, had insisted, saying I'd need help, but I wouldn't let them. Why, I wasn't sure. I knew Gramps needed the ranch, hated being away, and that he wasn't ready to retire anytime soon, despite being eighty years old and having Uncle Gerry to do most of the day-to-day stuff. He'd probably work until he couldn't anymore, and even then he'd hate it. He'd probably die on the back of a horse, and I had a feeling that he wouldn't want to die anywhere else, except perhaps in Grams's arms. I made them go home, even though I had no idea how I'd shower or get into the bathroom. How I'd get to and from the condo to the hospital to see Ever. How I'd do anything.

The one person who could help was the girl beside me, and something told me that wouldn't be a great idea. Mr. Eliot, maybe? I snorted.

"What's funny?" Eden asked, glancing at me.

I wasn't really all that keen on sharing my thought process, but I supposed I'd have to broach the subject at some point. "I'm just thinking about what I'm gonna do when I'm discharged from this place."

"What do you mean?"

I shrugged, trying desperately to sound nonchalant. "Well, I'm not exactly…mobile. I'm short an arm and a leg for a while, so—"

Eden frowned down at me as we boarded the elevator. "Cade. You're family. I know my dad might take some…convincing, but we're not gonna let you just…you won't be alone, okay?"

"Thinking about trying to enlist your dad's help is what made me laugh. I'm not exactly his favorite person, I don't think."

Eden made a you're probably right face, even as she said, "He'll come around. I'll make sure of it."

"You can't make him like me. I stole his daughter from him." The orderly glanced sideways at me in shock, then away, back to the opening doors of the elevator.

Eden made a sound of irritation. "The fuck you did. He lost her a long time ago. I wouldn't even really call what you and Ever did eloping, per se. You just had a really, really tiny wedding. At the last minute. Without Dad's knowledge or approval." She laughed. "That doesn't sound any better, does it? Look, Cade. Ever's relationship with Dad isn't your problem. He doesn't have to like the fact that you're her husband—he just has to deal with it."

"Yeah, but all that...it's not exactly the best footing for asking him to help me take a piss, or bring me to the hospital and back every day."

Ever ducked her head as we rounded the corner and approached Ever's room. "We'll figure it out, okay? I promise." She thanked the orderly as he parked me beside Ever and set the brake. When he was gone, she pulled up a chair, setting the cello case in the corner. "Hey, Ev. I thought I'd play for you. I've been working on Beethoven's sonata for cello and piano. I've got the first two movements down. Andy Minor is doing the piano pieces, and we're gonna present it together in a few months for the entire department. Andy is fucking sick talented, Ev. For real. He can slay pretty much any piece he wants. He's got the first four movements already. But you know how I am. I hate memorizing new pieces. Andy is kind of a freak, though. I mean, he's one of those musical geniuses who can barely remember to tie his shoes or zip his pants most days."

I listened to Eden talk, envious of her ability to hold a one-sided conversation as if Ever was responding, as if she was really listening. I couldn't do that. I never knew what to say, and I felt self-conscious talking to a silent room.

Eden continued talking as she withdrew her cello from the case, sat down with it, and adjusted the tuning slightly. "Andy is nice, though. He's polite, and he's not trying to get in my pants. Although I'm not sure he's batting for *either* team. He just doesn't seem interested, you know? Like, the only thing he thinks of is music. Which is kind of nice after working with Kyle Pinelli for that duet. Remember that? He was such a pig. Thought he was the smoothest fucking thing since greased cake pans. I must have turned him down a million times, and he never quit. I mean, he had that going for him, I've gotta say. He was persistent, and no matter how many times I said no, he was always convinced I'd come to my senses and let him fuck me in the studio. I didn't, I'll have you know." She shifted uncomfortably, as if remembering that I was there. "So yeah. I'm gonna play now. I'm not gonna play Beethoven, because it's not very exciting by itself. I played a piece from the Philip Glass/Wendy Sutter album for Dad earlier. He came to see me. Finally. Only took…well, all of this, for it to happen, though. So, I played that, and now I've got another piece from that album in my head. 'Song IV.' This one is for you, sis."

She rolled her shoulders, touched the bow to the string, shook her hair away from her face, and then closed her eyes, took a deep breath, and started playing.

I'd never sat and listened to anyone play like that before. Classical music simply wasn't a part of my world, not growing up, and not as an independent adult. I'd heard bits and pieces here and there, of course. I could recognize "Für Elise" and the Fifth Symphony part that everyone knows. But this...it was magical. Her fingers touched the strings gently, her arm drew the bow across in smooth strokes, and somehow, magic was created. The sound was like nothing I'd ever heard before, a deep, almost masculine voice, and the way she played it, the melody, the way the notes rose and fell, it created this rapturous spell over me. I couldn't *not* watch her play, couldn't take my eyes from her face, the way she seemed to be communing with her instrument, leaning into it, caressing sound from it, speaking to it, and it to her, her expression shifting and twisting and moving with the music.

I didn't dare even breathe, didn't dare move for fear of breaking the spell.

She finished, hung her head, breathing deeply. "How about some Bach? You can never go wrong with Bach." She seemed to be struggling, fighting against some well of emotion. I could hear it in her voice, even if she kept her face turned away from me. "You know this one, Ev. It's number five, the prelude. I know how you are about preludes. You always like the preludes best."

She began again, and I found myself closing my eyes to listen, to tune everything out but the pure sound. I heard the door open behind me, but I didn't care, didn't bother turning to see who it was. There was something mournful in the way she played. Perhaps it was the piece, perhaps it was in her playing itself, but I heard the sadness. She was playing with a purpose, not just to play, not to practice, but because she was mourning. I heard a pause, and then she began once more, and I watched her now, watched her sway, head bent toward her cello, her hair coming free from the braid along the side of her head, wisping around her eyes.

I almost thought I could feel Ever's soul somehow, feel her in the air, listening. I could see Eden sitting on a chair, playing, and Ever at her easel, washing the canvas with colors to match the music. I could feel her. Within me, around me. For as long as Eden played, I could feel her, and I never wanted it to end.

It was surreal being in the hospital, as if it were all a dream, a nightmare from which I'd wake up and Ever would be in our bed beside me, holding me, black hair a tangle, skin white in the darkness, peaceful in her sleep. And I'd be whole, no cast, no bandages, no metal rods or pins. Ever would be there.

I almost believed it, listening to Eden. I almost forgot reality, forgot that Ever was comatose and I was due for months of therapy before I walked or used my arm again.

And then Eden stopped and I had to open my eyes, and I saw Eden wipe at her face, run a finger beneath her eye, catching the tear as it fell, and then another trickled down, smearing eyeliner as it went.

I sensed the crowd. I turned around and saw a cluster of maybe thirty people standing around the doorway, huddled together, watching.

"I might've played the second and third movements, too," Eden said. "The fourth movement of the fifth suite is my favorite," she said, and I wasn't sure if she was talking to me or to Ever, "but if I played any longer, I think I'd probably lose it, and I just...I can't let that happen. I know you wouldn't want that." To Ever, then.

"I think...I think if you needed to let it out, she'd understand, though," I said, not sure where the words were coming from.

"Yeah, she would. But...I just can't. I won't. She'll wake up, and she'll need me to have my shit together. I can't...I can't just...I can't afford a breakdown. I've got that performance with Andy coming up, and I need to be focused. I've got to learn the rest of the sonata by the end of January, and I can't afford to break down. I can't afford it. I've got... I've got too much to do. And she wouldn't want it." Eden was chanting to herself now, convincing herself. "I'm fine. She'll be fine. Right? Yeah." She stood up, packed her cello away, and stood in the doorway, pausing to glance at me. "I've got to go. I've got homework to do."

"Sure. I'm good here."

She was gone then, and I was alone with Ever. The door was closed, the curtains drawn. I reached out and touched Ever's hand. She looked like she was asleep, just asleep, as if she'd wake up any time. Her skin was warm, her chest rose and fell ever so gently. Except...except the tubes, and the machines.

"Hi, babe. You never told me how talented she is. I mean, I guess I assumed she was good, but I never guessed *how* good. And I can't believe that her cello is, like, almost two hundred years old. That's kinda crazy, you know, to play something that's older than anyone alive? It's a piece of history, in a way. That's pretty cool, I think." I couldn't keep up the chatter. "I miss you, Ever. I miss you so much. I want you...I wish you could just wake up. I don't know how... what to do without you."

I fell silent then, and just sat with her until a nurse came in and brought me back to my room.

going home; cello in the dark

I stood up, with Nick's help, balanced, twisted in place, and sat down on my couch. Nick Eliot pushed the chair to one side and then stood in the center of the room, looking around.

"So…you need anything else?" He seemed at once uncomfortable with and interested in where Ever and I lived.

I'd been discharged, finally, and I'd asked Ever's father to bring me here. I had my papers for the out-patient therapy, and plans with both Eden and Nick to get me there. It would be every other day, initially, and then less frequently as I progressed, hopefully. I'd start therapy on my arm as soon as my stitches came out in a few weeks, but my leg would wait till it was out of the cast, which would be quite a while.

I shook my head. "Nah. I'm good." I then remembered that I wouldn't be able to get up on my own, at least not easily, and forced my pride to take a back seat. "Well, maybe the remote, and my sketching stuff from my hospital bag? The remote is on top of the TV."

Nick got me the things I'd asked for, and then stuck his hands in the pockets of his leather coat. "That's it, then? Sure you don't need anything else?"

I shook my head, because pride was too strong. "Thanks. I've got it." I met his eyes. "And…thanks a lot. I appreciate the help."

"No problem. So Eden's coming on Thursday to take you for the therapy thing, right?"

"Yeah."

"Okay. So. Yeah. Well, I'll see you on Saturday, then."

"'Bye." And then I was alone. I sat on the couch, arm bandaged and held in a sling against my chest, my leg immobilized in a cast.

I looked around. I hadn't been back here since the day of the accident, and it was strange. It felt… big, and empty. Silent. No music played; there was no Ever to fill the space. Her things were everywhere. A few of her paintings, framed and hung on the walls. Her favorite red cardigan, hanging on the back of a dining room chair. Her UGGs, flopped over by the door. Clogs beside those, and a pair of fancy shoes, not high heels, but with a kind of wedge. She wore those shoes when we went out for dinner somewhere nicer, usually.

I realized I'd asked Nick to bring me my sketchpad. It was sitting on the couch next to me, on my right side. I reached for it, fumbled it in my left hand. Dropped it, and finally managed to get it open on my lap. Even flipping the pages to a blank page was tricky with only one hand, but I kept on stubbornly. Getting my pencil case open didn't go so well. I scattered pencils everywhere, but finally got one out.

It turns out trying to even write my name with my left hand was nearly impossible. I was a child all over again, scrawling in sloppy, uneven letters. Trying to draw would be out of the question, clearly. I'd try, though. It might be months before my right hand and arm were back to where I could use them for art.

I spent the next several hours working on simply writing with my left hand, teaching the muscles to do what I wanted. All the while, my right hand seemed to be aching in jealousy. It twitched, throbbed, seemingly trying to take over, whispering, *I can do that*, but yet it couldn't. I wrote my name over and over again, and when I got sick of the sight of my own name, I wrote Ever's.

Ever Monroe. Ever Monroe. Ever Monroe.

A thousand times, until my hand ached and I couldn't hold the pencil anymore.

And then I had to pee.

I had a pair of crutches, which I couldn't really use without my right arm, but maybe I could mange to hobble over to the bathroom with just one of them. I slid along the edge of the couch, leaned as far as I could, and snagged one of the crutches from where they stood against the wall, just out of easy reach. I centered the crutch in front of myself, gripped it in my left hand, and pulled myself up. Or, tried to. I pulled, strained, pushed up with my left leg, and only managed to get halfway up. I hovered there, leg trembling, arm shaking. Shit. Why was this so hard? It shouldn't be so hard to merely stand up, should it? I pushed through it, forced myself up, then leaned on the crutch, panting. I was legitimately out of breath just from standing up.

I stared across the condo, which now seemed a hundred miles across. The bathroom was, under normal circumstances, only thirty steps away. I slid the crutch forward, leaned on it and took a step, then swung my cast-encased leg forward. And shit, that leg was heavy. By the time I was halfway to the bathroom, I was sweating and exhausted, and about to piss my pants. Which triply sucked, because there was just no way to hurry the process, and I didn't even have the ability to do the pee-pee dance; every muscle I had was being used to drag my sorry carcass across the fucking living room.

I got there, finally, only to discover the impossibility of getting even drawstring track pants down when the one useful arm you have is also the one you're using to stay balanced. Actually taking a piss felt like doing a Cirque du Soleil act, balancing on one leg—which meant leaning to one side to offset the weight of the cast—plus aiming…it was a wonder I managed it at all without falling on my ass.

And then I had to get all the way back across the living room. Which took just as long, and tired me out even further. And of course, as soon as I was sitting down, I realized my stomach was rumbling. Being an invalid sucked.

I thought of Ever then, lying all but dead in a hospital room, alone, unlikely to wake. My plight wasn't so bad, suddenly.

After a few minutes' rest, I worked myself to my feet and hobbled into the kitchen, only to discover that most of my food was spoiled. The rest of it required more cooking than I had the energy to do. This time, I stayed on my feet—or foot, as it were—and thought things through. I'd order pizza, unlock the door, and have the delivery guy bring it in to me. I placed the order, found the correct amount of cash, unlocked the front door, and then made my way back to the couch. I flipped on the TV, and started in on the DVR'd episodes of *Duck Dynasty* and *The Walking Dead* from the previous two weeks. Even that was nearly impossible to do without losing my mind. Ever loved those shows. They were *our* shows. Now I had to watch them by myself. When the knock on the door came, I called out a loud "Come in!", expecting the delivery guy.

I was surprised to see Eden come through the door with a box of pizza in one hand and bags of groceries in the other. "I met the delivery guy at the front door," she said, setting everything down on the dining room table. "I was on my way up with some things for you. Figured you might be out of food that was easy to make."

There was no reason for me to be so dumbfounded whenever she was in the room. But I was, and I didn't understand why. She showed up, and suddenly I was tongue-tied. It was idiotic.

"Thanks," I forced myself to say. "Here's cash for the pizza. How much was the food?" I'd kept my wallet in my pocket, intelligently enough.

She waved her hand. "Please. Don't worry about it. It's just some microwave burritos and ramen noodles."

"Eden, seriously. How much?"

"I don't want your money," she insisted, not looking at me as she stuffed burritos into my freezer, bags of shredded cheese into the fridge, and packages of ramen into a cupboard. "Just let me have some of your pizza. I'm starved."

She had her hair braided tight against her scalp, escaping strands plastered to her forehead and cheeks. She wore a pair of white spandex shorts, cross-trainers with ankle socks, and a black Northface fleece. Then she shucked her coat and tossed it on the table. All she had on up top was a sports bra. Purple. Tight. And… not quite up to the task of enclosing everything it was supposed to.

"Excuse my appearance," she said. "I was on the way home from the gym. Thought of you." She winced as if she'd said something wrong. "Thought of you, in the sense that I thought maybe the shit in your fridge had gone bad, since you've been gone for a couple of weeks, and it might be hard for you to shop, or cook, and—" She was rambling, clearly embarrassed. "Not that I'm just sitting around thinking of you, or anything…shit. This isn't going well. I'm—I'm just gonna gome. Gome? Go home. I'm going to go home. God, I'm such a fucking spazz." She grabbed her coat and scurried toward the front door. I'd noticed she tended to swear more than Ever, who only cursed when really upset, or in bed.

"Eden, wait. It's fine. You're—you're fine. Please stay. Have some pizza. I'm—I wasn't looking forward to eating alone anyway."

She hesitated with the door open and her foot on the threshold, staring down the hallway, as if it somehow held her rescue. "I should go."

I shrugged. Part of me was screaming, telling me to let her go. Let her leave. The other part was begging me to ask her to stay. She was company. A friendly face. Someone to talk to. "I mean, it's up to you," I said. "Just…I wouldn't mind the company."

She hesitated another moment, and then shut the door. She shut it slowly, letting it *click* closed with a certain strange finality. She set her coat back on the table. "Plates?"

I pointed at the sink. "Cupboard over the sink. There's some paper ones in there. No way in hell I'm doing dishes anytime soon."

She brought the box and a couple of plates and the roll of paper towels, and then went back for two cans of the soda she'd brought me. We ate in silence, both of us clearly hungry. We finished all but two slices of the large pizza, which kind of impressed me. I'd never met a girl who could eat like that. Of course, the only two girls I'd ever really known were Luisa and Ever, and both of them were light eaters. With all the talk Ever had done in her letters about how Eden was so figure conscious and health and fitness obsessed, I hadn't expected her to eat as much as she did, or be willing to be seen in public wearing what she was.

There was a thought I'd had, a question that I'd never had the courage to ask. Finally, I couldn't take the wondering anymore. "Eden? Did you know Ever was pregnant?"

She set her can down and wiped her hands on a sheet of paper towel. "No. Did you?"

I shook my head. "I was wondering if she'd talked to you about it."

Ever shrugged. "Not to me, no."

"Do you think she knew?"

Ever sighed. "I'd like to think no. I mean, if she didn't tell either of us, then I can't imagine she knew. That's not the kind of thing she'd keep secret. Not from me." She gave me an apologetic glance. "She might have kept it from you for a while, if she was scared to tell you, but…she'd tell me. And I'd have known something was up with her. I mean, we're twins. We know things about each other. We can sense when the other is keeping a secret. Sometimes I can tell when she's upset even when I'm not in the same room as her. That's happened a lot. I'll be in class or practicing and I just—I know she needs me."

"Did you—did you sense anything, when it happened?"

She shrugged again, but it was a tiny, uncertain gesture, and she kept her head down, her braid hanging over one shoulder. "Yeah. I knew."

"You knew?" I asked. "You knew what?"

"That something had happened." Her voice dropped to a murmur. "I felt…it felt like someone had stabbed me in the heart. I'm not kidding. It was physically painful. I swear I'm not making this up. I haven't—I haven't told anyone. I was in bed. I had a test the next morning, and I'd been cramming for it. I'd been up for, like, forty-eight hours. But I wasn't asleep yet. I'd just…just turned off the light. I closed my eyes and started to drift. And then I felt this… terror. Dread. Like…you know that feeling you get when something bad is happening? Like, right then, in that moment, that feeling you get when you know you can't stop it?"

My throat closed. "All too well."

Eden paled. "Shit…fuck. Of course you do. God, I'm so sorry, Cade, I didn't mean to—"

I waved my hand, focusing on not crying. The memory was so powerful, like icy claws in my gut, dragging horror up from the shadowy depths of my soul where nightmares resided. "It's fine," I choked out. "Keep going." I could sense she needed to say it, to tell someone. I didn't want to hear it. Not even remotely.

She took a deep breath. "I got that feeling. I was safe in bed, I knew I was, but I sat up and looked around, afraid. I mean, I think I honestly expected to see someone standing over me with a gun or something. Like the building was on fire or…I don't know. Something. It felt like I was in danger. It was that strong a feeling. And then I *knew*. I knew, Cade.

I knew something had happened to Ever. I called her phone. I must have called her phone a hundred times. It kept going to voicemail, straight to voicemail."

Ever's phone had been in her lap, and it had gone flying. Clean-up crew found it twenty feet away from where we'd first impacted, smashed into pieces.

Just like her.

"I didn't know your number. I called Dad, but he didn't answer, either. He was at work. He never answers his cell when he's at work. So I just—I went to the hospital. I knew, Cade. I knew." She blinked hard. Trembled. "I *knew*. I got to Beaumont about five minutes after the EMS truck. They...they wouldn't let me see her. They wouldn't tell me anything. Just that she was there, and so were you. They wouldn't tell me anything. I freaked out. They had to tell me that if I didn't calm down, they'd call security. I was losing it and I knew it, and I couldn't stop. I was screaming, kicking chairs over, demanding to see her, to know what the fucking hell had happened, but *they wouldn't tell me!* She's my twin, and I didn't even know if she was alive, what had happened." She was shaking all over, pale skin shivering, shoulders heaving. Barely keeping it together, about to crack.

I reached across my body and touched my palm to her shoulder. I didn't know what to say. I didn't say anything. She flinched from my hand, and then leaned into it. She sucked in a deep breath, sobbed once, then choked, visibly trying to stuff it down, to keep the tears at bay.

"It's okay, Eden." I whispered it. I wasn't sure whether I meant that things would be okay, to get her to stop crying, or that it was okay if she did cry. I knew the latter was probably what she needed. I just wasn't sure if I had the strength myself to comfort her. "It's—you can cry. I'm here."

She shook her head, "No, no…" scraping from her throat. But she leaned forward, face in her hands, and swayed toward me, into the chaste touch of my palm on the top of her shoulder.

I turned toward her, angling my body toward hers. I rubbed her shoulder, my hand touching the warmth of her back, the fabric of her sports bra. She quaked under my hand, and then turned into me, putting her forehead against my chest. I put my hand on her back, in the center, right over her spine, and held her as she cried. I closed my eyes and stared up at the ceiling, but I saw anyway the curvature of her spine as she bent into my awkward, one-armed hug.

The intimacy was disconcerting, right and wrong at the same time, comforting and terrifying, exhilarating and guilt-inducing.

She cried for a few minutes, and then the sobs trickled to a stop and she straightened, wiped her eyes with her forearm, sliding away from me, back across the couch, putting several feet between us once more, not looking at me. "Thanks," she murmured.

"It's hard," I said. "No one could go through this without crying."

She nodded, then got up and vanished into the bathroom. I heard the water going, and she returned with a damp face and less-puffy eyes. "I should go."

I nodded. She really should. "Thanks for the food."

"You have my number?"

"Yeah."

"Call if you need anything." She met my eyes. Hers, so green and so like Ever's, were conflicted, as if offering something she wasn't sure she should. "For real. Whatever time it is. Okay?"

I nodded. "I will. Thanks."

Awkward silence then, our eyes not quite locking, not quite looking away, aware of the moment we'd shared, the vulnerability witnessed, accepted. Holding someone as they cried bound you to them somehow. And we were already bound together, through Ever.

She slid her coat on and I stared out the window as she zipped it, facing away from me as she did so. I kept my eyes on the falling snow as she adjusted her shorts, tugging them down with a shimmy of her hips, kept my eyes on the heavy gray clouds thick with snow and darkening with falling night, on the

sidewalk going white, on the walls. Anywhere, everywhere, except Ever.

Except Eden.

Eden, not Ever.

Fuck.

Eden

I collapsed into bed, on top of the blankets, letting the cool air dry my naked body. I'd taken a long,
hot shower when I got home from Cade's apartment—from Cade and *Ever's* apartment. It was still
her apartment.

I tugged the blankets onto myself, but then got
too hot and kicked them off. Then I had to put on
a T-shirt, because for some reason, when I lay there
naked, all I could feel was the simple, innocent way
Cade had held me. It wasn't an arousing memory.
He'd held me while I bawled like a baby—how
embarrassing—and that was it. Only, I *never* cried in
front of guys. When I got dumped, I'd get pissed, I'd
scream and yell because I had a hell of a temper, but
I'd never cry. Not in front of guys. But I had, in front
of Cade. He'd made it easy somehow.

But I couldn't forget the feel of his palm on my
shoulder, strong fingers, hard and callused.

I forced myself to think of anything else. I
hummed the section of the Beethoven sonata I was

memorizing. Visualized the notes. Each individual stroke of the bow. Each movement of my fingers on the neck. Anything, everything. I thought of nothing at all.

I tried every trick I knew to get to sleep, but couldn't. I got out of bed and uncased my cello, sat on my chair, the cushion smooth and cold under my ass, my T-shirt slipping off one shoulder. The dark, varnished wood of Apollo's sides was cool against my bare thighs, and I felt the vibrations shiver through me as I drew the bow across his strings, not thinking, not playing anything specific, just playing to get my head straight, to give my confused, aching heart a reprieve. I played in the dark, not needing light to know where his strings were, how he felt, how to pull the music from within him, from within me.

I played until my wrist and fingers ached. Every note of what I'd played was stuck in my head, and I realized it was the next movement of my solo. I had to turn on the light to find my notes, and I scribbled madly, frantic to get the notation down while it was fresh in my head. When I had it written down, I played it again, and I knew it was brilliant.

It was deep, dark, slow and soulful and masculine.

It was the music of Cade's sad amber eyes, the sound of his sorrow.

I still couldn't sleep, so I put in my earbuds and turned my iPod to shuffle, lay down in the darkness, and listened to "Broken Crowns" by Portland Cello Project.

Finally, I felt my eyes grow heavy, focused on that feeling, on the slow floating away, falling under. Still, sleep was long in coming. And my dreams were fraught with strange, disorienting, painful images. Amber eyes, watching me and trying not to, the way mine were drawn to his and to him, in a way I hated and couldn't quite control. Dreams of Ever asleep, not asleep but in a coma, watching me from behind the veil of the spirit world. She watched me, watched Cade hold me as I cried, and I couldn't fathom her expression, couldn't quite see her; she was a silvery translucent ghost whose presence I could only feel as I cried, as I felt the comfort of Cade's arm around me.

Was it disapproval I felt from spirit-her?

How could it not be? Spirit-me resolved to be stronger, to keep my tears for my pillow, for the silence of my lonely bedroom.

percentage of miracles

Caden

I was covered in sweat, shaking from exhaustion. Everything hurt. Physical therapy was fucking brutal.

I'd withdrawn from school. I couldn't draw, couldn't write, couldn't focus; there was simply no point to going. I had enough money still left over from my father's life insurance that I could function for a while. I stayed home, read, watched TV and movies, and felt sorry for myself. Eden would come over every day after her last class and we'd go to the hospital together to visit Ever. We'd sit and talk, to each other, to Ever. I'd hobble out into the corridor, try to connect to the shitty hospital WiFi and browse the Internet, idly flipping through the day's galleries on The Chive or reading articles on Cracked, anything to get away from Eden and to give her time alone with Ever, to talk to her sister.

I felt Ever slipping away. I found myself less and less able to keep up the one-sided chatter that Eden seemed to produce so effortlessly.

Maybe it was I who was slipping away. I was retreating, I knew, back into the numb place I'd lived after Mom died, and even more so after Dad had. I was there again, and it was the only way I'd survive. I couldn't bear to miss Ever. It was too deep a cut through my heart. Talking to her made me miss her. She was there, breathing, heart beating, but she wasn't there. She wasn't listening. I wasn't sure if I believed she heard me or not.

I was slipping away.

Eden forced me into the present, into feeling. She made me feel strange things. I missed Ever when I looked at Eden, but I also saw Eden for herself, and I saw her as a friend, as a companion in misery, in missing Ever. I didn't see her as a sister, or as a family member. She was just Eden, and she looked so, so much like Ever, too much, and it hurt, but she also looked different enough to confuse me, to hit me where I couldn't fight it.

So I took every opportunity, whenever we were forced to be in the same room, to do anything but look at her, to be anywhere but close enough to touch her, even accidentally. I'd hold my pee for hours rather than let her help me stand up, and I'd make sure to not see her grief so I didn't have to touch her to comfort her.

It was tense and awkward.

Physically, I was a mess as well. I'd had rods and screws put in my leg, which meant being in a cast for three months. It was a long three months. I'd always been active, and to be a couch potato for that long was hellish. I grew dependent on fast food on the way home from the hospital, cafeteria food, easy-to-microwave meals. Unhealthy food.

I grew dependent on Eden. She drove me everywhere I needed to go, to the hospital and home, shopping. She was the only person who visited me, and the only person I talked to. Nick Eliot had dropped out of the picture again, as far as I could tell. He'd visited Ever a few times, I'd seen him when I was there, but I had no idea if he'd made any attempt to get closer to Eden as a result of all this.

Now out of the cast, I was in physical therapy several times a week, which Eden drove me to as well. She encouraged me when I wanted to quit, which was all the time. Never complained at my snappy attitude and ingratitude.

She'd infiltrated every aspect of my life, and I was confused by it, scared of it. I took to silence as a coping mechanism, responding only when spoken to, keeping my distance and my own counsel.

At the moment, I was sitting in her car, a two-year-old VW Passat. I was sweaty, stinking, hungry, and irritated. My thoughts were raging out of control, haywire. I thought of Ever, missing her, hating missing her, hating feeling like she was slipping away from me. I hated being so dependent on Eden, hated that I had to see her every day and fight how much she reminded me of Ever and yet how clearly she was her own person, so distinct and so unique that I couldn't deny having noticed it, having seen it every day for so many weeks.

Finally, as she parked the car in the guest spot of my condo complex, she sighed deeply and shut off the music, turned to face me. "You're not doing well," she said. "Emotionally, I mean." I shrugged, kept my gaze directed out the window. She grabbed my arm and turned me. "Damn it, Cade, talk to me."

"Why?" I snarled. "Say what? How am I supposed to be doing?"

"Well, tell me what's—god, I mean, I *know* what's wrong." She rubbed at her face. "I can't help you if you won't talk to me."

"Maybe there *is* no way to help me. I *miss* her, Eden. I—she's slipping away from me. I don't remember the sound of her voice. I don't—I don't remember anything. I can't—I can't feel her anymore."

Eden was silent. There wasn't anything to say.

"She'll come back." It wasn't even a whisper from Eden. "She *has* to."

"What if—what if she doesn't?"

"Don't *say* that!" Eden yelled, her voice an angry shriek. "She *will!* You have to believe. You have to *try*, Cade! You have to talk to her. You have to—to remind her what's here."

I heard those last words for hours after she left. *Remind her what's here.*

The next day, when Eden picked me up, I had a shoebox under my arm. Blue, with a red and white Union Jack. A Reeboks box. It was heavy, stuffed full. Eden glanced at it but didn't ask what was in it. Maybe she knew. She took it from me so I could crutch my way to the car. My right arm was healing enough to let me use crutches, but that was about it. My fine motor skills were basically nil, enough to let me open and close my hand, but not enough to hold a pencil yet.

At the hospital, Eden sat in the corner, and I didn't ask her to leave when I opened the top of the shoebox, revealing dozens and dozens of letters, sheaves of them bound together by rubber bands, a month's worth of envelopes together in each rubber band. I pulled out the bundle at the back of the box, set the box down, and unwound the rubber band. I found the first letter Ever had sent me. Her handwriting…god, it was so huge and loopy and girly.

I pulled the letter out, cleared my throat. "'Dear Caden,'" I read. "'How are you? I'm excited to be your pen pal. I've never had a pen pal before. I don't think I've written a letter to anyone before, actually. Not unless you count letters to Santa when I was in kindergarten. What should we write to each other about? Would you be interested if I told you about the painting I'm doing?'" I stopped, blinked hard. I could hear her voice. I heard a sniffle and knew Eden did, too.

I read the whole letter. The next one. And then I came to the letter in which she first referenced Eden. I stopped, lowered the letter, and made myself look at Eden. "I, um—she talks about you. In a lot of these letters. It might be—I don't know. It might be weird. It's—"

"Is she, like, making fun of me?" Eden asked.

I shrugged. "No. Not making fun of you, but it's just—"

"Private," Eden cut in. "I get it. Not meant for me to hear. I'll go get some coffee."

"It's not that I mind—"

She waved at me in negation. "I said I get it, Cade. Hearing what someone thinks about you when they know you're not listening, or whatever, it's not fun. I'd rather not know."

"She loved you," I said. "She wanted you to be happy. That's all she ever wanted."

I wondered if she noticed we were both referring to Ever in the past tense.

Eden squeezed her eyes shut and turned away. "I know that. I *know*. She's my twin. She's half of me. I know what it was about me that made her so mad. I'm fat. I hate the way I look. I hate that everything I eat goes to my ass. I hate that she could eat a whole cheesecake and not gain any weight, but if I even *smell* it, my ass gets bigger. She hated that I couldn't just be content with the way I look." She wasn't talking to me anymore, not really. "She hated that I was always comparing myself to her. I always have. I always will. She was—fuck, she *is* more beautiful than I am. And I hate that." She turned away from me, fists clenched, taking deep, harsh breaths.

"Eden, Jesus. You're not fat. You're…you and Ever, you're different people. Same basic genetic makeup or whatever, yeah, but still different. You can't—"

"Oh, shut the fuck up, Cade! What do you know about it?" She whirled on me. "You don't know me! She and I are ninety-nine-point-ninety-nine percent *the same exact FUCKING person!* But that one measly goddamn percent? It means I get fat and she didn't. It means I spend two hours at the gym every day just so I don't go all lard-ass, and she could work out once a week and eat whatever she wants and be skinny and beautiful and perfect."

"Eden, god, what—what can I—"

"NOTHING! You can't *do* anything. You can't *say* anything. It's how it is. I've been going to therapists for years about this, and you think in one conversation that you can just—just *fix* me?"

I closed my eyes and tried to think. "How did we get here? Why are we fighting? I just—"

She seemed to deflate. "I'm sorry, Cade. Shit. I'm sorry I blew up. You didn't deserve it. I can be a bitch sometimes—don't mind me. Just—don't read those letters around me, okay? They're private. Between you and her. They don't involve me." She left then, walking away, looking sadder than I'd ever seen.

"Eden, listen—"

"I'm fine, Cade." She paused, turned back to smile at me, a small, defeated smile. "I'm always fine. Don't worry about me. Just read to her. If anything can bring her back, those letters can." She was gone then, closing the door behind herself.

I stared at the door, at the place where she'd been just moments ago. That girl had some serious self-esteem issues, things that went bone-deep, soul-deep. I sensed that she really believed, in her heart of hearts, that she was actually fat.

How could she not see that she was beautiful? Had no one ever told her that? Had no one ever taken the time to make her *feel* beautiful? I knew I couldn't do that for her. Not the way she needed. But *someone* should. She didn't deserve to feel that way about herself, not as gorgeous as she was, not as talented and kind and unfailingly generous as she was.

The craziest part was, unless you really *knew* that about Eden, you'd never guess how deep those insecurities went.

I read on, stuffing one letter back in its envelope and pulling out another. "'Caden, or, I suppose I might actually address the letters 'Dear Caden' since you are dear. To me, I mean. Is that weird? Maybe it is. 'Dear' means, according to Google, 'regarded with deep affection; cherished by someone.' I hope that's not too weird for you, but I feel like you and I have a special connection. Do think so, too?'" I stopped, choking on the next part. "'I'm so, so sorry about your mom getting sicker.'" I couldn't keep reading. Being there in the hospital, it brought all that back. Days and days spent just like this, sitting next to Mom's bed, watching her die slowly. Except with Ever it was both better and worse. Better in that she wasn't getting actively sicker, but worse in that she wasn't healing and might never.

I swallowed hard, blinked away the tears, and continued. "'I can't imagine going through that. When I lost my mom to the car accident, it was the most horrible thing I've ever experienced. One minute she was there, alive and fine, and then the next Daddy was telling me she was dead…'" I made myself finish the letter, and the next one. When Eden came back, I tucked the letter I'd just finished back in its envelope, sniffing it for the faint scent still clinging to it.

Eden took a deep breath. "Cade, listen, I'm really, really—"

"Don't, Eden. Don't apologize. There's nothing to forgive. I know I have no idea what you've been through, how you feel. Any of that. And I probably never will. And I certainly know there's probably nothing I could ever do or say to fix you, and it's not even my job. But…just know that—as your friend, I mean—your insecurities are…misplaced." God, that was the most cowardly way to try to say that. I had to do better. Eden had done too much to help me to deserve less. "You're beautiful, Eden. You really are. You're perfect the way you are. I know that coming from me that may be weird, or it may not mean much, but you should know that. About yourself. Because it's true."

Eden tipped her head back and sniffed, then shook her head and laughed bitterly. "Thanks, Cade."

I tilted my head, confused by her reaction. "Did I just make it worse or something?"

She shook her head, seeming resigned now. "No. It's just…the first guy to ever tell me that without having an ulterior motive, and it has to be you. For real, thank you. That's very sweet of you, Cade."

"I'm sorry I'm not—"

She cut me off. "No, it's not you. It's…well, it is, kind of. But it's not your fault. You belong to Ever, that's all." She shrugged. "It's not that no one ever tells me they think I'm hot or whatever, it's just… when they do, it's because they want in my pants. So it doesn't count. Not really."

"Eden, just because they—"

She kept going, talking over me. "And you know the worst part? It usually works. 'Cause I'm just that easy and that desperate."

"Eden, you're not—"

"Not to be mean, Cade, but you don't know me." She moved to stand on the other side of Ever's bed, staring down at her sister. "She's the good one, the pure one. One boyfriend, and then you. And you, she fucking *married*. Me? If you only knew…" She shook her head, trailing off, then laughed, another bitter exhalation. "Why am I telling you all this? Jesus. Like you need to know how much of a fucking mess I am? God, I'm such an idiot. Forget I said anything. Forget I'm here. Just…give me a few minutes with Ev, and then we can go."

I hesitated, wanting to say something, to reassure her somehow, but she was right. I didn't know her. Not at all. For all that she'd been there for me, driven me places and kept me company, until recently all of our conversations had been light, aimless small talk as we drove or ate a quick lunch. I knew nothing about her, not really. I didn't know how she spent her time when she wasn't with me at the hospital. I mean, I knew she had sixteen credit hours plus cello mentoring or whatever it was called, practicing. But did she have a boyfriend? I'd always assumed no, but the way she talked about herself, it made her seem...I wasn't even sure what the word was. Loose? But she was so self-deprecating that I thought maybe she was exaggerating, the way she exaggerated about her weight.

Finally I simply left, hobbling out into the corridor and to the waiting room. Eden spent half an hour with Ever, and then she swept into the waiting room, stood beside me while I struggled to my feet. She never helped me unless I asked her to, and always had this way of walking slowly with me as if it was perfectly natural to walk that slowly, as if she strolled at a crutch-bound hobbling pace all the time.

The ride in the elevator, the walk to the car, the drive home, it was silent. At one point, I glanced at her, wanting to say something, but she just happened to switch the channel on her radio, find a song she liked, and turn up the volume. I took the cue and kept silent. When we got to my condo, I opened the door, but paused with my feet on the ground and my body inside the car.

"Eden, I—"

"Cade, please don't. I'm not your problem. I'm fine. For real. I get these downward swings every once in a while, but I always pull out of them. I like who I am, for the most part. And like I said, I'm not your problem. You need to focus on getting better, and on Ever."

"But I just—"

She stabbed the radio off with an angry punch of her finger. "I'm *fine*." She swung her head to look at me, hair swaying, green eyes daring me to say anything else. I didn't.

I levered myself out of the car, then balanced on one crutch and bent down to look at her. "Just know…I'm here, if you need to talk."

"I'll keep that in mind," she said. "Thanks. See you tomorrow."

Eden

Just shy of five months since the accident, and Cade was able to walk with only one crutch, and had almost full use of his right hand. He still had trouble with drawing, which I gathered was excruciatingly hard for him. If I couldn't play the cello for five or six months…I'd go nuts.

I'd learned to keep my damn mouth shut around Cade, finally. No more embarrassing explosions, no more blurting out my deepest fears and insecurities to the one single person on the planet who couldn't really do a damn thing about them. We visited Ever, took turns with her. He read the letters she wrote him, and then found that she'd kept his to her in a similar box, hidden in the back of their closet, and he read those, too. I never listened. I was too much of a coward to face that. He loved her, and he always would. He didn't need to see how jealous I was of their love, of Eden for having him, for having love like his.

Then, one sunny but cool spring afternoon, Cade and I were sitting in Ever's room, both of us having had time alone with her. We were about to leave when a doctor came into the room. Ever had nurses come in while we were there, check on things, maybe move her a little, change a bag of liquid. But never a doctor. He was tall, thin, gray-haired and ramrod straight. He grabbed the rolling stool and sat facing us.

"I'm Dr. Overton, with the neurosurgery department. We've been monitoring Ms. Monroe for some months now, and we—the team assigned to her case—have decided it's probably best for her to be moved to a long-term care facility." He said this calmly, easily, smoothly.

Cade didn't respond right away, and when he did, his voice was much too even, much too careful. "So basically…you're giving up on her?"

Dr. Overton didn't even blink. "No, son—"

"I'm not your son."

"Sorry, Mr. Monroe. But no, we're not giving up. But…she's been in a coma for almost five months now. Her brain activity hasn't altered in all that time. Essentially, she's showing no signs of changing, and a long-term care facility can provide the best quality of life for her. I believe this eventuality was discussed with you some months ago, Mr. Monroe."

"Yeah, I just—I hoped—"

"And please, don't give up that hope." Dr. Overton leaned forward, elbows on his knees, fingertips pressed together. "Here's a very honest truth for you both: We know very little about comas, about the human brain in general, really. There's little we can do at this point but keep her body healthy and hope that she comes out of it on her own. She may, I'm not saying she won't. Miracles happen. I've seen it. But…medically, statistically—"

"You're saying it would be a miracle if she does." Cade seemed more fragile than I'd ever seen him.

I took his hand and squeezed; I couldn't not. Sometimes you just need the touch of another human, no matter who it is.

Dr. Overton sighed. "It's very unlikely that she will wake up, yes." A pretty young nurse came in then, with a folder in one hand. "This is Ms. Jackson. She'll go over your options with you."

Nurse Jackson was quiet, but efficient. She listed various facilities in the area equipped to deal with Ever's condition, explained that the cost of her care would be borne by the state, and then left us with the packet of information. Left us to choose in which nursing home we'd put my comatose sister.

We went through the motions of discussing the various facilities, and picked one. Cade seemed to be simply going along at this point, blindly accepting. We fell silent, and Cade stared at Ever for a long time, almost as if not seeing her.

"What—what if she never wakes up, Eden?" His voice was a ragged whisper. "What do I do?"

"I don't—I don't know."

"I—she's my *wife*. I love her. I don't know how to—I don't know what to do. I miss her. I need her."

I wanted to cry for him, for the brokenness I heard in his voice. "I know, Cade. She's my sister, my best friend."

"But she's my wife. She's all I had. Should I just… live as if she'll never wake up? Move on? Go back to school? Just keep on going? Like…like she's dead? But visit her like she's alive?"

I heard what he wasn't asking, what he wasn't saying. "I don't know, Cade. I don't think anyone can tell you that. You just have to do what seems right to you."

"But—I don't know what *is* right. How can I? She's not dead, but she's not alive." He seemed to be barely hanging on suddenly.

"Let's go, Cade. Let me take you home."

He nodded and followed me to my car, silent all the way.

things you can't unsee

Caden

Ever,

My love. It seems like it's been forever since I wrote you like this. Since I sat down with pen and paper and expressed my thoughts to you. So much has changed since then.

Everything has changed. I don't even know where to start. We met IRL (I didn't know what that phrase meant, way back when you first used it, you know) and we fell in love and we got married. God, all that seems like a lifetime ago. I don't know who that was, that Cade who was with you back then. I'm someone else now. This... hole in the world, man-shaped. Me-shaped. A vacancy.

I can't pretend like you're going to read this, like you're going to write back. I'm sorry, but I just can't.

You're in a coma, and you might never wake up, and I'm alone. You promised, Ever. You promised you'd never leave me. I know you didn't want to, you didn't mean to. But you still did, and I'm back to being numb and floating through life, through every day.

Except now I don't even have you, have your letters to keep me tied to the earth.

It's been six months. It's summer, and it was the day before Christmas the last time I heard your voice. The last time I saw your smile and your eyes.

I have to make some decisions now. Finish school? Keep the condo? Do I pack your things away? Do I hang up the sweater you left draped over the kitchen chair? I haven't yet. Do I put away your shoes that are by the door? Do I put all of your stuff in a box like you've died?

I can't. I know I should. Seeing your stuff just like you left it on December 23rd, it hurts. Every day, every time I see it all there, like you left it. But I can't bear to act like you're never coming back. I have to hope that you will. Because you will, right? You'll wake up. You'll come back to me. You love me, and you're just…lost. Somewhere out there, trying to come back. Like Odysseus fighting to get back to Penelope.

I don't know how to live without you, but I have to try. Don't I? If you were to wake up and I've given up, just stopped living, you'd be so mad. You'd kick my ass.

So I have to keep going. I have to pick myself up, and live. I don't know how I'll do it, but I will. For you. For US.

I love you, forever and always.

Cade

I lowered the letter, rested it on my knee. A bird chirped outside the window, hopping on a tree branch just beyond Ever's window. I stared out, watching the bird, struggling to keep it together. I'd decided to keep our deal, from back when we were writing letters to each other. I'd write whatever was in my heart and head, and I'd never erase or hold back. And I read them to her, out loud. Every word, no matter how painful.

I was driving on my own now, and able to use a pencil again. I could draw and write. It was going to take months of work yet to get my hand back to the skill it once had so effortlessly, but I could function. I could walk, I could drive. I'd never run the hundred-meter dash, but I could move around without much problem. Getting the ability to drive back meant I wasn't dependent on Eden anymore, but we still saw each other at the nursing home a few times a week. That was…bittersweet.

"I have another one," I told Ever. "So I'll read that."

Ever,

I finally got the insurance company to pay for a new truck. A Jeep Grand Cherokee. Brand new. You'd like it. It's green. Almost the color of your eyes, but a little darker. I wish I'd had you there to help me decide what to get. I wanted to pick something you'd love, but I just...I didn't know what. I almost picked another F-150, but I've had enough of those. I needed something different.

Your hair is getting long, you know that? They had to shave it all off when they did the surgeries on you. And now it's almost to your chin. I think it's actually a little darker black somehow. I think I remember reading that when you shaved your head, sometimes the hair would change a little. But then I read somewhere else that that wasn't actually true, it was just the ends of the hair being different or something.

I miss you so much, Ever. I miss talking to you. I miss waking up next to you. I miss the way you'd smile at me first thing in the morning. Sleepy, sexy, hair messy, like seeing me was the best way to wake up. I miss watching you put on your lotion. The way it made our bedroom smell like vanilla. I miss sleeping next to you. Jesus, I miss, most of all, the way you sounded when we made love. Your voice. How dirty you'd talk to me.

I'm going nuts, baby. Six months without you. Six months without touching you or kissing you. Six months, and I don't know what to do. About how horny I am. How I ache. For you. I wake up at night sometimes, and I've dreamed of you. Sex dreams of you. And I'll be on the verge of coming, just from the dream, but I always wake up, and then I remember that you're gone and I can't get the dream back, can't get the feeling back.

I miss your skin. Soft, smooth, warm.

I miss you so much sometimes that I could cry. But I can't. Don't. Won't. It's stupid, maybe, but if I don't mourn you, don't cry for you, then part of me thinks maybe you'll come back. And I won't have to.

Come back to me, my love. Please. Come back to me, and make love to me.

Forever yours, and yours beyond forever,

Caden

I heard a noise behind me, swiveled to see Eden standing in the doorway. Her hand was over her mouth and she was crying, bright silver tears sliding over her cheekbones.

"Sorry," she murmured, "I didn't mean to eavesdrop."

"It's okay," I said, as though part of me wasn't mortified that she'd heard my confession. As if she hadn't learned that, with Ever in a coma, I was still somehow able to go on having physical needs as if she were fine, as if my life hadn't ended with hers. I shouldn't want anything but for her to wake up. I shouldn't be so selfish as to want her to wake up so she could satisfy my desires.

Eden wouldn't quite look at me. "I can go, if you're—if you need more time."

"No, I was done. I was gonna go."

She held up a vase of daisies. "I've already been today. I just wanted to drop these off. She likes daisies. She always says they're—"

"Happy flowers," I finished.

"Yeah. Happy flowers." Eden set the vase on the windowsill, where the flowers could get the most sunlight.

Neither of us moved to leave, and neither of us spoke or looked at each other. Tense, thick silence hovered between us, freighted with the things we knew about each other that we shouldn't.

"I'll see you—"

"Do you want to grab some dinner?" Eden spoke at the same time as me. I gestured for her continue. She swept her fingers through her hair, flipping it back over her shoulder. "I was just thinking, you know, we're—there's no reason we can't talk, right? Hang out? We're…in some ways, we're all each other has."

I hated the reminder. "Yeah. That's true." I hated how part of me jumped at the opportunity to be around her. It wasn't her, really. It was anyone. I spent far too much time alone, and Eden and I were bound together, like she'd said. "Sure. That sounds good."

We ended up at a little Italian place in Birmingham, sharing a loaf of bread and sipping red wine while we waited for our orders to come up. Conversation was easy as long as we stayed to light, neutral topics. We both liked the same kind of movies, and generally kept the talk to actors and actresses, favorite scenes, quoting lines from movies we'd seen a thousand times. There was always a layer of awkwardness, a constant thread of tension, the feeling that somehow this wasn't quite acceptable in some subtle way. It was just dinner and conversation, though. Nothing else.

Dinner that night turned into dinner at that little Italian place twice a week, Sundays and Wednesdays, after we visited Ever. We ate, we had a couple glasses of wine, and we talked. We never lingered after the meal was finished. It was company, companionship. The chance to interact with someone who knew what the other was going through. We shared an unspoken commiseration, a missing of Ever Eileen Eliot Monroe. We knew, we felt it, but we never acknowledged it out loud. We never discussed meet-ing twice a week for dinner; it just happened, all by itself.

And then one Tuesday, Eden asked me if I'd drive to the restaurant. She didn't feel up to it, she said. She seemed…out of it. Lost in her head. I drove, and as soon we sat down at our usual table in the corner by the window, Eden ordered not a glass of merlot, but a bottle. That was unusual. One, maybe two glasses apiece, that was it, always.

I glanced at her. "Are you okay?"

She shrugged, ripped a piece of bread off and dipped it in the oil, all without meeting my eyes. "Yeah. Fine."

"That's convincing."

She waited until the server poured the wine and left to respond. "Sorry. Just…I had a bad day. No big." Except her eyes, downcast, conveyed otherwise.

"How about the truth, Eden? I'm your friend. You don't have to act fine with me, of all people. I'm the least okay person on the planet, probably."

She laughed, a sniffling giggle. "Quite a pair, aren't we?" She took a long sip of the wine. "You want the truth? I got dumped."

That stung in a way I didn't dare examine. "That sucks. What happened?" I hadn't known she was seeing anyone.

"The usual." She waved a dismissive hand. "Guy seemed nice. Guy seemed cute. Guy seemed nice and cute until he got what he wanted from Eden, and then Eden gets dumped. It's a routine by this point. Every few months, I do this to myself."

"Talk about yourself in the third person?" I asked, joking.

"Ha-ha. No. You know what I mean."

I sighed. "Yeah, I guess I do. Why do it to yourself, then? If it's a routine and you're aware of that fact, then why not try to change it?"

She gave me a look that said, *are you dumb, or joking?* "I don't go out there looking for this to happen. I just pick the wrong guys. I just have shitty radar, I guess. Like I said, I met this guy, Ryan, at a show. He's a stand-up bassist in a band. I went with some girls from the program. They just kind of dragged me along, you know? Ryan was nice. Took me out, paid, opened doors. And then as soon as I put out, he stops answering his phone."

I winced. "That fucking sucks."

"Tell me about it." She swirled the ruby liquid in her glass. "I'll be fine. I just…someday, I keep hoping I'll meet a guy who's after more from me than… that." I opened my mouth to speak, but she wasn't done. "You know, it's not like I'm going home with these guys on the first date, either. I give it time, you know? I try to be smart. I try to make sure they seem like decent guys. And they always seem that way, right until I get burned. And I get fooled every time. I mean, is it the way I look? What is it about me that makes me such an easy target?"

"Maybe they're just douchebags."

"Yeah, that's a given. But there's got to be something about me. I mean, a couple times, okay, bad luck. But an ongoing problem? Every time I date a guy, this happens." She was halfway through her second glass already, and we hadn't gotten our food yet.

I had no idea what to say. "Maybe…I don't know. Maybe don't…go there at all? I mean, not *never*, just see how much patience the guy has. If he sticks around for a while without that, then maybe he's actually interested in you."

Something about this conversation was making me want to hide, run, talk about anything else. It was too much; it was wrong somehow. I shouldn't hear this about her. I didn't want to know.

Eden laughed. "Yeah, that seems great in theory. Not so easy to do in practice."

"Yeah, I guess it wouldn't be."

"Sorry," Eden said, pouring her third glass. "This is probably TMI. But you *did* ask."

"Yeah, I did. It's okay. We're friends. We can talk about things, right?"

She peered at me, her gaze sharp. "Is that what we are? Friends?" Her tone suggested doubt.

I didn't like where this was going. "What else would we be?"

She drank yet more, too much, too fast. Our food arrived and she dug in, answering after her first mouthful. "I don't know. But 'friends' isn't the right word."

"Why not?" I asked.

"You choose friends, right? You meet someone, recognize something in them that you like, that you identify with." She gestured between us with her fork. "You and me? We're something I don't think English has a word for. We're thrown together by life. My sister is your wife, but…brother-in-law, sister-in-law, that just describes the…the on-paper way we're connected. It doesn't describe the way our lives have intertwined. You know? How our journeys have intersected. We're fate-companions. Path-mates. That's something. It's more than friends. Even good friends, you hold things back. You share good times, bad times. Get drunk together, maybe fight about something. But this? You and me, bonding over Ever's coma? It's something else. Something… thicker, realer than all of that. Does that make any sense to you? Would we be friends if it weren't for Ever? I mean, are we even compatible, as people? I don't know. Yes, sometimes. No, sometimes." She was rambling, but it was coherent, coming from some raw truthful place, drawn out or let free by the wine.

I set my glass down, not daring to drink any more. "I get what you're saying."

"But there's more, isn't there?" Eden wasn't done. She ate, spoke, drank, repeat. On a roll, unstoppable.

"You know there is. I've blurted shit about myself that I wouldn't even to friends. I have friends. At school. I do. People I play music with. We drink together sometimes. Talk about life. Philosophy. Movies. Guys. Typical college girl bullshit. Classes, profs, music. Always music. We talk about entire movements, try to describe how it feels to let the music rule you. It's different for everyone, you know. But it's not…it's not real. With them. I wouldn't ever tell them how I feel about my body. I hide that. I act like I'm confident. I dress confident. I *am* confident, most days. But when the doubt hits, it's all-powerful. It's like depression, but worse. I should know, because I get depressed, too, but that's separate. I get it from Mom. Ever does, too. Or…did. She'd lock herself away and paint until it passed. When she was in her studio for, like, days without eating or anything? That's her depression. For me, I play through it. But that's just…a Band-Aid. Not a fix." She poured the last of the bottle.

"Just so you know, I'm not gonna stop anytime soon." She held up the wine glass. "I'm getting wasted. It's what I do now. How I deal. If Ever was…around, I'd see her. We'd watch *Love Actually* or *Notting Hill* or *Sleepless in Seattle*. Eat ice cream and cheesy chips and salad with lots of ranch and shredded cheese and drink, like, a gallon of wine, and she'd make sure I'd snap out of it. Now…I think I'll just skip right to the wine."

"I'm not Ever—"

"No shit, Sherlock."

I ignored that. "But we could watch a movie. Under the circumstances, I could probably stomach a chick flick. If…if it'll help."

She peered at me. "Why? Why would you do that? Help me get over some asshole after I've been humped-and-dumped?"

"Well" —I wasn't sure why, myself— "because, friends or not, or whatever you want to call this, like you said, we're all we've got. And I like ice cream."

So we ended up at the condo. After stopping for another bottle of wine and mint chocolate chip Breyers. The whole time, my head was telling me to take her home, that someone else could help her through it. That she'd get drunk and pass out and wake up and deal with it, same as she always did.

Instead, we watched *How to Lose a Guy in Ten Days*, and Ever got colossally wasted. I sat on the opposite edge of the couch and got more slowly and more carefully tipsy. We didn't talk, just laughed and drank and passed the gallon of ice cream back and forth, each of us with our own spoon.

She fell asleep at some point, and I left her there, covered her with a blanket. Only, she woke up, sat up, peered at me blearily. "Hot. Gotta pee." She lurched to her feet, stumbled three steps sideways. I caught her, held her by the shoulder and guided her into the bathroom. She stood facing the toilet, swaying in place. Then she glanced at me with one eye. "This could be tricky. Too many toilets."

"Need help?" I was tired, more drunk than I wanted to be, but not enough to let me be unaware of the tension coiled between us even now.

She turned slowly in place. "Nah. I got it. I think."

I turned away as she fumbled with her jeans. I rummaged in the kitchen, hunting for aspirin. When I found it and a glass of water, Eden was stumbling out of the bathroom, tripping over her jeans, which were trailing behind her, stuck on one ankle. She was wearing a red thong. I looked away, blinking to clear my head of the image. I had known this was a bad idea. I could handle it, though. It was fine. I kept my eyes on the wall, the floor, the thin fabric of her Cold War Kids concert T-shirt. Handed her the aspirin and the water, not once looking down.

"Thanks," she mumbled, but I had to catch her as she swayed in place while drinking, spilling the water down her front. "Shit. Now I'm wet."

"You could borrow a shirt." I didn't say whose, because we both knew whose.

"'Kay." She lurched to the couch, flopped onto it. "God, I'm hammered."

"No kidding."

"You mad, bro?" she asked, then giggled as if that was a joke.

I shook my head and wove carefully into my bedroom, stood with my hand on the knob of Ever's T-shirt drawer. It hadn't been opened in months. I didn't want to open it. I did anyway, and found a shirt Ever had often worn with comfy pants, a loose, soft orange V-neck. I brought it out to Eden, and immediately regretted it. She was facing me, her shirt half off, struggling comically to get it off while swaying drunkenly.

I swallowed hard, kept my eyes on her dyed blonde hair, helped her get her shirt off. "Here." I set the clean shirt on her lap without looking.

"Thanks." She was in bra and panties, in my living room.

Red push-up bra, red thong. Nothing else. Why? Why had I noticed what kind of bra she was wearing? I turned away and moved toward my room, needing to either sleep or drink more.

"Wait...I'm—I'm stuck. I can't reach." I sighed, turned back around, staring at Ever's painting on the wall. Eden was standing up, spinning in place as she tried to unhook her bra.

God, no. No. There was no way in hell I was helping her with that. "I...um. Just leave it on?"

She groaned in frustration. "I can't. I need it off. I can't sleep in a bra. Just unhook it. That's it."

I closed my eyes and counted to ten. I wanted to sleep. I didn't want this situation. I stopped breathing and closed my eyes, and reached for the red hook-and-eyelets. Only, I couldn't do it without looking. As soon as the last hook was freed, Eden had the bra off and was tossing it on the floor, and she was between me and my room, and there was nowhere I could go to get away from her. I turned around, but Eden was giggling, laughing, and I risked a glance to see that she'd fallen down. White skin, red thong, curves, blonde hair, her laughter, drunk and silly. I turned away, fished a beer from the fridge, and wrestled the twist-top until my palm was bleeding, only to realize it was a pop-off, and Eden was still on her hands and knees, crawling toward the clean shirt, which had ended up across the room somehow, and now she had it, and as much as I tried to look away, knew I should, I couldn't. She was sitting cross-legged on the floor, the shirt on her lap, her spine straight. All of her, on display. Her eyes on me. Watching me, her gaze swimming but lucid. It was one of those moments that you can't ignore, can't ever forget; you know in the moment that it's occurring that it means something significant.

She stared at me, and my eyes were on hers, on her eyes, green and somehow haunted, staring at me with a wealth of emotion that I couldn't decipher and didn't dare try to. I couldn't help but see her. Her bare breasts, full and swelling with each slow breath.

I was frozen and I couldn't breathe, couldn't look away, knew I'd never unsee this.

And then I managed to blink and break the spell and flee to my room, beer open and untouched.

Eden

I came to consciousness but didn't open my eyes while I took inventory. Drunk. Still had my panties on, which meant I hadn't had sex. Probably. Wasn't wearing pants, or a bra. I was on a couch. I opened my eyes and glanced around, and it took me a minute to realize I was in Cade's apartment, on his couch. I looked down at myself. I was wearing Ever's favorite comfy-clothes T-shirt.

Everything came back in a flash. Dinner. Spilling about Ryan. Getting drunk. Watching *How to Lose a Guy in Ten Days*, and getting even more hammered. Mint chocolate chip Breyers—my favorite kind.

Stripping in front of Cade.

Sitting on the floor in nothing but my tiny red *got dumped and need to feel sexy* thong, staring at Cade, his eyes warring between my eyes and my tits, his emotions clearly a raging mess of contradictions. I'd seen anger at me, confusion, and, yes, desire.

But surely that was just because I looked like Ever. I was her twin, and he was seeing her in me, and probably hating me for the reminder.

I sat up, which was a mistake. My head swam, my stomach lurched. Oh, god. Wine hangover. So fucking horrible. There was a hot spike being driven through my skull. I groaned and wished, not for the first time, that I could go back and undo the previous night's events.

"Headache?" I heard Cade's voice. I nodded, which hurt. I felt his hand brush my shoulder, and opened my eyes to see his palm in front of me, containing two aspirin, and a glass of water in the other hand. He wasn't looking at me. Probably couldn't bear to.

"Thanks," I said, after taking the pills and drinking all of the water. I glanced up at him, squinting in the bright sunlight streaming through the windows. "So. Do you have a hole I can borrow?"

He finally looked down at me in confusion. "Hole?"

I shrugged and tried to smile, didn't quite succeed at it, either. "To crawl into and disappear."

He turned away, went to the kitchen, and started making coffee. God bless him for that. "Why would you need to crawl into a hole?"

I found my jeans on the floor, leaned forward, and snagged them, tugged them on. "Last night was—god, I'm so embarrassed—"

"Shit happens. Nothing to talk about. Nothing happened." He bit out the words brusquely, harshly. Obviously he didn't believe that any more than I did.

I saw my bra on the floor as well, and set about putting it on without taking off my shirt. Ever's shirt. He turned to look at me while I was in the middle of this process and promptly spun back around, rattling dishes in the sink. When I was dressed completely, I gathered my courage and went into the kitchen. The Keurig sputtered, and he pushed the mug of coffee toward me, gestured at the cream and sugar he'd already gotten out, then set about making his own coffee.

After a careful sip, I touched Cade's shoulder. He glanced at me, stepped back out of reach. It wasn't even a disguised move—he simply moved away so I couldn't touch him, so I wasn't so close. "Look, Cade, I'm not into pretending nothing happened. It did. I got drunk and made an idiot of myself. I don't really have any excuse, and I'm sorry."

He shrugged, setting the Keurig to brew a second time, filling his mug the rest of the way. "It's fine. It happens."

I didn't think I'd get much more from him. "It was stupid of me. I shouldn't have—it shouldn't have happened." I ducked my head, sipping my coffee. "That's just…me, though. It's how I am when I get drunk. I get overheated and…when I decide I'm gonna go to sleep, I end up taking my clothes off and—"

Cade swore, setting his coffee down. "Burned my mouth," he explained. His eyes, however, spoke of…

remembering. "We're both adults, right? It happened. No big deal. Let's just move on."

"Right."

"Okay." I finished my coffee and he took me back to my car, which had a parking ticket, and I went home.

I noticed, in the days that followed, that he was even more reserved around me, keeping his eyes on mine, or, more likely, anywhere *but* me. Oddly, our Sunday and Tuesday dinners continued, but he was careful to never drink more than one glass of wine, and so was I. We established a status quo, and never talked about that night again.

I wondered if he remembered any of the things I'd said while I was drunk.

I knew I did.

letters unsent; cutting loose

Caden

Ever,

School starts in a week. I'm registered for four classes. Talked with a counselor about the best way to make up for the lost time. That was his phrase: "make up for lost time." I heard that phrase and I hated it, hated him for saying it. Lost time.

You can't make up for what's lost. Especially not time. This time that you're gone, we'll never get it back. It's lost. Time with you, lost. Love and life with you, lost.

I don't want to move on, act like things are fine, like life continues. It doesn't. But it has to, right? So I'm registered for classes, and I'm going to focus on making up credit hours and finishing this degree. Not long to go, really. Six semesters, I think? Not much.

My hand is back to normal finally. Or as normal as it can get, I think. It'll never be the way it was.

Oh, hell. Nothing will ever be the way it was. I won't, you won't. You may never BE again, period. I lose hope sometimes. I can't help it. I try—I fight against it. Every day, hour by hour, I fight to keep hoping, to keep believing you'll wake up. But sometimes I lose hope. I start to wonder if you will. If you'll just lie there in that bed, growing old without really living, and I'll visit you, and love you, and it'll be some kind of life lived in limbo. That's what this feels like, life lived in limbo. But I hope, even if I have to fight for it. You are my love, my best friend, my forever. And you WILL wake up. You have to, because I can't keep up this limbo act forever. Something will have to change, somehow, someday.

I love you so much, Ever. I miss you. Dear Jesus, I miss you. Come back to me.

For forever, and after forever,

Caden

My hand trembled as I folded the letter I'd written to her just yesterday, tucked it into the envelope marked, simply, "EVER," and put the envelope into the shoebox. It was a new box, from a pair of heels she'd bought a few months before the accident but never got around to wearing. Black heels, low, strappy, with little pieces of fake crystal on the straps. She'd have looked so sexy in them, the way heels made her legs look like they went on forever.

God, she was like this frail thing in the huge bed now. Like she was vanishing day by day.

I'd forgotten the sound of her voice. I called her voicemail just to hear it, but the mailbox was full and I couldn't even hear the recording. I cried then. Briefly, quietly, in the bathroom of my condo.

It was *my* condo now. Not *our*. But her things were still there, just…out of sight. I'd put her sweater away, her shoes. Put it all in the closet. Cleaned up once in a while, and when I cleaned, a few more of her things would get put away, out of sight. I left her paintings up, left her clothes in their drawers, hung up on their hangers in her half of the closet. Left her makeup container on the counter, her shampoo and conditioner in the shower, her lotion on our dresser.

Sometimes I opened the cap of the lotion and sniffed. Inhaled the scent of Ever.

Now, in her room at the nursing home, I closed the top of the box and set it on the little stand next to her bed. The box was filling with letters. An envelope per letter, unaddressed but for her name, bundled together with all the letters I wrote her each week, and again with those belonging to each month. So far there were three months' worth of bundled letters. I didn't write her every day. Sometimes twice a week, sometimes four or five times. Sometimes I'd write her two letters in one day. Those were the days when I missed her so badly I wanted to just crawl onto the bed beside her and sleep beside her forever, just quit trying to pretend it was okay, that I was okay, that ANYTHING was okay.

I never did, though. If I lay down beside her, I knew I'd never leave. I didn't have the courage to keep living. All I had was force of habit. Wake up, out of habit. Eat breakfast. Get dressed. Go to class. Eat lunch. Go to class. Sketch. Sketch. Eat dinner. Go to bed. Repeat.

I needed something else in my life. Something not class, not the condo, and not the nursing home. "The Home," as Eden and I both referred to it. I even envisioned the capital "H." The Home. *Have you been to the Home yet today?* she'd ask me via text. I'd call her from my car: *I'm on my way to the Home.*

Never *to visit Ever.*

After class one Monday, I decided to get a job. Something exhausting. Something that I'd not be able to think while doing. I spent two weeks filling out applications and going to interviews before I found something that filled my criteria: unloading in a UPS warehouse. It was perfect. It fit my limited hours, being from 5 p.m. to 8 p.m. Monday through Friday, and it paid enough to be worth the time I spent there. And it was hard work, nonstop motion for three hours straight. I'd clock in at five exactly, hit the first truck in line, step into the diamond-plate interior and grab boxes, throw them down the move-able chute, one after another. Empty the truck, push the chute to the next truck, empty it. Repeat at top speed until there were no more trucks left.

While I was unloading, I was able to turn off my brain, lock out my heart, and simply *move*. My arm and my leg always ached at the end of the shift, but I'd gotten clearance from my doctor before taking the job. No one talked to me while I was unloading, except for the occasional checkup from Rick, the supervisor, or a quick hello from the driver. I worked in silence, in solitude.

I took to visiting Ever after my shift, which was a good thing, since it meant I'd be able to visit her on my own, as Eden had class until nine every day this semester. I was actively avoiding her at this point. I didn't want to be rude about it, but it was simply necessary. After the episode in my living room, it was just too weird, too strained to see her very often. We still had dinner together on Sundays after a joint visit to the Home, but that was it, and I never let those dinners stray out of the restaurant itself, never let conversation go anywhere serious.

There was something dangerous about Eden, about the way we were together when we let our guards down.

This became the new norm. Life settled into a pattern, which was its own comfort in a way. Fall semester progressed, and I completed some new pieces for my portfolio. After the accident, after I got the use of my right hand back, my style as an artist shifted. Before, I'd done largely still-lifes, nature scenes, hands, eyes. I'd even started experimenting with hyperrealism, the kind of pieces you see online, like, *this is a drawing, not a photograph kind* of thing. Now, simply due to the shift in my muscles and the need to basically relearn how to use my hand, I found my style and subject matter changing.

I drew a grinning white skull, snakes curling through the eye sockets, the background black but writhing with shadowy shapes not quite visible. A rosebush, floating in a stormy sky. A tornado, held in a palm. Dark imagery, distorted viewpoints and twisted perspective.

Thanksgiving was a non-affair. I bought a small precooked rotisserie chicken from Costco, ate it alone. Eden came by, and we watched the Lions game, ate some of the pumpkin pie she'd brought with her. Avoided discussing the pathetic nature of our holiday.

Eden's dad called her phone while she was over, and she ignored it. I glanced at her, watched her check the screen of her phone, sigh, and hit the "ignore" button, stuff it back in her purse. It rang twice more, and she deleted the voicemails without listening to them.

I should have said something. I knew I should. He was her father. But I remembered the fight Ever and I had gotten in about this very subject, and Ever was far more even-tempered than Eden.

"Say it already," Eden said, dipping a tortilla chip into the salsa. "I can feel you stewing over there."

"I'm not stewing."

"Yes, you are. And I know why. I'm not gonna answer. I don't want to see him."

I held up my hands. "I didn't say anything."

"But you were thinking it."

I blew out a frustrated breath. "Yeah. He's your dad. He's all you have." Before she could say anything, I continued. "Look, I know there's history there. The worst argument Ever and I got into was about this, and I learned my lesson. It's your business. But…family is important."

She nodded and shrugged simultaneously. "Yeah. True. But I don't really have him, do I? He made a tiny little effort after the accident happened. He visited me at school once, visited Ever a couple of times. Then he vanished again. He's a coward, Cade. He can't handle grief. I haven't seen him in months. He hasn't visited Ever at the Home once. Not once. She's his *daughter*, and he doesn't visit her. I know it's hard. Obviously I do, but he *owes* it to her, to me. If he made an effort, I'd be there. I'd forgive him, best I can. But he's not, okay? He's not trying. So I don't want to talk to him, I'm not going to his house. Not now, not for Christmas, not at all. Not until he proves he's willing to try." She set the salsa on the coffee table and brushed her hands together, stood up. "And he's not gonna do that, so…fuck it. Fuck it, and fuck him."

She went into the kitchen, rummaged in my fridge. More for an excuse to get away from me, to hide her emotions than anything, I think. She came back with two beers and hurt, angry eyes.

"Fair enough," I said, taking one. "Happy Thanksgiving, huh?"

"Yeah. Happy fucking Thanksgiving." She held out her bottle, and we clinked.

We finished the game, ate more chicken. Watched *Skyfall*. Drank more beer. I'd picked up a case of Harp lager on the way home from work the day before Thanksgiving, which, in hindsight, was probably a mistake. I'd intended to make it last for a few weeks, one or two every once in a while, when I had a hard time getting to sleep. Just a couple of beers to take the edge off.

Only now we were each three beers in, and I was putting on my dad's aged DVD copy of *Dr. No*. That led to two more beers each, and *From Russia With Love*. There was little conversation, as was typical with Eden and me during movies. It was strange for me. Ever had been chatty during movies. She liked to cuddle close to me and talk throughout the whole thing, a constant chatter about the movie, about the actor or actress, about school or her latest piece or whatever was on her mind. I'd learned to listen to her with half an ear, her running commentary simply part of watching a movie with Ever.

Eden, she sat on the opposite side of the couch, leaning against the arm with her knees tucked underneath her to one side, beer in her left hand, dipping into a bag of veggie sticks with the other. She kept her mouth shut, watched the movie, and that was that. It was odd. We were there together, but it wasn't really like two friends watching movies together, nor like boyfriend–girlfriend.

As she'd said that night she got naked-wasted, we were something that didn't fit into any easy category, something I didn't have a word for.

After *From Russia With Love* ended, I made my way to the bathroom, breaking the seal after seven beers. I was tipsy. Maybe more than tipsy. Time to eat something. I put together leftover turkey sandwiches while Eden did something on her phone. I turned on *Goldfinger*. We washed the sandwiches down with… yes, more beer. This was a bad idea. I knew it but didn't care. It felt good to be loose, to let myself go a little. I kept myself under tight rein most of the time.

Kept my emotions locked up, kept to my routine and never altered. Keeping the routine was how I kept going, day after day, without Ever.

But sometimes you had to cut loose. And it was just more fun, more satisfying to cut loose with someone else than it was by yourself. Getting drunk alone was shitty. I'd learned that the hard way.

Ever got up, visited the bathroom, and when she came back and sat down, it wasn't on the opposite end of the couch. She sat next to me, space between us, but closer than normal.

I got up, got more beer, sat down, and the space between us shrank again. The food had reduced the intensity of my buzz, but now it was coming back. I should slow down, I tried to tell myself. But I didn't.

It was past midnight, and we'd been watching movies since three in the afternoon. There was no school the next morning for either of us, so I put in *Thunderball* and got two more beers. I was definitely drunk at that point, having to focus on each step, each motion. I sat down carefully, and as my weight hit the couch, Eden fell sideways into me. I didn't push her away, and she didn't sit up.

I closed one eye after a while, and decided I was done. I finished the beer, realized I'd lost count. I knew there were only, like, four beers left—or was it two?—which meant I had to have had eight? Ten? Too many. I felt great. Dizzy, loose, emotionally numb.

A little heavy, though, and a little tired. I stuffed a throw pillow behind me and slid down, laying my head on the armrest. Somehow, Eden went with me, and now she was between me and the back of the couch. There was something odd about that, about the fact that she had her head on my chest. I couldn't quite remember what it was that was so odd about this position, though. It was comfortable. Comforting. It had been far, far too long since I'd felt this kind of physical comfort.

My left arm was going numb, squished by Eden, so I wiggled it free and draped it over her shoulders.

"You produce a lot of body heat," she mumbled.

"I'm kinda drunk." I wasn't sure if that was meant to be an admission or an answer to her non sequitur.

"Me, too."

After a while, the credits rolled.

"One more?" I asked.

"Sure."

Except neither of us moved to get up. My eyes drooped, sagged, closed, and I let them close. I heard the home screen repeating, and cracked an eye open enough to find the "off" button for the TV, then dropped the remote on the floor. Felt myself float away, enjoying the warmth of another body near mine, a head on my chest, hair tickling my nose. A soft body pressed against mine. Somewhere in the back of my head, a tiny voice whispered, but the words were lost in the haze of onrushing sleep. It was something about Eden, about falling asleep like this. Something about *bad idea*.

I let myself float, ignoring the voice, unable and unwilling to move. The room spun, my head spun, but Eden kept me rooted to the couch, kept me from spinning away.

Sleep hit, sucked me in.

I woke up suddenly, having to pee. The clock on the cable box said 3:10 in red letters. I slid out from beneath Eden, stumbled to the bathroom. I was still really, *really* drunk. Maybe more so than when I fell asleep. I found some aspirin, washed them down with handfuls of water.

Eden shuffled into the bathroom while I was slurping water from my palms, and I didn't think it was strange how she didn't wait until I'd left the bathroom to pee.

"That couch is not very comfortable," I said. "I've never slept there before."

"No. It's really not," Eden agreed as she washed her hands. Water sloshed everywhere, and she fumbled the hand towel, dropped it on the floor.

We both bent to reach for it, bumped heads. Laughed, hanging onto each other for balance as we each held our foreheads. I blinked away the dizzy throb and saw that Eden was watching me, rubbing her head idly.

"Do I have to sleep on the couch?" she asked.

I shrugged. "I'm too drunk to care." I stumbled into my room, leaving Eden in the bathroom.

I changed into a pair of gym shorts, no shirt, and slipped into bed. I felt the other side dip, and felt Eden wiggle under the covers.

"Is this a bad idea?" she asked.

I felt warm skin brush against my leg briefly, and I wondered if she was wearing pants. "Yeah," I said. "It probably is."

"I'll stay over here," she said, rolling away from me.

"Me, too," I said, rolling the other way.

Only it didn't work that way. I never slept deeply when I was drunk. It was a weird idiosyncrasy of mine, but I always woke up a dozen times. The first time I woke up, Eden was curled up against me, shivering, the blankets on her side tangled and twisted away. I tugged them back over her and slipped back toward sleep, trying subtly to slide away, to give her space. She shifted closer, and I fell asleep with Eden's hair tickling my chin, her face pressed against my arm. Her hand on my chest. Her thigh brushing mine.

Definitely not wearing pants.

Every time I woke up, we were tangled more together, and I was still too drunk and too sleepy to do anything about it.

When I woke up the next morning, sun was streaming through my window, and the clock read 10:52 a.m. I couldn't remember the last time I'd slept that late. I didn't remember the last time I'd slept that *well*. For once, and despite my burgeoning hangover, I felt more rested than I had in months. Eden was draped completely over me, head in the nook of my shoulder, leg over one of mine, arm across my stomach.

She snored, just a little.

A bolt of panic shot through me, along with a rush of desperation. I *needed* this. It felt wrong, but right.

It was comfort. For the first time since the accident, I didn't feel so horribly, miserably alone. Nothing had happened but sleep. I knew that. And yet…there was guilt. This was wrong.

Eden snorted, stirred, stretched against me. And then, like a cartoon or a movie, her hand touched my skin, my chest, my face. Her leg shifted. She was taking stock, realizing where she was, and then she gasped, realizing with whom.

"Shit." Her voice was rough, scratchy with sleep.

"Yeah."

Neither of us had moved. My arm was still around her shoulder. Thank god she was wearing a shirt.

"You and I should *not* get drunk together," Eden said.

"No, we shouldn't," I agreed.

"I slept *really* well." Eden stretched against me, and I hated myself for liking, more than a little, the way her breasts crushed into my chest. I hated myself for almost needing the physical contact, for not wanting to let go, to get out of bed.

"Me, too."

"You have anywhere to be?"

"Work at five. You?"

She shook her head. "Nah."

My eyes were still heavy, and I felt myself drowsing again. "Should get up," I mumbled.

She moaned, stretching again, and now her thigh slid over mine, hot and heavy and soft. "Why?"

"'Cause this...it's—"

"I know," she interrupted. "It is. But...not yet. I like not feeling alone."

"Me, too."

We slept again.

When I woke up, I was on my side, facing the middle of the bed. My head was partially on the pillow, and mostly on Eden's shoulder. My hand was touching flesh. Her shirt was hiked up, baring her stomach, the blankets shoved down around her hips. She was wearing blue underwear, not a thong this time, but the kind that were cut high up around her legs, a long, deep "V" of fabric. My hand was on her hipbone, my leg across hers.

Not good.

I glanced at the clock: 4:55 p.m. Shit. Shitshitshit. I rolled over and grabbed my phone from where I had, at some point last night, plugged it in. I called work, explained that I was running late, started apologizing.

Rick interrupted me. "Actually, I was gonna send you back home when you got here. It's dead today. Shitty weather, slow pickups. I'm gonna run a skeleton crew. So just stay home, bud. And thanks for calling in."

I had never, not in my entire life, slept so much. The only time I'd ever been in bed at five o'clock in the afternoon was sex. And as that thought ran through my head, I felt my body waking up. It wasn't morning, but I had morning wood, and Eden was pressed against me, her leg just beneath my groin, her hand on my stomach, low, dangerously low. She'd rolled with me when I moved to grab my phone, and now she was waking up and stretching. She was very…feline when she stretched. She groaned in satisfaction, arching her back, muscles shivering, and then her hand fell back down across me. Right on top of my accidental erection.

I felt her freeze. I glanced down at her, shifting away from her, going red with embarrassment. "Sorry. God, sorry—"

She colored, too, shrugged. "It's fine. It's natural. I didn't mean to—to…" She was talking, explaining, but she hadn't moved her hand.

I grabbed her wrist and pushed her hand away. I was painfully hard, her touch having catalyzed something inside me. I'd been fairly successful at forgetting that aspect of life. I'd focused on work, on school, on art, on anything except the ache inside me, the occasional throb of my body and the need, on some molecular level, for release that I'd never get.

And now, after one accidental touch, all that was reawakened, and I was pulsating, aching with need.

I slid out of bed, turning away to hide the fact that my shorts were tented. "I'm gonna…um. Make some coffee."

Eden watched me; I felt her eyes on me. "Sounds…" Her voice cracked. "Sounds good."

I had to pee, but that was impossible at the moment. Eden stayed in bed while I went into the kitchen, and I spent the next few minutes trying to put any thought into my head that I could, anything that would ease the throbbing hardness. It wasn't working. I kept seeing Eden's face, feeling her body as we slept, and then, fucking hell, I saw her as she'd been that night a few months ago, right over there. Sitting cross-legged on my living room floor, flushed, topless, eyes on me. That was *not* helping. I ran cold water and scrubbed my face, but then I just had a clean face and was still painfully erect.

I had one recourse, I decided. I poked my head around the doorpost, caught a glance of Eden in my bed, scrolling through her phone. "I made coffee. Yours is on the counter. I'm gonna take a shower."

She didn't look up, just nodded. "'Kay."

I made my way to the en suite bathroom, shut the door behind me, ran the water hot as I could stand it. I tried to bring up an image of Ever. I thought of her sitting on our bed, naked, rubbing lotion on her body. I visualized her, saw her clearly, imagined her eyes on mine, imagined her beckoning me to her, kissing my chest as I stood between her thighs. I imagined it was her hand on my cock as I touched myself. I hadn't done this in years, not since I was a horny teenager with Internet access and no adult supervision. I'd not needed to, not after I met Luisa, and then Ever.

I closed my eyes and pictured Ever's hand around my cock, stroking me. But…as I furthered the fantasy, imagined her fair skin and swaying tits, somehow Ever's black hair was blonde, and her eyes a slightly lighter shade of green, and her body as I pictured it was a little curvier, her breasts bigger and the areolae wider and darker, and suddenly it was Eden I was seeing in my head, and then I came, all over the wall of the shower, stream after stream, and I felt dirty, felt horrible, felt confused and guiltier than ever.

I finished my shower, but even though my body was clean, I felt dirty inside. I wrapped a towel around my waist and wished I'd thought to bring clean clothes in with me. Eden had left the bedroom, thank god. I didn't think I could meet her eyes, not after what had just happened.

I dropped my towel and stood in the doorway to the bathroom scrubbing my hair dry. Only, when I tossed the towel aside and stepped into the bedroom to get my clothes, Eden was standing in the doorway with a mug of coffee in each hand and a surprised expression on her face.

"I—I—" Her gaze flicked up to my face, and then back down. She was still in her T-shirt and underwear.

I was in the middle of the bedroom, no towel, all my clothes on the other side of the room. She was staring at me, stunned into paralysis, and so was I. Her gaze had me twitching down below, and I had to do something. I had to get away from her gaze, from the obvious desire I saw in her eyes.

I turned around, forcing myself to move, and then I heard her close the door. I dressed quickly, and when I emerged, Eden was dressed as well and putting on her coat.

"I'm—I should go." Her coffee was untouched on the counter.

"Eden, listen, it was an accident." Why was I protesting her departure? She absolutely should go. We'd slept in the same bed. We'd now seen each other naked.

"Yeah, I know. I'm sorry, I—" She shrugged, clearly at a loss for words.

What I couldn't seem to ignore, couldn't seem to dispute the significance of, was that she hadn't looked away immediately. Hadn't turned around. She'd kept looking.

"Just…finish your coffee." I couldn't seem to stop the words from tumbling out. "We're both adults. It was an accident."

"Now we're even," she said, trying to lessen the awkwardness with a joke.

She shed her coat and sat down at the table, wrapped her hands around the mug. I had a flash of the fantasy I'd had in the shower, of hands wrapping around me, Eden's hands. I blinked hard, wondering what the hell was wrong with me.

Eden was watching me, and I couldn't help but wonder if my thoughts were obvious. If somehow she could see what I'd been thinking, what had happened in the shower.

"Are you okay?" she asked.

I shrugged. "Yeah. Fine."

"Why don't I believe you?"

I went for broke. "We keep…crossing the line. Pushing the line further and further."

Eden closed her eyes briefly, and then opened them and met my own with a frank, conflicted expression. "Is there a line, though? And what is it? Where is it?"

"I don't know. But last night—"

"We slept in the same bed. That was it." She traced the rim of her mug with her index finger.

"It was more than that, though. Wasn't it?"

She shrugged. "Maybe. Sure. But…we didn't do anything wrong." She seemed like she was trying to convince herself more than me. "We're both…going through a lot, and we were drunk."

"Anytime alcohol is involved, one of us ends up seeing the other naked," I pointed out.

"Both times were accidents."

"And both times, we were both…slow to look away."

"We're lonely. And you've got to be…frustrated."

"That's no reason for—"

Eden stood up, a quick, angry movement that sent her chair skidding across the floor. "Quit tearing yourself up, Cade! We slept in the same bed. We held each other. It was mutual comfort. It's fine. We're fine. You're fine." She sighed. "Look, I'm confused, too, okay? But both of us feeling guilty all the time, about this, about whatever…this…is between you and me…I can't live that way. And neither can you."

She finished her coffee, set the mug in the sink, and put on her coat. "I'm going. And I'll be honest. I had a good time last night. I slept better than I have in months, and I don't think that's any accident."

On impulse, halfway out the door, she turned back, crossed the space between us, and wrapped her arms around my neck, hugging me. I stood in shock for a moment, and then my arms went around her, embraced her in return.

"You're…you're all I've got, Eden," I whispered into her hair, "and I don't want to mess that up. And I can't betray Ever."

She breathed deeply. "I know. You're all I have, too, and you haven't betrayed anyone."

Not yet, I thought as she finally, actually left.

Not yet.

song of mourning

Eden

Snow arrived around mid-December, and I found myself constantly wondering how Cade was doing. If he was having trouble driving in the snow. If he was going to have a breakdown on the one-year anniversary of the accident, which was in less than two weeks.

We'd been chaste and careful ever since Thanksgiving. No physical contact, no movie nights, no alcohol. I was so conflicted about that. Part of me had relished it. Had felt nearly whole while he held me. Had slept like a baby in his arms. And the next day, when he got out of the shower…I'd wanted him. I'd been able to admit that much to myself.

I shouldn't, because he wasn't mine, but I did, and there was no point denying it.

And…there was something deep in the darkest corner of my soul, whispering to me. Musing, wondering. Asking *what if.* I denied those thoughts. Kept visiting Ever at the Home, talking to her, playing for her. Hoping she'd wake up. But I wondered, deep down, late at night alone, what would happen if she never did. What that would mean for Cade. For… me.

And then I berated myself and hated myself. Exorcised the guilt with hours of penance at the cello. Composing. One good thing that had come from all this turmoil and conflict surrounding my bizarre relationship with Cade was that it was all being changed and turned into music, catalyzing inspiration. My cello solo composition was flowing, movement after movement flying out of me whole cloth.

The day before the one-year anniversary, I texted Cade. *What are you doing tomorrow?*

He responded after a few minutes. **IDK. Visiting Ever?**

Together?

Sure.

We met in the parking lot. It was snowing hard, the way it had that day. Cade looked haunted, staring up at the falling snow as he waited for me to park.

He seemed...lost. The way he'd been immediately after the accident. He nodded at me, not even trying to smile. We went together into Ever's room. I'd decorated it for Christmas. Sprigs of fake holly on the walls, strands of white lights around the perimeter of the ceiling. A tiny tree, multicolored LED lights, standing on the table beside her bed.

Cade sat in one chair, I in the other beside him. Neither of us spoke for a long time. Finally, Cade glanced at me, and then dug an envelope out of his coat pocket. His hands were red with cold, and trembling. I recognized the letter for what it was and started to stand up. He shook his head, put his hand on my arm.

"Stay. I can't...I can't do this alone. Not today." I didn't even think. I threaded my fingers through his and squeezed. He blinked hard, smiled small and sad at me in thanks. He unfolded the letter. "Ever, my love. Today is one year. You've been in a coma for an entire year. Three hundred and sixty-five days unconscious. Gone from me. I don't even know how to hope anymore. How to believe that you're coming back. That you'll wake up. I'll..." His voice cracked, gave out, and he had to pause, try again. "I'll never give up, Ever. I'll visit you every day. No matter what. Until I'm old. Until you're—you're old. I love you, Ever.

"I can't believe it's been a year. One whole year without you. I still…" His voice wavered, but he went on. "I still don't know what I'm doing. Just…going through the motions is all, really. It's all I can do. I miss you so much. I tried to draw you yesterday. I wanted to bring you a sketch, as a Christmas present. But…unless I'm here, it's almost like I don't know what you look like. This you, the you in the bed, it's not you. It doesn't look like you. And I wanted to draw you as you were, before the accident. Before I let this happen. And I couldn't."

"I couldn't." He dropped the letter, sagged forward against the bed, taking her small, thin, lifeless hand in his, sobbing.

I put my hand on his back, held his hand in mine, leaned forward shoulder to shoulder with him, and cried with him. His heartbreak was…ruinous.

When I could take his tears no longer, I unpacked Apollo, brought him into perfect tune, closed my eyes, and summoned the piece I'd written for her.

He quieted as I began to play, a soft stroke across the strings, a high note. Her song was all high, mellow notes. Slow and sorrowful, quick and joyful, lovely, complex and changing. I played it for her. For him. For all three of us. I cried as I played it, for it was a song of mourning. I mourned for her, with my cello. Apollo sang her song, deep-throated notes of sorrow, long, twisted melodies of loss.

As was the case whenever I played here, there was a crowd around the door. The aged residents, doctors, nurses, family members. Some were crying.

"What was that?" Cade asked.

"It's something I wrote. It's called 'Song for Ever.'"

"Is there more?"

"Yeah." I breathed in, called to mind his song, which I'd titled "Cadence." I played it through for him, seeing his face in the deep, tragic notes, the entire movement played on the lower strings. "That was your song."

"Don't stop playing, please?" He couldn't look at me, couldn't seem to lift his head.

"Excuse me?" This was from an old man in a wheelchair, liver spots on his scalp, a few wisps of hair, palsy-trembling hands, sharp, lucid eyes. "I was a cellist. My wife...she loved the fourth suite." He obviously expected I'd know what he meant.

"Which part should I play?" I asked.

He responded without hesitation. "Sarabande. That was her favorite."

I played the fourth suite Sarabande, and then, because once I start playing the suites I just can't stop, I played the Bourée. I watched the old man as I played, and I watched his fingers follow along with mine, watched him sway, watched his face shift in the rapture of a musician.

Eventually I had to stop. When I stilled my bow, the old man beckoned to me. I leaned down to him, and he hugged me.

"Thank you, my dear. My Lily would have been in heaven if she could hear you play." He let go, and wheeled himself away slowly.

I noticed one of the nurses eyeing him in surprise. "What is it?" I asked her.

"Well, it's just that Ralph, he's—his dementia is so bad he often doesn't even know himself most days. He never talks about his wife. I didn't even know he'd been a cellist, and he's been here for ten years." The nurse watched him go, shaking her head in amazement. "Wonders never cease. I've not seen him that lucid, that much himself in all the years he's been here."

"Music can do amazing things," I said.

"That it can," she agreed. "Merry Christmas."

"Merry Christmas," I said to her. When I turned back to Cade, he was sitting up, wiping his face. "Are you okay?" I asked him.

He shrugged. "No. But then, I never am." He stood up. "You want some time?"

I shook my head. "No. That was my time."

I packed Apollo into his case, and we left together. We were tugging on hats, gloves, and scarves when one of the doctors emerged from an office, saw us, and held up a hand to stop us. I didn't like the look on his face, and, judging from Cade's expression, neither did he. I left my scarf unwound, tugged my gloves back off.

"Mr. Monroe, Ms. Eliot, I'm glad I caught you. I've been meaning to speak to you both for some time." He gestured at the office door he'd just left. "Do you have a moment?"

We followed him into his office, each of us taking one of the chairs opposite his desk.

"What is it, Dr. Murphy?" Cade asked, his voice weary.

Dr. Murphy hesitated, straightening already neat stacks of file folders. "Have you thought of Ever's quality of life?"

Cade narrowed his eyes. "Quality of life?"

"Well, yes. Meaning, have you thought about her future, long-term? She's only able to survive with a ventilator and feeding tubes. And sometimes, you have to ask yourself what kind of life that is for her."

"What are you suggesting?" Cade's voice was sharp as razors.

"Merely that you consider all the factors. Ever is not showing any sign of brain activity. It's been a year, and there has been no sign of change. It's true that with the ventilator and feeding tubes she can remain technically alive indefinitely, but…*should* she? She may not, and likely will never, emerge from her coma, Mr. Monroe. That is simply a sad but unavoidable truth. I'm only suggesting that maybe you consider other options. Organ donation, for example. There are waiting lists extending into months and years for healthy organs, and Ever could save many, many lives if you chose to donate her organs."

"Don—donate her *organs?*" Cade asked. "Are you—are you fucking *kidding* me?"

The doctor frowned. "I apologize if that seems harsh, or uncaring. I assure you, I care very much about Ever's welfare. I've been monitoring her condition since the day she arrived, and I only want what's best for her…and for you. Ever is in what we call a persistent vegetative state, or a persistent non-responsive state. We have no way to bring her out of it, no way to know what long-term damage has been done to her brain. In the process of saving her life, the surgeons had to act quickly to stave off what would have been a fatal aneurysm. That, in turn, led to a stroke."

"I know all this, Dr. Murphy. The surgeons told me all this a year ago." Cade spoke carefully, his words clipped and far too calm.

"It's my job to consider all avenues, Mr. Monroe, Ms. Eliot. And I think you should at least consider what would be best for everyone."

I knew Cade well enough to know he was on the verge of throttling Dr. Murphy where he sat. "Thank you, Doctor. We'll keep that in mind." I touched Cade's arm. "Let's go."

Dr. Murphy stood up with us, extended his hand to shake Cade's. "Happy holidays to you both."

Cade ignored the outstretched hand with obvious derision. "Yeah. Happy fucking holidays."

Dr. Murphy dropped his hand. He opened his mouth to speak, but I pushed Cade out the door before he could say anything else. The timing of doctors was sometimes unfathomable.

"Are you going home?" I asked Cade, once we were outside.

"I don't know," he said. Cade stood outside his Jeep, watching the snow fall. He finally turned to look at me. "I can't—I can't go back there. Not today."

"So come home with me. I've got some gin."

He just nodded, and got into his car. I worried about him. He seemed absent, and I wasn't sure he was okay to drive. I didn't stop him, though. I got into my Passat and led the way, out into the evening darkness. The snow was a white veil obscuring all the world. As we drove, I watched him in my rearview mirror. He seemed okay, and then, nearly home, he swerved, slowed, and cut across onto the shoulder. Panic hit me, but he seemed in control, sliding to a stop in the inch-deep accumulation on the shoulder. I jumped out of my car and ran to the passenger side of his Jeep. He fumbled with the lock, and I got in.

The heat was blasting, the interior a sweltering sauna. The radio was off, and Cade was slumped against the steering wheel, hyperventilating. I turned the heat down, cracked my window, put my hand on his back.

"Breathe, Cade. Deep breaths. In and out. Deep breaths."

"I can't—I can't. I thought I could do it, but I can't. The car, it came out of nowhere. I didn't see it. I didn't see it until it was too late. But…maybe if I hadn't overcorrected, she'd…she'd be okay." He'd never talked to me about the accident itself. "I keep seeing it happen. Over and over. The gray Hyundai stuck in the ditch. Spinning. Hitting the asphalt. We flew so far, and then we hit. Right on her side. I wish—I wish it had been mine. Should have been me. I couldn't stop it. We rolled and rolled, and she wasn't screaming. She should be screaming. Why isn't she screaming? She shouldn't be so quiet. There's so much blood. I can see bone, god, her bones. Pieces of bone. Pieces of her…her fucking *head*. Floating in the blood. Why didn't she just *die?* Why did they save her, just to leave her half-alive?"

"Cade, stop, stop." I leaned forward, but he wouldn't look at me. "Stop, Cade. Try to breathe. Try to calm down."

"I CAN'T CALM DOWN!" he screamed, spittle flying from his mouth, eyes manic and wild, wet and red-rimmed. "She's gone! But she's not dead, and I can't mourn and can't forget her and can't move on. I can't bury her, but I can't have her! I can't do anything! I'm coming apart, Eden! I'm going crazy, don't you understand that?" He pulled his hair, rocking back and forth.

I didn't know what to do. He was rocking, rocking, crying, pulling violently at his hair.

"I couldn't get to her. If I could just—just reach her. But I can't. My arm is stuck. Something—something has my arm. She's not crying. Not doing anything. Just lying there. Goddammit, Ever...Ever. No. Wake up. Wake up! WAKE UP!" He looked at me, not seeing me. "She won't wake up. They're taking her, but they won't tell me if she's dead. She's not dead, is she? Just TELL ME!"

I grabbed his shoulders and shook him as hard as I could, desperate to stop him. "CADE! STOP!" I grabbed his face, his stubble-roughened cheeks. "Look at me, Cade."

His eyes found mine. Hope welled. "Ever?"

Oh, that hurt. That hurt like a knife. "No. It's me. It's Eden."

The fading of hope into haunted loss hurt even worse. "Eden?"

I didn't let go of his face, my nose touching his, watching his tortured amber eyes. "Yeah, Cade. It's me, it's Eden. You're okay. Right? You're okay? Come on, Cade, talk to me. Snap out of it."

He blinked. Seemed to crumple. I caught him, held his face against my breast and tangled my fingers in his hair as he sobbed with wrecked abandon. Cars whooshed by intermittently, rocking the Jeep, and Cade wept. His tears wet my shirt, and he clutched my shoulders with bruising strength, shuddering, wracked by the kind of sobs that come from absolute agony.

I held him, stroked his head and his shoulders, his broad back.

He eventually sat up. "Sorry, god—sorry, I just—"

I put my hand over his mouth. "Don't apologize. Never apologize. Not to me."

"I—I—Eden, I can't—I don't know what to do anymore. I don't know how to keep doing this. It's a half-life. It's the worst guilt I've ever felt, but sometimes, I—I wish she'd just died. Wish she'd just die. So I don't have to keep this up, keep pretending to live. I tell myself, one day at a time, but I can't…I can't do it anymore."

"Cade, please, no. Don't talk like that. She'll wake up. She will. Don't give up." I hunted his eyes with mine, saw the horror there, the despondency. "You're not—you're not considering suicide…are you?"

His hesitation was enough to make my stomach heave. "It's not that I want to kill myself. I just don't—I can't keep living like this. I don't want to *die*, I just don't want to be alive anymore, not if this is all it'll ever be."

"You *can't*, Cade. Please. Don't talk like that." I brushed his hair out of his eyes. It was too long, down past his cheekbones. "You have to keep hoping. You have to believe. She'll wake up, Cade. She will."

"SHE WON'T!" The words were a ragged cry. "She won't. She won't."

"She has to."

"What if she doesn't?" He looked at me, desperate for answers, for hope I didn't really feel.

I shrugged miserably. "She will. She will."

He seemed to understand that I didn't have anything else to offer, no more hope, no more reassurance. He stared out the window at the snow. "I hate snow."

"Me, too." A plow truck roared past, thrown snow blattering against the window, salt pelting the door. "We should go. It isn't safe here."

"Okay." He wiped his face, rolled his shoulders, and took a deep breath. "Okay. I'm good. I'm... good."

"I can drive. I'll bring you back to your Jeep later."

"Nah. I'm okay. Promise."

"Do you want me to follow you back to your place? Or are we still going to mine?"

He shrugged. "I can't…I don't want to be alone. And my place…there are too many memories. Especially tonight."

"All right." I leaned into him, wrapped him up in a hug. When we pulled apart, our faces hovered inches apart. I swallowed hard, forced myself to get out of the car. "We're close. Just…drive safe, okay? I'll see you in a minute."

We made it to my dorm without issue. I was on full alert the whole way, watching him in my rearview, paranoid, but he stayed two car-lengths back and kept it between the lines. We parked, and the wind battered us, cut us with slicing shards of snow. Cade took my cello from me, and I let him, although it made me queasy to let anyone else touch it.

My roommate was from Virginia and she was back home for the holidays, so I had the place to myself. When Ever had moved from an apartment into the Cranbrook dorms, I had gone with her. Just to be closer to her. Being so far apart had felt impossible.

Cade gave me Apollo back and I took him with a sigh of relief, set him in his place in my room, then shucked my coat and boots. Cade was sitting on the couch, still in his coat, hat, and scarf. I sat beside him, pulled his hat off, smoothed his hair down. He swallowed, met my eyes.

"Is this okay? Me, being here?"

"Of course. I don't really want to be alone either," I confessed.

"I'm sorry I lost it—"

I shushed him, my hand on his mouth. "Don't. I told you, don't. Not with me." My hand didn't leave his mouth right away, and he stared at me, my hand on his mouth, his eyes wavering.

He let me take his coat, kicked his boots off. Bits of snow melted on the threadbare carpet. "Can you believe that guy?" He rubbed his face, then ran his hands through his hair. "'I think you should let your wife die. And give her organs away. Oh, and merry Christmas.'"

I didn't answer right away. "He was kind of an idiot for bringing that up today, of all days."

Cade's gaze went sharp with suspicion. "You don't…*agree* with him, do you?"

"No! Of course not. I just…I think he had a point in saying that maybe we should at least…*think* about—"

"About what? Killing her off? Letting them harvest her organs?"

"No, Cade. Just…" I trailed off with a sigh. "God, that is what he was suggesting, wasn't it? Just in doctor-speak."

"I read some stories online. About coma patients. People have been in a coma for twenty years and come out of it, just all of a sudden, wake up perfectly aware. I can't just let her go like that. Not when she could come back any day. Any moment, she could wake up."

"But what if it is, like, *twenty* years, Cade? It's been *one* year, and we're both going crazy. This isn't a sustainable life. Not for me, not for you. For you, most of all."

"What do you mean, me most of all?"

I stood up, tossed his boots by the door, and went into the kitchen. I opened the freezer, found the bottle of Bombay Sapphire I'd been saving, poured two fingers each into glasses with ice. And then realized I didn't have anything to mix it with except orange juice. My roommate, however, had a bizarre obsession with Capri Sun. She bought two or three boxes every week, and there was a brand-new box in the fridge. I took out two pouches, cut the tops off, and poured the strawberry-kiwi flavored liquid into the ice and gin. I sat down beside Cade, handing him one of the glasses.

"What is this?"

I shrugged. "Gin and Capri Sun. It's all I had."

He sipped at it. "Surprisingly good."

I laughed. "Gin goes well with just about everything. Especially when it's Sapphire."

"Are you a gin snob?" he teased.

"Absolutely," I said, grinning over my glass. "Wine, pour me a glass of whatever. Beer? Don't care,

I'll drink anything. Whiskey? Yuck. But for whatever reason, the only gin I like is Sapphire. Call me crazy."

"Crazy." We sipped in silence for a few moments. And then Cade leveled a look at me that told me he hadn't forgotten my comment. "What did you mean, me most of all?"

I blew out a long breath. "Just that…you're stuck. You can't go forward. With life. With…love."

"So I'm supposed to pull the plug on her so I can be with someone else? There *is* no one else. She knows everything about me. Knows what I've been through. I could never…I couldn't explain my life to anyone else."

"So you're supposed to live on the edge of nothing indefinitely?" I rubbed at the condensation on my glass. "It's no way to live. You said it yourself." We were both empty already, so I mixed us each a second one.

"But what's the answer? How can I just…give up on her? I can't. Not when there are literally thousands of stories of people coming out of comas, or persistent vegetative states, or whatever." He hung his head, leaning forward with his elbows on his knees. "It's all so impossible."

I knew what he meant all too well. Daily life without her was impossible. She'd been the constant in my life. We'd made up a secret language as little girls, and had even used it as teenagers a few times, in a public situation. It had been years since we'd used it together, though. What I felt in Ever's absence was beyond missing. It was something worse than merely missing her.

I moved closer to him, rested my head on his shoulder. "That's all I'm saying. And as much as he came across like a callous asshole, I think that's all Dr. Murphy was saying. It's impossible, and we have to at least *consider*, as horrible as it seems, all the angles."

"I can't examine *all the angles!*" Cade said, his voice quiet but intense. "I love her. I'll always love her. How can I just…let her go?" He clenched his fists, pressed them into his eye sockets. The next words came out in a hiss. "And what does it say about me that I *have* considered that? Every day that thought passes through my head. What would I do without her? Would it…*fuck*…would it be easier if she was…was gone? How *horrible* does that make me?" He knuckled his forehead so hard, so violently, that I grabbed his wrists and pulled them away.

"It doesn't make you horrible, Cade. It makes you human." I didn't let go of his wrists. My cheek rested on his shoulder. "It's okay to think about your-self. You have to give yourself permission to be okay."

He turned his head, shifted his torso toward mine, and suddenly we were face to face. The scant inches between us, between our faces, crackled, thick with some tension I couldn't bear to name. I wasn't breathing, and neither was he. Our eyes locked, too close. I smelled the gin on his breath.

And then he was up, rocketing to his feet, crossing the room and slamming his fists into the refrigerator door. "I don't know *how.*" He slammed his drink, the ice clinking, falling against his mouth as he drank, clinking again as he set it down on the counter with a groan. "The only thing I know for sure is that I'm... lost. And I don't know how to find myself."

I stood up, set my glass beside his. Stood behind him. "You're not lost, Cade. You're hurting. You're... you're here. With me. For whatever that's worth."

He turned in place, and suddenly I was standing looking up into his amber eyes, his conflicted, angry, hurting eyes. "But what does that mean?"

"Does it have to mean anything? Sometimes, maybe...sometimes there's no right or wrong. Sometimes there's just...surviving."

"Surviving?" He was close, so close to me. Tall, huge. Strong. But...somehow fragile, and in need of someone to...shelter him.

"Surviving." I couldn't get a full breath. His gaze on mine was unwavering, and I felt dizzy, felt the gin rushing through me.

"I survive by keeping it all...in. Down. By holding on so tight. I'm holding on, just...holding on. With all my strength. And I'm running out of strength. But…what happens when I can't hold on? When I let go?"

We both stood on the edge of something. I sensed it, and so did he. I felt something building, something that had been burning, an ember glowing deep down, setting slow hot fire that spread, spread, and it was consuming me. Consuming him. I'd been denying the fire, denying its heat, denying its voracious teeth sunk into me.

There was no space between us now. We were flush, but still not touching. Touch was a match lit in a room full of explosives. I didn't dare move for fear of striking that match.

"Eden," he whispered. I only blinked in response, looked up at him. "What is this?"

"I don't know."

"I'm holding on for dear life, Eden. What happens if I let go?" He wasn't talking merely about hope, about belief, or about survival, I somehow knew. He was talking about the ember burning between us. It was just a single spark, a tiny point of light in a world of darkness.

But a spark held so much potential. A spark contained all the heat and violence of a wildfire.

I don't know which one of us moved first, but it was sudden, aggressive.

It was a violent, gin-laced kiss, soaked in desperation.

the maelstrom

Caden

There are moments in life when you know, irrevocably, that you've given in, come undone. That you've slipped, lost your balance, and fallen over a cliff's edge, that there's no climbing back up, there's no slowing the fall. You never forget those moments. They get burned into the fabric of your soul, imprinted on you, tattooed on your consciousness.

Kissing Eden Eliot was that moment in my life. It was giving in.

It was only lips on lips at first. Surprise, tasting like gin. Heat, tasting like strawberry-kiwi. And then her fingers curled into the sleeve of my flannel button-down, clawing at my arm. Gripping me for dear life, her fingers like daggers in my skin. My hands, once at my sides, now became tangled in her shirt, brushing flesh. Dug into her back, her waist.

The kiss was push and pull, give and take. Pressure mounted in the kiss, heat spiraling to a thousand degrees Celsius within a heartbeat, aggression in the bruising crush of our mouths. Her hand rose, touched my cheek, trembling with furious energy. Slid over my ear, into my hair, tangled and gripped, clawed.

Breath exchanged, a single gasping breath, and then our mouths met like glaciers colliding, and my fingers curled like talons into the soft, supple flesh of her waist beneath her sweater and pulled her against me, jerked her flush against my waist, so every curve of her body pressed into the hard lines and angles of mine.

We kissed like devouring.

Heat and need and gin warred for dominance in my skull, but a single mote of reason flashed into sudden brilliance, and I pushed her away, unapologetically violent. She stumbled backward, cheeks flushed, panting, hand over her swollen lips, eyes panicked, needy, raging with volcanic heat, searching me.

"Cade…*fuck*…what just happened?" she gasped, her voice grating, scraping in her raw throat.

I shook my head, taking a tremulous step away from the counter. Away from the counter, meaning…

toward her. Wrong direction. I slid along the counter's edge, shuffling away, as if trying to escape the hungry gaze of a predator stalking me.

But it was just Eden, watching me.

I turned away from her, unable to tolerate the expression in her eyes. The fiery blaze of need, matching the animal fury pounding within me. I couldn't breathe, couldn't see. All I could feel was the scintillating imprint where her hand had touched me, as if I was scarred by the softness of her hands. I felt her lips on mine. I fought the shivering, fought the pulsing need, fought the sweetness of the way she'd tasted.

But I felt her behind me, felt her presence. "Cade?" Her voice broke on the single syllable.

I shook my head, denying even the sound of her voice, but I was on fire, I was lost in the grip of a drug. Desperation is a chemical, a narcotic. I was desperate for anything, for any emotion other than what I'd been living with for the last year.

I couldn't help but turn around, shying away from her intoxicating proximity, the guilt of her very scent in my nostrils, the knowledge of her on my skin, seeping into my pores. Her gaze locked on mine, green like barium-fed flames. I resisted. Fought against it. Against her. Against needing this, *needing* her. It was primal need, animal hunger. I stared at her, gripping the counter edge in my hands until I heard the laminate creak and crack, my fingers aching from the pressure.

She lunged at me, pouncing like a lion, both hands in my hair at the back of my head pulling me, jerking me into the kiss, and I did not go willingly. I kissed her back with anger. Tangled my fingers in her hair, grabbing a handful of blonde locks and tugging her head back, kissing her off-balance, holding her by her waist, one arm around her, keeping her up.

She went limp in my arms, and I tasted blood from the force of the kiss.

I righted her, let her go, broke the kiss with a curse. "Eden, we—we *can't!*"

She backed away from me, turned to the freezer and poured way too much gin into each glass, mixing it with the remnants of the ice and gin and juice. She swallowed it pure, and I took mine, followed suit.

She paused in drinking, rested her wrist against her mouth, the glass against her cheek and temple, staring at me sidelong. "We can't...but I can't *not.*" She slammed the rest. Poured more.

I drank, gin burning and mixing with the flames inside me, fueling the fire. The gin was supposed to help me make sense of it all, but it wasn't. It was only swallowing that mote of reason. And I knew, understood about myself that I was drinking the gin to drown that atom of logic. It was the last shred of my fingernail upon the cliff face, holding me aloft with such excruciating pain, such agony. And giving in, it would be pain, further agony, new torment, but I couldn't take the horror anymore, the longing for something I'd never have, the longing for Ever when I'd never have her again.

I'd lost all hope. When the doctor had spoken of "considering all options," I'd lost hope. When I even considered entertaining other options, the one truth binding me to the shredded notion of hope evaporated.

And when I lost hope, I lost the will to hold everything in. To hold back. Hope was all I had, and with it gone, I was lost. So lost. I'd been lost my whole life, and Ever had been my one true north. With her gone, taken from me, I had no compass. All I had was Eden, there in front of me.

Watching me, needing me the way I needed her. I didn't want to need her, but I did.

I had no north, no direction, no hope. All I had left was this, giving in to this.

"I'm lost…" I whispered.

"Me, too." She set her glass down, carefully, gingerly, as if wary of startling a wild animal. I was that animal, caged and tensed, poised to spring. "I'm lost. You're lost. But if we have to be lost, can't we…can't we at least be lost together?"

She was begging me to make it okay. I couldn't give that to her. I had nothing to give. I could only take, and even that was impossible. Everything was impossible.

I couldn't look away from her, from the way the thin blue cashmere of her sweater clung to her frame, clung to her curves, to her breasts that swelled with each breath. I couldn't not see the bell of her hips and the muscle of her thighs beneath the khaki of her slacks. I knew the sight of her flesh beneath her clothes, and I knew the taste of her lips and I knew that I needed *something*, and she was there, all that was there, the only thing in my life that was sure, a one true thing in a hurricane world. The only breath I could catch in the battering pound of waves all around.

She stood before me, and we both gasped for breath, panting beneath the weight of resistance. I shook, every muscle trembling with the force of denial. My hands clawed, my skull throbbed, my stomach churned, my heart pounded. I was holding back, staring down at her, my chest burning as I tried to deny the gravity of need, its pull upon me.

"I can't hold on any longer," I whispered. "I'm drowning."

She took the glass from me, empty now, although I had no memory of finishing the gin. "I'm sick of fighting it. I can't anymore."

"Me, neither." I meant to say something else, I didn't know what, but all that emerged was a choked, strained sob.

And then I was falling, letting go, letting go. Knowing I was drowning now and that I'd never see light again, that I was descending into some dark place from which I'd never return.

This time, the kiss was slow with fragility, no less desperate for all that, both of us trembling and unable to breathe, unable to stop this. I felt her tongue at my teeth, tasted the gin and felt her breath in my lungs and heard the whimper in her throat. We stumbled across the room, dizzy and breathless and limbs tangling, bouncing off walls and doors. She pushed me, and I pulled her. Blue cashmere bunched in my hands, fingers at the edges of the V-neck. I heard the rip of cloth, felt my fists part, and her sweater tore down the middle, fell away. Her hands pushed at me, clawed at the collar of my flannel, found where the buttons joined, and I heard buttons pop and clatter off the drywall, felt the shirt open, and we were moving again, breathless in the kiss, frantic and furious and fumbling, falling. I felt something hit the back of my knees. We were in a darkened room and her bed was behind me, tumbling me backward, and I was suddenly horizontal with Eden above me, on top of me. I felt the soft skin of her belly against mine, felt the slinking slide of her bra and the squishing crush of her tits against my chest. Nothing could stop the kiss, the incandescent driving sun-hot press of our bodies, the need for release from the pressure within us.

Hands tore, slid and scraped and ripped and clawed, and palms arced and spines arched and lips met, and her weight was so deliriously what I needed in that moment that even though I knew I was committing some crime, I knew as well that I could never stop this until it was completed. I knew the direction of my fingers as they danced up her body, crawling one by one along the flesh-hidden knobs of her spine to the strap of her bra, and my fingers knew in the darkness their work of releasing hook by eye by hook by eye the catches, so that the full glorious heft of her tits fell free, and her arms twisted and she lifted and the bra flew aside. She moved so she was kneeling astride my hips, our frantic and desperate kiss as yet unbroken, mouths devouring and tongues exploring, and her hands fumbled at my belly, at my hip pockets, at the fly, finally found the button and tore it open, tugged at my jeans and remembered the zipper, lowered it, pushed and pushed and I wiggled with her and somehow her hands caught my underwear as well, and I lifted my hips and kicked the last of my clothes away. I repeated her hurried, hungry scramble to unbutton and unzip her pants and they were gone, but her panties remained, and I fumbled with them. She arched her hips up and I tugged at the lacy material, but it defied us, catching around her hips, so I growled into her mouth and gathered handfuls of lace, ripped them at one leg opening, ripped them at the other, and tugged the fabric free from beneath her ass. And then we were naked together, still at the foot end of the bed, my feet hanging off the edge.

I tasted tongue and gin in my mouth, felt miles of skin and miles of curves pressed against me, and I couldn't help a moan from escaping. I slid my palms everywhere they would reach, following the line of her side to her hip, over the taut, muscular, generous bubble of her ass, up her spine, then curled my hands around her shoulders and tangled my fingers in her hair and kissed her with everything I had left within me, which was nothing much at all, but what I had I gave away, needing nothing but anything that wasn't misery and loneliness and agony of missing something forever lost.

Eden arched her body into mine, coiled her body, drawing her core up to my belly, dragging her damp opening over my erection. There was nothing to say, no drawing it out. I caught her hips in my hands, bit her lip between my teeth and sucked it into my mouth and shifted my body, poised my aching cock at her entrance. She took over then, not waiting for me, not taking it slowly, simply plunging herself down around me, and we groaned in tandem, and I knew I was spiraling away, drowned completely now, down in the deepest trenches of this bottomless sea that was my dark and hopeless existence, a thing not worth calling life.

I felt her breath catch, felt our kiss finally falter, and I couldn't breathe, either, could only claw my fingers into the flexed cheeks of her ass and pull at her, frantic for more, for the finish of this. All the weight and the pressure and the boiling heat that had been building in me, between us, it was coming free now, finding vent, and all we could do was ride the plume as it spewed us into delirium and fever dreams and panting furor.

Her mouth stuttered away from mine, pressed open lips to my clavicle, and she drew her body up, gathered her knees beneath her weight and lifted up, providing slick friction, and then crashed down. Whimpered. Her shoulders shook, trembled. Her hands on my sides were crushing claws, digging into the spaces between my ribs, and she gasped in a sobbing moan as she lifted up again, hovered with her weight suspended on bent, powerful legs, and then sank down once more. I couldn't bear it, couldn't take the billowing fractious pressure. I felt as if I were cracking at the seams, all smoldering embers and sharp edges and weak pressure points.

I was buried hilt deep, our bodies joined fully, and now she slid her hands up my chest, tracing the contours of my face in the darkness, feathered her hands in my hair in a gesture all her own, then clutched my skull for support as she lowered her chest to mine. My head arched backward, her mouth was on my chin, my hands were on her hips and pulling her up my body, and then together we crashed her down, and she cried out once, loudly, her whole body spasming and the walls of her pussy clenching around me and her fingers trying to crush my skull. Her mouth found mine, and she was crying, shaking.

She suddenly rolled with me, pulled me down over her and wrapped her legs around my back, clinging to me. Her hands pulled at my ass and her mouth sucked at my tongue, and then she shoved my head down and thrust her nipple into my mouth. I sucked hard and rhythmically as I began to move inside her, and I didn't hold back, attempted no finesse or tenderness, only furious pounding need, a fiery plasmic need in place of my blood.

After a few hard strokes I lost my rhythm and found only the crush of body against body, and Eden used her hands and her feet to pull me harder, an unvoiced plea for more, begging me silently to go harder, to give all.

Mad, frantic, furious.

Silent.

Then she could stay silent no longer. I felt her body clenching, spasming as she came again, and each breath was a ragged whimper in the back of her throat, rhythmed to the wild pound of our bodies meeting, and now I could only groan in the same rhythm, raw grunts torn from me with each stroke into her.

I came with a long, low growl, a spasmodic release so hard it made me dizzy, made me weak.

I collapsed on top of her, and she took my weight without complaint. When I could summon enough strength to move, I slid downward, curling back onto my knees, finally sitting up on my shins.

She lay spread out, arms flung aside, legs wide, core bared and slick, breasts huge and heavy and pulled to each side by gravity. Her skin was lit dull silver by the thin glow of the moon through the wind-blown snow. She trembled all over, a quaking aftershock that jiggled her tits.

And then, as I watched, her face contorted and her eyes squeezed shut. Tears leaked from the corner of her eyes. She pressed her fists to her eyes, sucked in a harsh breath, but couldn't contain the tremoring sob.

The reality of what had just occurred juddered through me. I fell forward, crashing to the bed beside her.

"Caden..." Her voice was thick, low, tattered with guilt.

She never, ever, called me Caden.

She lay on her back beside me, hands covering her face. I was struggling to simply breathe, to expel the air caught in my lungs.

"What have we done?" she asked.

I could only shake my head, my eyes burning, heart aching in my chest. "We…" I wanted to find some way to mitigate, to deny, to erase. There was nothing. "God…what did we do?"

Panic hit me. Flowed through me like magma rising in the conduit of a volcano. I sucked in a breath, finally getting a lungful of air, and then it left me in a rush of moaning, whimpering, panicking horror. I scrambled away, unable to see, shaking all over. Full-scale panic attack.

I had no idea where I was suddenly, only knew that I was on fire, that I'd done something I couldn't take back, that I couldn't breathe, and I was breaking apart, shivering, bones rattling. I felt a small soft careful hand on my back. Sliding up my spine, pulling my head against her breast. I could hear her heartbeat, a mad pounding to match my own.

"Don't cry, Cade, please." Her voice was a tiny seed of sound. "Breathe, Cade. It'll be okay. Ssshhh. Breathe for me."

I realized I was sobbing, I wasn't breathing, only expelling the wracking grief and guilt within me. "Can't…can't…"

She took my face in her palms and twisted my head so I was forced to look at her. "Cade…look at me. Take a breath in." I forced air into my lungs, a shuddering inbreath that made me dizzy with the sudden influx of oxygen. "Good. One more. Good. I'm here, Cade. You're not alone. You're not in this alone. We're in this together."

How was she so calm?

"What *is* this?" I pushed away from her, from the wall. I was in the corner between the bed and the wall, huddled on my knees.

I crawled onto the bed, lay on my back, and covered my lower half with the sheet. Eden climbed up beside me, pulled the sheet up over her chest, sitting on her knees and staring down at me. Her hair was loose and wild, blonde strays and tangles wisping in her face, in her mouth, across her eyes.

"I don't know what this is. But...we can't take it back." She ducked her head. "I'm not—I'm not sure I'm capable of even *wanting* to, if you want the truth."

I sat up and looked at her sharply, puzzled, shocked. "Don't you understand that we—we—we betrayed—"

"*I KNOW!*" she screamed. "I know what we did! Do you think I don't know? How could I not know what we just did? But it was...*fuck*...it was the best sex of my entire life."

It wasn't for me. I couldn't say that, of course. But it was one of the most intense moments of my life. And that's saying something huge.

She kept going. "Don't—don't say anything. I don't expect you to...I know it wasn't for you what it was for—for me. It was a betrayal, I know that. But I can't escape the other truth."

"What other truth?"

"That…that she might never know. That she might never find out. That she might never wake up. That—it makes me a horrible, horrible person. But that's just my life." She laughed bitterly.

"What?" I asked.

"It's just so perfectly ironic. The best, most intense, most meaningful sex I've ever had, ever experienced, and it's…it's nothing but a mistake for you. Meaningless."

"It wasn't—"

"*SHUT UP!*" she screeched, shoving at me, angry, furious, dropping the sheet and not caring. "I know what that was. What this is between us. It wasn't love. It wasn't even fucking. Like everything that's ever happened between you and me, there's no way to put in a box what we are, what we do, what we are to each other. You don't love me. You'll never love me."

"Eden, I—"

"I said *shut up,*" she hissed, on her hands and knees, a feral animal, teeth bared, all skin and claws and bright angry eyes and hunger and something primal and furious. "You don't, won't…*can't* ever love me. I know. You know. But…we need each other. Now, in this. We need each other. We're the only thing we have in life. We're orphans in a huge, scary world.

We're alone. We're lost in the darkness together. And we have to stick together—we have to hold on to each other. I can't face life completely alone, Cade." She knelt in front of me, gripped my arms, her eyes exposing every raw nerve in her soul, every fear and all her vulnerability. "Don't lie to me. Don't tell me what you think I want to hear. But don't...don't tear yourself to pieces over this."

"How am I supposed to be okay with this?"

"I don't know. Maybe you're not. But don't lie about what it is, either."

"You keep saying that. What is it, then? What is this?"

She wrapped her arms around herself. "It's necessary, Cade. No one can go through life completely alone, and this, what we're going through, there are no rules for it. There's no map or guidebook, or anyone to tell us what's right or wrong, or how to act or anything. There's just you and me and this thing between us. We don't know the future. How things will turn out. And I don't know about you, but I need *some* kind of comfort. You...you comfort me. You make me feel good, when the rest of my life is... lonely and painful."

I couldn't bear the fragility in her voice, the pain. I slid over so our naked hips touched, pulled her against me in a hug. The embrace turned into leaning back against the wall, and her head rested on my chest. All of my muscles tensed, part of me wanting to relax and let the tension fade, enjoy what I could while I could, but the other part of me was too aware of who it was I was in bed with, what we had just done together, and how it could possibly destroy me, ruin me, ruin everything.

She shuddered then, as I held her. I felt the tension in her body, matching mine. But she shivered, trembled, and then began to cry. Not sob, not gasp or weep, just to softly, quietly cry, shoulders shaking, sniffling. I sensed a lifetime of complexity in her quiet tears. I didn't dare ask what it was that made her cry so, with such isolated, self-contained agony. It wasn't just us, this guilt-riddled tryst of ours.

I held her and she cried, *sotto voce,* for a long, long time. I felt her still, felt her breathing slow and even out. I couldn't sleep. I wanted to. I wanted to close my eyes and forget everything. There was no trace of the gin left in me, having been burned away. But I held her, unable to let go of the tension within me.

Eden had been strong for me. She'd been a friend, a companion, a constant source of support throughout the last year. Tonight, she'd handled my panic attack—not just one, but two, at that—with calmness and kindness, even though I knew she'd been fighting her own emotional demons. She'd spoken the truth without flinching, she'd faced the fucked-up situation we'd just created without cringing away from the hard facts. I wanted to run, to bury myself in the darkness, to drown myself at the bottom of a bottle the way my dad had, so many years ago now. But I owed it to Eden to provide strength back for her, to give her *something*, even if it couldn't be love, or even real affection. She'd been all too right. I'd never be able to love her. Not the way she deserved. Even if—god forbid, and god forgive me for even considering it—I pulled the plug on Ever and let her die completely, I'd never be able to love Eden. This wasn't love between us. It wasn't just sex, either, which immensely complicated things. She'd always remind me of Ever. She'd always remind me of what I'd lost. I'd never be able to see her without seeing Ever's sweet, innocent green gaze.

My thoughts whirled and swirled in endless circles, trying to sort out what this was with Eden, what I was supposed to do about it, how I was supposed to visit Ever without dying from the acid burn of guilt.

I also wondered, deep down, how I was going to get through each day without Eden. Now that I'd tasted the illicit comfort she offered, need for it raced through my bloodstream like a narcotic.

I fell asleep at some point in the smallest hours of the night.

shaken

Eden

When I woke up, Cade was gone. Not in the bed, at least, although his side was still warm. I lay on my back, staring at the ceiling with the covers rucked around my hips, wondering what my life had come to. At least this was my apartment, so I didn't have to do the walk of shame. But...I still had to face the fact that Cade was probably going to bolt now. He'd run, curl inward, and grow distant.

No guy I ever fucked had stayed the night. Not once, not ever. They never stayed to talk. Never stuck around to even pretend like it had meant something. That's at least part of why I'd cried for a long time last night. He'd stayed to hold me, and it had been the sweetest, most tender moment of my life. He hadn't asked what was wrong. He hadn't kissed my tears away. But at least he'd offered silent strength. I'd known he'd be gone in the morning, and I knew that I'd never get another moment with him that wasn't freighted with guilt and awkward, tight-strung tension.

I couldn't keep my thoughts from returning to how we'd been together. It had been raw, almost angry. Starvation-desperate, violent. Yet, for all that, it had been as far from empty fucking as I'd ever had with anyone. It had meant something. I felt tears slide down all over again as I realized that. It had *meant* something huge to me. Cade had given me some part of himself last night, and he'd taken what I'd offered him of myself.

I heard the bathroom door open, and Cade entered my room, still naked. I hurriedly wiped my eyes and sniffed away the self-pity. He saw me, just as I was wiping one last errant tear away, and his amber eyes went soft with concern.

"What's up?" he asked.

I shrugged. "Nothing. I'm fine."

He lifted an eyebrow, obviously not buying that line. I swallowed hard as he climbed onto my bed. His torso rippled with muscle, biceps shifting, abs cut and hard, thighs thick. I couldn't look away from him, and didn't try. I had a gorgeous, naked man in my bed, and I wasn't about to waste the opportunity to devour him. With my eyes at least. My hands itched to clutch his huge hard muscles and feel the rippling power in his body, but I didn't dare. Didn't dare move from my spot on the bed.

I felt his eyes on me as well, and his hands curled into fists on his thighs as he sat half on the bed, one foot still on the floor. "Bullshit," he said. "'Fine' never means fine."

I blinked hard, not knowing what to say, what to tell him. "Just…everything." Maybe that would throw him off the scent.

"I'm not a coward, Eden." Apparently not. "I may…what we did might have been wrong, but I'm not going to vanish the next morning."

How the hell did he know that's what I was thinking? Damn the man's insightfulness. "Everyone else does."

"I'm not everyone else."

"Clearly."

He scratched his bicep. "Where do we go from here?" His eyes slid down from mine, raked over my body and then quickly away.

"We just…keep going forward. One day at a time. Same as we've been doing."

He flopped the rest of the way onto the bed. "That's not what I meant."

"You and I, you mean?" I asked, turning my head to look at him. He nodded, and I rolled a shoulder. "I don't know. I really don't."

He sighed, more of a groan than anything else. "Way I see it, we have a couple of choices. We can go back to acting like nothing happened. Call it an accident and be more careful. Or…something not that."

I laughed. "Something not that?"

He laughed with me. "That's as far as I'd thought it through, I guess."

"So, we act like nothing happened." Why did that thought make my eyes sting and my heart ache with the pain of rejection?

"Well, no, I mean, we can't act like it didn't happen. It did. But…we just have to be careful not to put ourselves in that position again."

"You mean vulnerability? Weakness?" That came out a lot more sarcastically and bitterly than I'd intended.

"I mean drunk and careless."

"That's not fair and you know it, Cade." I felt my temper heating up. "It wasn't like we just…oopsed. We didn't fuck by accident. There was intent there, on *both* sides, and if you try to deny that, then you *are* a coward."

He rubbed his face with both hands. "You're right. Fine. God, you're right. I'm sorry. But am I supposed to go, 'oh, okay, it's fine'?"

"No, but don't act like I seduced you. Like it was just the booze making us stupid. It was more than that." I couldn't stop the words from coming out like an avalanche. "It may not mean to you what it did to me, but *don't you dare* cheapen it that way, Cade."

"What did it mean to you? That's what I don't get."

"I'm still trying to figure that out, honestly, but I know it *did* mean something. Like I said last night, it was…comfort. It was something real. A moment of complete vulnerability between two really fucked-up people." I sat up further, tugged the sheet up to cover my boobs. "What was it to you? Honestly."

He didn't answer right away, and when he did, he spoke slowly, as if parsing the truth from a briar-tangle of thorny confusion. "It was that for me, too. It was…release." He glanced at me apologetically. "I'm just telling the truth. It was release. I'd had so much… tension, and frustration built up. Life tension and… sexual tension. Anger. All that."

I knew I'd hate the answer to my next question, but I refused to shy away from the truth, no matter ugly it ever became. "Was there…was there anything in it that was…me? About me?" I couldn't meet his eyes.

He covered his face with both hands, spoke past his palms, his words muffled. "Yeah. There was." It sounded as if the admission hurt like a knee to the gut. "I wanted it. With you. Is that what you want to hear? The most horrible truth about this whole fucked scenario? You aren't your sister, and I knew that, and I still wanted you. *You.* I didn't—I *don't*—want to want you. And no, I'm not in love with you and I never will be, but that doesn't stop me from being a shallow, selfish asshole. Clearly." The bitterness in his voice was directed at himself, but I couldn't help feeling like he resented me for making him want me.

"I'm sorry I'm such a problem for you," I heard myself say. He didn't deserve that, but I was hurting, and he was the only target.

"*Don't*," he growled, rolling toward me. "*You* didn't seduce me. You didn't do anything wrong."

"Oh, so it was all you? All the guilt in this is on you?" Anger and sarcasm warred for dominance in my voice. "I was just a helpless little thing, right? How could I possibly resist you, how could I possibly keep my legs together when faced with—"

"Oh, don't be a bitch, Eden," Cade spat, "that's not what I meant, and you goddamn well know it!"

"Well, that's how it sounded to me!" I yelled back.

Somehow, we were sliding toward each other, like the matching energy of our anger was a magnetic force drawing us together.

"I just meant I should have made sure we didn't—"

"And so should I!" I shoved at him, but my palms on his chest barely moved him. "I'm not going to let you make this all about you! I'm just as complicit—I wanted it just as much."

"But I'm the one who—"

"You want to know something? I've *always* wanted you. From the very first time Ever introduced you, I was attracted to you, and jealous of Ever for having you. All those letters, the way you just... showed up and rocked her world? Do you have any idea how fucking romantic that was? How jealous that made me? She had Billy and then she had you, and I've never gotten a guy even half as amazing as you to even *fuck* me more than once! And she got Billy to stick around for almost two years!"

"He broke her fucking heart!" Cade yelled, and he was so close now that I could smell him, feel the heat from his skin. "I wouldn't be jealous of him if I were you. He was a selfish bastard who lied and cheated on her for months. He treated her like an extra piece of ass. If that's what you want, then good luck to you."

"I know what he did to her," I said. "But it's still more than I've ever gotten."

"You've never had a serious relationship?" Cade asked.

I shook my head, feeling suddenly small. "Nope. I'm not relationship material, obviously. None of the guys I ever fall for want anything but a good fuck. And that's all I am, all I've ever been, and all I ever will be." I slid down to a lying position and rolled away from him.

"You're selling yourself short, Eden. You're worth a fuckload more than that."

I didn't bother looking at him. "Yeah, and how do you know?"

"Because it's obvious to anyone who isn't a blind dickwad!"

I felt him move closer to me, felt his presence behind me. Felt his hand on my shoulder, brushing my hair away from my face. I felt his thighs rub the back of mine, his chest against my back. The slightest wriggle of my hips pressed my ass against him, and then I felt him harden in response.

His hand slid down my arm, touched my side. My hip. And then he hissed in frustration, rolled away from me and fairly leapt off the bed.

"We can't, Eden! Not again."

I flew off the bed, cornering him, standing facing him. "And why not? Why can't we?"

"Because it's wrong!" He backed away.

I followed, and he backed up to the wall, pressed his palms flat against the wall, and then his fingers curled as if scrabbling for purchase, for something to grip instead of me. I wanted it to be me.

"I know it's wrong, but tell me what's right! Maybe it makes me a shitty person, but at least I'm willing to admit that I want it, that I don't want to keep fighting it! I know it's temporary! I know it's never going to be anything more than what it is, but I still want it! I still want you! I want what I can get, and I'm not afraid to admit it! I know how desperate and—and *pathetic* that makes me, but I don't care!"

"What about the cost? What about the...what about *her*?"

"She's *never* going to wake up, Cade!" I screamed the one truth that lurked in the darkest hole of my heart, the thing I feared the most.

"But what if she does?" He wasn't touching me still, but our bodies were scant millimeters from each other's.

"Then we'll face the music. We'll—we'd figure that out if it happens."

"And until then?"

"Until then?" I shrugged, and his eyes followed the sway of my body. "Until then, we just..." I couldn't find the right phrase.

"Take what we can get?" he filled in.

I didn't answer. None was required. We stood face to face, my nipples brushing the dusting of hair on his chest, his hands curling and uncurling at his sides, both of us panting, anger not forgotten but banked, hurt not banished but buried, pain not healed but merely shoved aside, denied.

There was silence, and it crackled with electricity.

His eyes wavered, locked on mine as if refusing to look elsewhere, refusing to allow himself to see me, to look at my naked body. So I held his gaze. And then, as if stubbornly relinquishing a tenuous finger hold, his amber gaze flickered down to my tits, to my thighs pressed together and hiding my core. I held my head high and endured his scrutiny. Let him look. I watched his eyes for the disappointment when he saw the extra flesh at my belly, my hips, my ass, the weight I couldn't lose no matter how hard I tried. That disappointment always came. They'd undress me eagerly enough, and then once they got a good look at me, at what my clothes hid, I'd see the disappointment, the disgust or dissatisfaction, or whatever it was. And I waited for it to enter Cade's expression.

It never did.

"You're beautiful, Eden. You are. You have to know that."

I shook my head. "I don't."

"I wish I could show you."

"Not your job. Not your problem."

"Gotta be someone's."

"But not yours." I let my gaze trace the contours of his torso, and finally let my eyes settle on his cock.

God, it was a beautiful thing. Straight, thick, hard as a rock.

I wanted it.

He was still at war with himself. And I? I fought myself as well. Fought off the desire to wrap my hands around him. Fought the urge to go to my knees and suck him dry. I was good at that. But I wouldn't. I'd talked a good game, like I wasn't afraid to admit that I wanted him, that I wanted to feel him again, but the reality was that I was terrified. I was terrified that I'd give in to wanting him and he'd push me away, like all the others had.

And so the silence reigned again, electric silence, just like it always was between Cade and me.

He growled, deep in his throat, and grabbed me around the waist, fingers digging painfully into my sides as he jerked me against him, crushed his lips to mine. Demanded my tongue. I gave it to him, feeling my core ache and grow damp. His cock jutted hard between our bodies, and I slid my hand between us, grabbed him, squeezed, letting my own inner war translate into aggression the way he clearly was doing.

His mouth ravaged mine, and his cock throbbed in my hand.

I wondered, briefly, how this would feel with him if it was gentle, but I knew that wouldn't happen.

He broke the kiss, backed away, panting, but I refused to let go of him, and his back was to the wall

anyway. I met his eyes, daring, stubborn, and deliberately stroked his length. A challenge.

He drew a long breath, resisted, held still, as if trying to push me away without touching me. And then
he hung his head. "Fuck." He rumbled the word, the
curse a vented sigh of defeat. "I'm so fucking weak."

He bent to kiss me again, and this time his hands
held my hips, and then his fingers slid between
my thighs and touched me, demanding entrance. I
opened my thighs and let him in, let him touch me,
let him bring me to the edge, as I brought him to the
edge. I kept my eyes shut, clamped my mouth shut.

I hated being his weakness, being something he
had to concede to. But I was the same, needed him
even though I knew I shouldn't want him, and giving
in to this was a surrender, painfully sweet.

I refused to even breathe a sigh as he touched me.
He wasn't quite there, wasn't quite finding me where
I needed friction, so I put my hand on his, my fingers
around his and showed him. He, in turn, wrapped his
other hand around mine on his cock and showed me
how to stroke him, how to make him tremble.

I came first. But then, coming had never been
my problem. I had a hair trigger, not needing much
to devolve into paroxysms and whimpers. But this…
it was a powerful, debilitating, clenching climax that
stole the strength from my knees. My fist squeezed
him and stroked him with involuntary speed as I

quaked in the grip of the orgasm. Finally, I couldn't stand up under the power of it any longer, and I had to let go of him and wrap both arms around his neck, holding on for balance as tremors shook me. I panted through gritted teeth, and then I felt him lift me up, and I liked the way his hands felt on my ass, gripping tight and hard. I bit his shoulder to keep silent as he pivoted with me, and I couldn't help gasping in surprised pain as my back slammed against the wall, and then the gasp turned to shocked pleasure as he drove up into me with unapologetic violence.

"Oh…*fuck*…" I hissed, resting my forehead on his shoulder blade.

"Shit, I didn't hurt—" Cade started to say.

I didn't let him finish. In the middle of his sentence, I lifted myself up, locking my heels around his ass and my arms around his neck, and then I sank down on his cock with the same violence as he'd pierced me. He groaned in equal parts pleasure and pain, and then I repeated the act, and he nearly dropped me. Only, I was impaled on him, clinging to him. He stumbled, shoving my spine against the wall, leaning on me, crushing me. I arched back, pushing hard, and he straightened his knees, found his balance, and discovered that he didn't need his hands to hold me up. His fingers pinched my nipples, cupped my tits, squeezed and kneaded, imparting painfully perfect pressure. I could take anything he had to give, and give it back. He bucked into me, and we both moaned, and then I planted my palms on his shoulder blades, lifted up, held myself aloft with just the tip of his cock inside me.

"Look at me, goddamn it," I snarled.

His eyes snapped open and his head pivoted up, and his eyes were fire, wide and superheated. I made sure he was looking at me, and then I let myself fall, pierced and impaled and filled, and I felt a groan rip through him, and then he was rocking into me, thrusting and pumping with fierce power. I met him stroke for stroke, sinking down onto his up-thrusts, and now I was moaning in my throat with each body-jarring fuck of his hips, my tits jouncing and bouncing, and I knew he was watched them move so I arched my back and made them bounce harder. He was groaning, growling, gasping.

He slammed into me once more, one last time, and then I felt him go up on his toes and I was filled with his hot wet seed, felt him come and come and come, and then I was overtaken as well. My body was squeezed and wrung, my insides shivering, my muscles tremoring, and I was gasping high-pitched whimpers, the noise of my orgasm a breathless whine.

He held me and I clung to him, both of us shaken.

When I slid off him, the look in his eyes was haunted.

I knew the feeling. Whenever we finally gave in, we were both possessed by something primal. It was all sheer aggression, raw hunger, mixed with threads of anger and pain and confusion.

I could tell he needed to get away from me, and honestly, I was exhausted from the intensity spiking every moment we were together. "I'm gonna go to the gym," I said.

He nodded, but didn't look away from me, and I didn't look away, either.

"Eden, I—"

"Don't. I'm sick of talking about it." I looked up at him, still quivering and sore and out of breath. "Where we go from here is up to you. I'll follow your lead."

He sighed and ran his hands through his hair. "I—" He seemed to be on the verge of starting the whole circular discussion over again, but then he shook his head in denial and started again. "I'll see you later."

At the gym, I punished myself until I could barely walk. Of course, walking was already a little tricky, as sore as I was, but that was a kind of sore I'd never minded. I was dripping sweat and trembling all over by the time I finally left the gym, having done more reps on all the weight machines than was probably advisable. I'd even run flat out on the treadmill for almost twenty minutes, and I hated running.

Other days, instead of all that, I'd hang the heavy bag from the hook I'd attached by hand to the ceiling in my studio space, and I'd wrap my knuckles the way the personal trainer had shown me so long ago, and I'd work the heavy bag until I couldn't move my arms or legs.

It still didn't quiet the war of voices waging in my head, the angel on one shoulder and the demon on the other.

Caden

I'm so fucked up, Ever. Such a mess. There's no up anymore. I'm just tumbling through life without any up or down. You were my up. You were my direction. I'm barely passing my classes, and even my art is all fucked up, dark and twisted images that make no sense. You are my light, Ever. Or you were, and now I have none.

Do I even have hope anymore? I don't know. I used to. They're talking about the chances of emergence, organ donation. Quality of life. Quality of life for whom? You? Me? God, I don't know. I know they're talking about you, but...it should be me. I'd donate my organs. I have no chance of emerging from this. I'm in a coma, too, Ever, just like you. Only I'm walking and talking, and you're in a bed.

I visit you every day still. Regardless of what they say, I come see you. I write you letters, just like we used to. Unlike then, I sit at your side and read them to you.

I miss something different about you every day. Today, I miss your painting. I miss going into your studio and seeing you in that fucking shirt, the white button-down with all the paint splatters. That shirt is such a mess. But it's so you. And you're always naked underneath it, your long thin legs naked and so white. I miss how you can be so quiet, but fill any room. So gentle, so tender, but so fierce when you want to be.

I'd give anything, anything in the whole fucking world to be able to just sit and talk to you, just once. I'd pillage the whole earth if it meant talking to you. I'd fucking raze cities to the ground if it'd bring you back. I'd sell everything I own. I'd go homeless. I'd starve. Just to have you look at me one time with your green eyes. Just to hear your quiet voice. You have such a musical voice.

I never understood how much I loved you. I didn't. You know how we talked about our love, how it was this thing that was EVERYTHING to us? It was everything to me, Ever, every last goddamned motherfucking thing, and it's gone. You're gone. And I needed it even more than I knew then, when I had you.

Will you know me if you wake up? Will you love me?

For you, Ever,

Caden

My hand shook uncontrollably, clutching the letter, and I felt the paper crumple in my fist. "Shit," I mumbled. I straightened the letter, smoothed it against the silver metal of the railing on her bed, folded it, tucked it into the envelope. Put it with the others. Too many letters.

I closed my eyes and breathed, focused on keeping it together.

I failed.

Falling forward, I felt her frail cold hand against my forehead. "Goddamn it, Ever," I whispered. "If you're there, if you're in there, show me. Move your finger. Something. Show me you're there, so I can hold on. I'm losing it, baby. I'm losing it."

I lifted my head to watch her, looking for any sign, a twitch, a blip on the machines, a finger wiggling, an eye moving beneath the lid.

"Please, baby. *Please.*" I was cracking. "I can't do this without you. I can't...keep going. You have to... you have to wake up, baby."

I didn't deserve to call her that. I didn't deserve her anymore.

Everything I was, everything I knew, it was all breaking apart. I'd tried to draw Ever the other day, and instead, I'd drawn a horrific, distorted Noh mask, white as bloodless flesh, with Ever's brilliant eyes coruscating green but somehow sightless and menacing, fine black strands of hair flying about like storm-whipped tendrils of purest darkness.

I wasn't sleeping. I'd dream, and wake up. A dozen times a night I'd dream I was with Ever, in bed with my Ever, and then it would all twist as dreams do and it'd be a lifeless husk I was clutching.

Once, the corpse in my bed was Eden.

Once, it was a two-faced nightmare creature, reaching for me with pale hands and talon fingernails painted blood red, or red with blood, and it was my blood. I'd looked down and saw jagged claw marks ripping open my chest, and there had been no heart beating in my ribcage, and one face was Ever's and that one was weeping great hot jade tears that drained her eyes of color, and the other face was Eden's, and she was grinning with filed cannibal teeth and laughing and cackling. The body, the two-faced creature's body had been a chimera, part Ever's body, part Eden's. I'd known the difference. The creature's breasts had been Ever's; I'd known it as an immutable truth, I'd been able to recognize them, recognize their shape and their size, and I'd known each dimple on the areolae. Its hips and legs had been Eden's, and between its legs it had been Eden as well, and I'd known that with just as much surety, and in the dream I'd shut tight my eyes but had still seen, still been forced to see the creature I'd wrought with my sins.

I'd woken screaming, alone in my bed, and I hadn't gone back to sleep that night, nor the next night. I'd doze off in class, exhausted, and I'd dream then as well. I'd jerk awake or be prodded by a classmate. I'd doze off at home, on the couch in front of the TV, which I watched listlessly.

I'd always known in the back of my head that Grams and Gramps were there, but there was nothing they could do. They couldn't wake up Ever. I didn't need money. They couldn't come and stay with me, and I couldn't move there to live with them. But… they were there. A fallback, if I ever hit absolute rock-bottom and had nowhere else to go. But until then, I was alone.

I spent Christmas Day alone. I spent New Year's alone. I didn't dare catch so much as a whiff of Eden, because I knew I had no place, no right, no control.

I ached. I dreamed of Eden. Sometimes they were normal dreams, strange conversations and aggressive sex. Other times, they were nightmares in which I'd be with Eden and Ever would be crucified to the wall, awake and watching and unable to look away.

When I woke from those dreams, I'd be weeping, and I'd be unable to stop for hours, more tears than I'd ever cried in my life, even as a baby, surely. And I'd be unable to sleep again after that. I'd draw and let the images take over. I'd draw my dreams, and those pieces were things I wished I could burn but didn't dare because they were evidence of my torture, witness to my ongoing penance.

I'd drop to the floor and do pushups until I couldn't lift my face from the carpet, and then I'd roll over and do sit-ups until I was about to vomit, and then I'd stand up and do squats until I collapsed, dripping sweat. I made myself eat, but food was ash in my mouth, tasteless.

Every day, I was tormented by the need to see Eden. To get a fix. I refused, refused, refused.

This went on for nearly a month, and by the end of January I was hallucinating while awake, living on coffee and protein bars and vitamin supplements and fast food. I'd gained more than ten pounds of muscle in my arms and chest, because instead of sleeping and risking the dreams, I'd do pushups, wide-stance to work my pecs, make a triangle with my fingers directly beneath my chest to work my triceps. Crunches, squats, lunges, wall-squats, every at-home exercise I could think of. I'd eventually sleep, and after a few hours the dreams would come and I'd be desperate to wake up, and when I did, I'd wake more tired than ever.

Finally, I could take it no longer.

between sin and suicide

Can you come over? I sent the text.

It was two in the morning and I'd had a nightmare, spent the last hour working myself into exhaustion, sweating and trembling and unable to do one more pushup. Yet still I was pacing the living room, near tears from exhaustion, nightmare images flashing through my head. I ached from the need to find release. As many nightmares as I had, I suffered equally from wet dreams of Eden, of Ever. Once, horribly, of both of them at once.

I'd vomited after that dream and drunk myself into a stupor, missing an entire day of classes and work.

But the wet dreams continued, just like the nightmares, and I could never ejaculate in the dreams, and

I'd wake up hard, on the verge of coming, but unable to finish it, unable to bring myself to touch myself. So I ached, exhausted, weak, seeing Ever in every face, Eden in others.

Sure. B right there, she texted back after ten minutes.

She rapped softly on my door twenty minutes later, and I let her in. Wearing a torn gray Champion sweatshirt and red knee-length spandex, hair in a sloppy braid, dirty white cross-trainers, she looked like she wasn't in any better shape than I was. She stank of sweat, and her eyes were heavy-lidded, exhausted. I shut the door behind her, went to the fridge, and got her a Gatorade. She took it, uncapped it, drank greedily.

Lowering the bottle, she eyed me as she wiped a wrist across her mouth. "You look like shit."

"Feel worse."

"So you call me?" She sounded resentful.

I drank from my own bottle, wiped sweat off my forehead. "I tried not to. For as long as I could."

"And now?"

"I'm not sleeping. I have nightmares."

She laughed bitterly. "Me, too." Her eyes roved over my shirtless torso. "Looks like you're coping the same way I am. You've put on muscle."

"So have you." She had, too. Her legs, encased in skin-tight red, were pillars of defined muscle, and even under the baggy sweatshirt I could see that she'd been working out as hard as I had been.

She just snorted. "Yeah, right. I've been pigging out as often as I go the gym. I ate half a pizza by myself yesterday. Then ice cream. Pie today. Lots and lots of booze. It's a miracle I don't need a forklift for my ass." She sidled past me to throw away her bottle, and my eyes were drawn to the ass that she claimed required a forklift.

"Your ass looks pretty tight to me." Might as well admit it.

She'd been in the act of drinking the last drop of Gatorade when I spoke, and she froze, then slowly and deliberately dropped the bottle into the trash can. "Now we come to it." She turned around. "You think my ass is tight?"

I shrugged. "Yeah."

"And that's why you texted me, right?" She glared at me, her hair coming loose from the braid.

I frowned. "I thought we weren't going to pretend?"

She took an angry step toward me. "But that doesn't mean you can avoid me for a month and then text me at two in the morning like I'm a cheap piece-of-ass booty call!"

"Jesus, Eden. That's not why I asked you to come over. I just needed—"

"Yeah, you needed. I *know* what you needed. That *is* why you texted me."

I turned away from her, tempted to put my fist through a wall. Instead, I whirled back, pointing at her with an accusatory finger. "Yeah, well, you're here, aren't you?"

Her eyes filled with tears. "Yeah. I am. I'm here. I knew what you wanted, and I still came running. So you might as well get on with it." She ripped her sweatshirt off, revealing a sports bra that matched her pants, red and tight.

She curled her fingers under the bottom edge of the bra and started to peel it off. I lunged across the space between us, grabbed her wrists, and forced her hands away, pulled her to me. Or, I tried. She exerted all her strength, pushing me away. Holy fucking hell, the girl was a goddamned powerhouse. I bared my teeth and felt a feral energy ripple through me. I curled her inward, to me, drawing her inexorably to my chest, and she didn't give an inch, her entire body an unbending iron bar.

Her eyes were furious, snapping with electricity. "*Let…me…go.*" She began to push back, and was very nearly able to do so.

"No. You're not cheap. That's not how this is." I held her in place, but it took all my strength to do so. "Goddamn it, Eden. I'm sorry. I'm sorry. Fuck, I'm sorry."

That broke her anger off at the knees. "Wh-what?" She didn't give, though, refusing to close in.

"I said I'm sorry. I didn't mean to make you feel like...like it was a booty call. Like I only care when I need...that."

"It's the truth, isn't it?"

"No!" I let go of her wrists and wrapped my arms around her shoulders. She was still hard and tensed, and she tilted her head up to meet my eyes from within the circle of my arms. "I swear it's not. It's...you. I can't get away from the fact that I need... you. You're all there is, and I...need you. It's fucked up. *I'm* fucked up. I can't sleep, and I—I sleep when I'm with you. Whatever it is between us, as fucked up as it is, it's all I have that's not...the craziness."

She finally went soft. "The craziness?"

I swallowed hard. "I'm losing it, Eden," I whispered. "I haven't slept more than a couple of hours at a time in—in a fucking month. I'm seeing shit. If you could see the pieces I'm drawing, the dreams I'm having...it's fucked up. Crazy shit. I'm—*fuck*. I'm scared." Those two words were an admission torn from the shredded core of my soul.

"Me, too." I felt the words whispered against my bare chest rather than heard them.

"What are you scared of?"

"You. This. This...ending." She leaned against me now, rested her cheek against my breastbone. "I'm afraid I need it too much. I'm afraid because I know, whatever happens with you, with Ever, this will end for me. And I don't know what I'll do. You've never pretended that what we do is making love, but I'll still never be able to go back to cheap sex and quick fucks. I'm afraid because all this has changed me, and I don't know what I'll do when it's over."

"Listen to me, Eden." I let her go and touched my finger to her chin, lifted her face so she looked me in the eyes. "Part of me…some part of me wishes I was…free. So I could show you how much you're worth." It was so, *so* hard to say that.

She ripped her face away, tucked her chin down and wept. "Goddamn you, Cade. You can't say shit like that to me. It's not fair."

I had nothing to say in comfort, nothing that would change the truth. So I did the only thing I *could* do. I took her damp cheeks in my palms and lifted her face to mine, kissed her. That kiss, it was a dangerous kiss.

It rode some fine, nearly invisible line between sin and suicide.

But I, lost in the foolish tidal swell of her pain, drowning in the mad oceanic power of my desperation, kissed her anyway. It was a long, slow kiss, bordering on sweet. I kissed her because I wanted to push away her agony, even if just for a moment; I couldn't take her pain on top of my own. I couldn't handle what was inside me, much less take anything else from her, so I sought instead to kiss away the hurt that plagued both of us.

When she was breathless and needed oxygen, she shivered away from my kiss and sobbed into my mouth, touched my face with her fingertips as if blind and seeking to know my features by touch. Her hands trembled, and she was panting for breath, gasping for control of tears I didn't quite understand. And then her gentle fingers turned into demanding claws, pulling my face to hers and scouring my mouth with hers. My hands drew down her face, brushed away the tears from her cheeks and smoothed down the back of her neck, beneath the braid. Her shoulder were bare, and I touched them. Her waist was bare, and I touched it. Up her spine, to the strap of her sports bra. She kissed me, and I kissed her, and I peeled away the crimson barrier between our flesh. She lifted her arms, and her heavy tits fell free from the pinioning fabric. Her palms skated over my deltoids and down my spine, and then found the elastic waistband of my shorts.

Our kiss reached a plateau, and we pulled away, both of us topless. Her eyes searched me, and then I watched as renewed emotion ravaged her expression, soul-searing vulnerability and some fierce hunger I knew I'd never be able to sate. She slammed into me, her teeth crushing my lips and her hands roving my body. I met her, slid my palms down her ribs to her hips and began rolling down the second skin of her workout pants. She kicked off her shoes as I broke away from her mouth and kissed down her body, between her breasts, and then she was naked but for ankle socks, which she toed off clumsily, holding my head as I kissed the hollow where hip met thigh and over to her soft mound.

Before I could taste her, she was sinking down and bowling me backward to the carpet. She landed on top of me and kissed me, missed, her lips landing on the corner of my mouth, and then she was jerking down my shorts, pulling the elastic away from my erection, and then before I could react she had me in her mouth, deep, hot and wet and tight and sucking.

I curled forward, wrapped my arms beneath her armpits and jerked her bodily up my torso, on top of me, to me. Rolled with her, hovering over her, pinning her arms above her head. I lowered my face to hers, kissed her far, far too gently, feeling her soft, pliable flesh beneath me, her lush curves that sheathed iron muscle. I let go of one of her hands, and that hand found the back of my neck, tangled through my hair in that uniquely Eden gesture, and I found the tail of her braid, tugged the hair tie free and carefully worked the braid undone as our kiss reached a fevered pitch. She lifted her head off the carpet as I combed through her hair with my fingers and spread it out beneath her.

My palm cupped her cheek, her fingers in the hair at my nape, and then we slid our hips together in unison and I entered her, and we were moving together, sinking slowly together there on the carpet, kiss unbroken, bodies moving in near-perfect sync. And then she arched her spine and tipped her head back, and I kissed her throat, burying deep with a slow hard stroke. She pushed my head down, and I sucked her turgid nipple into my mouth, and she held me there, heels digging into the carpet to find purchase, seeking to push harder against me, to sink me deeper.

"Oh, god, Cade…yes…" she whispered—

—and then gasped, a sound of horror, and I lifted my face to look at her. She was moving with me still but staring at the ceiling, brows furrowed, fright her only expression.

"No. No…" She shook her head. "Off, get off! Not like this." She pushed at me, shoving frantically.

I slid out of her and backed away, confused. "Eden, what—?"

She rolled to her stomach, drew her knees beneath her belly, a position of supplication, and then lifted up on all fours and turned to look at me over her shoulder. "Like this."

I was sitting on my shins behind her, aching, throbbing. "Eden…" I rose to my knees, touched her ass. "I don't understand what's wrong."

She hung her head in frustration, then lifted it again to look at me. "Don't you understand what was happening? What we were doing? Are you really that oblivious?" She shook her head. "Never mind. Come on. I need it. I need to come."

I shuffled forward, flush against her. She pushed back against me, then reached back between her legs and found my erection, guided me, slipped the tip inside her, then rocked back to sink me deep. I groaned, rocking forward. She went down to her elbows, raising her hips so I was even deeper, and rolled back to meet my thrusts.

And then, like a bolt of lightning, I realized. I faltered in my rhythm. "Shit, Eden."

She pushed into me. "Now you get it. You see what was happening?" I started to pull away, but she rocked her body. "Don't stop. Not now. Just…finish. Like this."

I hesitated. "Eden, I—"

"God*damn* it, Cade! Shut up and fuck me!"

I pulled out, abrupt, and stood up, backed away from her. "Just wait a second! Not like this, Eden."

She stood up, following me. She stood face to face me, both of us panting. She was angry and I was, too, only it was mixed with hurt and confusion.

"This is where we are, Cade." She swept a hand at the floor. "That...it can't happen. I can't let it happen. *You* can't let it happen."

"Maybe we shouldn't—" I took another step back, away from her, toward the kitchen.

She followed me, not letting me get away. "You think we can just...stop? We've tried. You've tried." She pointed at the floor where we'd been, her finger stabbing angrily. "*That* was fucking dangerous. But I know you, and I know me, and I know that, right now, we can't get away from each other. Nothing has changed."

"But it has changed." She pushed me, hard, and I stumbled backward. My knees hit a kitchen chair, and I sat down. "We can't keep doing this."

She stood over me. "So you want me to leave?"

I thought of watching her dress, watching her leave, knowing she wouldn't come back. Knowing, if she went out that door right now, it would be a knife severing the tenuous thread binding us. And I couldn't bear that. "No." I was a coward, a goddamned coward and a fool. "Don't go."

She took a step forward, her eyes on mine, and then straddled my knees. Put her hands on my shoulders and her feet on either side of the chair. Pushed me down, and I knew her game. I took her waist in my hands, and she lifted up on her toes. We both paused, hesitated, and then I was driving up into her, sinking in, and she was settling down onto me. She put her feet on the rungs of the chair that ran sideways between the front and back chair legs, hands on my shoulders for balance, and lifted up. Sank down. Head tipped back, eyes on me, she arched her spine, shoving her tits toward me. I cupped them, let her move.

She didn't rush, didn't allow herself to go crazy. She kept an even rhythm, sliding up and down my cock, using only the strength in her legs to push up. Her eyes never wavered from mine. Some spark in them, that chasm-deep hint of vulnerability, it was gone. Hidden.

I felt myself going close, gripped her hips in my hands and started to move her, pull her down.

"No." She took my hands in hers, pulled them away from her hips, and replaced them on her boobs. "Not yet. Don't come yet."

We never spoke during sex.

I held still and focused on control, on holding back. She kept the rhythm, slow and steady, eyes locked on mine, hands on my shoulders, just holding on. Moving. Stroking slowly. Sliding with controlled grace. I didn't dare look away, didn't dare move, because if I did, I'd lose it. I was holding back by sheer effort, teeth grinding, muscles tensed.

"Not yet." Her fingers turned to talons on my shoulders, nails digging in. "Not yet."

It was nearly impossible to hold back now. I gripped her waist and let my fingers crush her. I forced myself to loosen my grip for fear of bruising her skin.

"No, it's fine. Hold on tight. Not yet." Her movements began to grow powerful, forceful, still slow but harder and harder. "Hold onto me. Not yet. Not yet."

"Fuck. Fuck." I was shaking, and I knew my hands must be gripping her hips with vise-like strength, but her fingers were clawing down my chest and she was tipping forward, leaning into me as she began to lose control of her motion, to lose the grace of her strokes.

"Almost. Almost." She fell forward, all her weight on me now, only her hips moving, gyrating and grinding, and her fingers clawed my back, gouged my skin, left trails of fire.

I focused on the pain, struggling to wait. I was groaning now, pressure like an overloaded boiler within me, needing release so bad it hurt, it burned, it ached. "I can't…I can't—"

She was jerking herself by her hands now, shoving her body down, groaning through gritted teeth. "Almost…not yet, god, not yet."

"I can't wait. I have to—"

"No, no, wait, wait—"

"Fuck, *fuck*, I can't wait."

She sank her teeth into the round part of my shoulder and growled, lifted up, hovered, and then sank down so hard it hurt, and with that I could keep it back no longer, I exploded with convulsive force.

A short shriek left her throat. "Yes, now, *now!* Fuck, *fuck* yes—"

I bit back the roar that rumbled in my chest, gripped her hipbones in my hand and let myself go, let myself fuck up into her hard, harder than I'd ever fucked in my life, and I found her breasts brushing my face, found her hard nipple scraping my mouth, and I took it between my teeth and bit down.

Eden screamed between clamped molars, her forehead pushing at mine; she raked her fingers down my chest, rising up away from my downstroke, and met me with enough force that our hips jarred and our flesh slapped, and the force of my orgasm was wrenching, dizzying, unrelenting, painful in its power.

Three more times we collided like that, both of us coming so hard we couldn't breathe, could only grit our teeth and grip each other and ride the tsunami crest.

And then she went limp and I couldn't hold her up, couldn't do anything but rest my hands on her thighs and take her weight. We breathed together in silence, and then I levered myself upright, dragged my feet under me, held on to Eden's back with both hands and pushed myself to my feet, holding her weight, took a shaky step, locked my knees, and then moved with us to my bedroom. Eden clung to me, and then when she felt the bed beneath her she crawled away from me, found the pillow, and burrowed under the covers.

"Spoon me," she mumbled. "Please?" The last word was a ragged, broken plea.

I slid behind her, fit our bodies together, and we slept.

Eden

I woke up with full awareness of whose bed I was in, what we'd done the night before, what our desperate, needy sex had almost become. Cade was still behind me, spooning me, both of us having been so exhausted we'd slept without stirring. Dawn filtered through his windows. A bird chirped. I heard his breathing falter, felt him start to wake.

I felt his cock wake up, too. It hardened right between the cheeks of my ass. I'd never had sex in the morning. I bit my lip, then went for it. I knew he wasn't awake yet, but I also didn't care. Everything between us up to that point had been about losing ourselves in mutual need. This was about something I wanted, something just for me.

Remaining on my side, I threw my top leg over his, wriggled and shifted so the tip of his erection touched the suddenly damp folds of my core. I heard him groan, felt him shift his hips in response. I hesitated, wondering if maybe I should wait until he was fully awake. But then if I did that, he'd probably want to talk about last night, and I just couldn't handle that conversation.

So I curved my back into his chest, then straightened so he sank into me. He groaned, and I bit my lip so hard I tasted the tang of blood. I rolled my hips, and a whimper was torn from me as his cock touched me briefly in just the right place. I sought that contact again, the angle that had him striking me just so, and he was groaning, stretching even as he moved with me. His hand gripped my hip, tender and gentle. His lips touched my shoulder. No. No. Not good. I craned my neck and saw that he was blinking awake, pulling at my hipbone to get deeper. I moaned, unable to stop it. He was hitting me deep inside, and I was, within minutes, on the verge of coming.

And then he spoke, a soft murmur. "Ever? God, you feel good."

I cried out, curled into myself.

He started, and I felt him falter. "Oh…oh, *shit.* Eden. I—fuck, I was…I was dreaming. I thought it was a dream."

I shook my head, wanting to tell him it was fine, but not capable of it. I scrambled out of the bed, aching inside, feeling the impending orgasm building

and hovering on the verge, potential energy teeter-
ing on the brink of becoming kinetic. I tripped as
I ran for the *en suite* bathroom, elbowed the door
closed, but it only shivered and touched the jamb,
not latching. I didn't care. I sank down onto the toilet lid, buried my face in my hands, and fought for
breath and for control. I sobbed, choked it down.

I told myself he hadn't meant it. He'd been half-
asleep and dreaming. Of his wife, naturally. Thinking
it was her, thinking it was a dream. He'd told me
he'd been having dreams. Maybe he'd thought in his
sleeping mind that all of what had passed between us
had been the dream, and that he was waking up to
her. What a wrenching wake-up that must have been.

My pussy throbbed, needing the finish to what
I'd begun. I was on the edge of hysteria, cut deep by
Cade's accidental slip, and still burning with the need
to come. I sat back on the toilet, stretched my legs out
and spread my heels wide apart, dipped two fingers
against my clit and circled it, swiping in slow, measured strokes, seeking the right amount of pressure.

There, god, there it was. I whimpered. It was
unsatisfying, but better than going through the day
aching with the snarling frustration of an unfinished
orgasm. There was little worse, to me. I *had* to come
once I started, or I'd be a mess all day. I let my head
rest against the cold porcelain of the back of the toilet and brought myself back to the peak.

I heard the hinges creak and couldn't stop myself as he threw the door wide, mouth open to apologize. "Eden, I'm so sorry, I didn't mean—oh, shit…um…" He was still hard, too, bobbing from side to side as he stumbled to a stop in the middle of the bathroom.

I couldn't stop now. I was there, right there. If I stopped now, I'd never get it back. But look at him, painfully hard, slick and glistening with juices.

He started to back away, but he was clearly unable to tear his gaze from watching me touch myself.

"Don't go," I gasped. "Watch."

"Eden…"

"Come closer." I crooked my finger at him, and he took a few steps toward me, as though my finger was tied to a string around his waist. He stopped, standing between my legs. "You, too." I pushed his hand onto his cock.

He grasped himself in his fist, touched himself, slowly at first. "I didn't mean—"

"I know," I interrupted. "It's fine." It hurt; it wasn't fine.

But I was on the verge of orgasm and didn't care, not then. Especially not as I watched the plump mushroom head of his cock turn purple as he squeezed himself, then slid his fist down his length, and his eyes were on me, watching my two middle fingers circle madly in my pussy, my other hand at my boob, pinching my nipple, twisting and tweaking it.

I came. It was a slow and roiling climax, pushing through me like a mudslide. I gasped, breath caught, and my hands worked my body until I couldn't come anymore. Cade was still going, stroking himself hard and fast, standing over me, eyes hooded, watching me with his head tipped back, lip curled in a snarl.

I watched him, watched his balls clench and his eyes close, watched his motions go frantic, and then he jerked his fist down his length violently, once, groaning hard. A thick stream of come spat out of him and coated my tits and my belly, and I took his cock from him, leaned forward swiftly and wrapped my mouth around the soft springy head of his cock and sucked as he came again, spurting into my throat, sliding my fist down his length as fast and hard as I could, and he groaned, thrust involuntarily. I stretched my head forward and opened my throat and took the thrust, felt a third spasm shoot down my throat.

He cried out and pulled free. "Jesus, Eden." He turned and sagged against the opposite wall. "That was crazy. I've never done anything like that."

"Me, either," I said.

"I came in here to apologize," he said, "not to—"

"It wasn't your fault. I shouldn't have done that while you were asleep. I should be the one to apologize."

He scrubbed his hand through his hair. "I just…I thought I was dreaming. I do that, I have these really intense dreams, so real, like I wake up and I can't figure out if I'm awake and the dream was a dream or if I'm still asleep and the dream was reality…I get so confused, and I thought I'd been dreaming what happened with us—"

"I know," I said, pivoting on the toilet seat. "I shouldn't have done that to you. I'm sorry." I couldn't look at him, mortified at what he'd watched me do, now that I was out of the grip of the moment.

"That was kind of…crazy," Cade said, seeming as embarrassed as I was.

It was strange for us to be embarrassed. We'd seen the worst in each other, and often brought it out. But that, it had been a strange and intimate tableau, and neither of us knew how to deal with it.

"I've never done anything like that. I've never watched anyone—"

"I haven't, either," I rushed to admit.

Silence, heavy and awkward yet again.

"Why don't you take a shower?" he suggested.

I grimaced. "God, that would be fucking amazing."

He turned away. "I'll—I'll put out some clean clothes for you. You can borrow—"

I cut him off, spared him having to say her name. "Thanks."

I took a long, hot shower, scrubbed myself raw while I tried to make sense of what my life had become. Things with Cade were getting out of hand. The more we gave in, the more I wanted it, needed it. And last night, I'd started to *feel* something unfurling in my chest, deep at the root of my heart. Something that simply could not be.

But I knew simply staying away from Cade wouldn't help. As long as our lives continued in this impossible no-man's land of pain, unable to mourn and unable to move on, unable to help or do anything but wait, we'd keep falling into this. Staying away wouldn't help. We'd tried that over and over again. One of us would break. I'd been close to breaking his door down myself when he texted me while I was at the gym. I'd been on a stationary bike, pedaling for all I was worth, and my phone had gone off. I'd seen his name on the screen, the four little words. I'd left immediately, knowing exactly what would happen and wanting it. But I'd made myself wait to text him back, not wanting to seem eager. And in that time I'd worked myself into anger, resenting him for pushing me away. Well, even anger couldn't stop us. Anger seemed to exacerbate things, if anything, making it that much more intense of a high.

It really was a drug. The more I got, the more I needed. And I didn't know where the endpoint was. I was afraid I'd reached the event horizon, the point from which I'd never escape the inexorable gravity of needing him.

After I stepped out of the shower and dried off, I examined myself in mirror. I noted finger-prints bruised into the skin of my hips where he'd gripped me, dark bruises as reminders. I didn't mind the bruises, oddly. I wrapped the towel around my chest and left the bathroom, found Cade sitting at the kitchen table wearing nothing but a pair of shorts, the ones from last night, I was pretty sure. I approached him from behind, and winced as I saw four parallel scratch marks on both shoulders. He heard me, turned around. I gasped; I'd gouged his chest even worse. I hadn't noticed while he was in the bathroom with me.

"Holy shit, Cade. I didn't realize I'd scratched you that badly."

He glanced down, making that strange face we make when trying to see something just beneath our chin. "Yeah, you got me pretty good." He looked up at me. "Did I mark you at all?"

I pulled aside the towel, showing him the bruises on my hips. "A couple of bruises. Nothing *that* bad," I said, gesturing at the claw marks on his chest.

He leaned forward, examining the bruises. "Shit, Eden. I'm sorry. I knew I shouldn't have—"

"It's fine. We've both got marks."

"Is it both sides?"

I tugged up the edge of the towel at my other side, showing him the matching bruises. He was getting a good long look at my pussy in the process, but at this stage there was no point in bashfulness. "They'll heal," I said. "I bruise easily, and they always go away in a day or two."

I watched his eyes flick from the bruises over to my privates, and then he sat back and turned to his sketchpad. "Well, I shouldn't have left marks. I'm sorry."

I traced a finger down a scratch on his back. "I'm not."

He slowly swiveled to face me again. "You're not?"

I shook my head. "I'm trying to make sense of all this. Of you and me. And while I was in the shower, I realized something." I sat down in the chair kitty-corner to his, crossing my legs in some vague and probably stupid attempt at modesty.

"What's that?" he asked.

"We keep resisting this, acting like…like each time is an accident. But unless something changes, unless one of us either removes ourselves from the equation completely, or Ever's condition changes, I just don't think we'll be able to stop. We've tried, Cade. I stayed away from you the past month, too, you know. I could've asked you to come over. I almost did. If you hadn't texted me, I would've shown up at some point." I ran my still-damp hair through a wringer of my fingers, and Cade's eyes followed the trickle of water as it sluiced down between my breasts. "I feel like...you're a drug, and I'm addicted. And I don't—I can't even pretend anymore. I can't keep acting like I don't want it."

"Addicted. That's a good way of putting it." Cade tossed his pencil down on the table, closed the pad, and turned to face me. "So what's gonna change?"

I shrugged. "I don't know! Maybe nothing." I picked up the pencil he'd put down, toyed with it idly. "Are you going to leave? I mean, are you going to leave Ever? Quit visiting the Home, start over somewhere else?"

He reared back, shocked. "NO! I can't—I wouldn't—"

"And neither can I! She's my sister. She's your wife. Neither of us can just...leave. So that means something with her has to change."

"You're saying just...*not*...isn't an option. That we're both so weak that we can't quit each other."

I sighed. "Yeah, that's what I'm saying. I'll admit it. I'm too weak. I don't have that much self-control. You make me feel good, and that...it's the only good thing in my life. Cello...it's part of me. It doesn't provide relief. It gives me...I don't know how to put it...*expression*, I guess. But that's not the same." I leveled a hard look at him. "Can you stay away? Can you go day to day, see me at the Home, be around me, go about your business without slipping up?"

He groaned, leaning back in the chair and scrubbing his face. "No," he admitted miserably. "I've tried that." He flung his hand out and tapped an impatient rhythm on the table.

"Yeah, and how well has that worked?" I put my hand on his. "You either avoid me completely, or if you're around me and trying to act like you don't need this with me as much as I do, then you shut down, barely talking, barely responding. Neither of which works." He sighed and turned away without answering. I pushed at him. "Go take a shower."

He got up and moved toward the bathroom with the slow shuffle of someone who's lost all will and all direction.

event horizon; exhaust the demon

Caden

I don't know who I am anymore, Ever. I'm a cast-away. Lost. Drowning. I love you. That's the only true thing I know, and it's all I have to hold on to. I love you. I'll love you forever. Until the day I die, and I'll love you in whatever world comes after this one.

Cade

It was the shortest letter I'd ever written her. I'd sat, struggling, for hours to write her. But everything got stuck, bottled up. Eden had left not long after I took a shower, and I'd spent the rest of the day consumed by her words. Eventually, in an attempt to forget them, I'd decided to write Ever and then visit her. I hoped that visiting her would clear my head, would give me some clarity. But she lay there, same as always, as if she never moved. I knew, intellectually, that the nurses rotated her and did all sorts of things to keep her muscles from atrophying and to keep her from getting bedsores. But to me, she was always there on her back, eyes closed, hair neatly smoothed behind her ears. No change. No change. No brain activity. No signs of waking.

"I don't know what's happening to me," I whispered to her. "I don't know what I'm doing. I don't know how to stop. I love you. I don't want you to think I don't. I love you more than ever. I love you so much it literally wakes me up with my heart aching for you. And I don't want…what's happening. When I'm not here."

I couldn't bear to say it, even though I didn't really believe she was in there, that she heard me. It was easiest to believe she was asleep.

"Do you hate me? For letting this happen to you? Jesus, Ev. How can you not? If…*when* you wake up, I know what'll happen. And that's what I dread the most. But I still can't seem to…to find direction. To stop. To not keep fucking everything up, again and again and again. I know you'll never love me again. After you find out. But if you wake up, at least you'll be alive and I'll know how to live. If you hate me, it'll destroy me, but right now that's better than this. This…nothingness, this emptiness, this hell of stuck-between. It'd be better. Better than you, lying there like that. Forever." My whole body was wracked by a silent sob. "You have to come back, Ev. You have to rescue me. Come save me. God, Jesus, please save me." Was I praying? I didn't know. If I was, it was to Ever. It was a plea, regardless of the object.

I sat there, hunched forward, unable to cry but unable to sit up from the weight of the grief and the guilt weighing down on me. I forced my eyes open, forced myself to look at Ever. If I loved her like I claimed, why couldn't I stay faithful? Why couldn't I just…be a good person? If I loved her, I wouldn't be doing what I was doing with Eden.

Had I ever loved Ever? Doubts assailed me, struck me like hail, like lightning. Had I lost her? Had I lost my love for her? Was I hanging on out of stubbornness? Holding on to the knowledge that I'd loved her, even after I'd ruined it? How could I love her and do what I did every time I saw Eden?

What kind of horrible person was I?

I clawed at my face, tore at my hair, feeling everything inside me being ripped apart. I'd always had the fact that I loved Ever as the sole focus of my identity. And now I doubted even that.

I'd lost everyone in my life. Everyone.

Except Eden.

And Grams and Gramps. I struck on an idea. Maybe if they came here to Michigan, they'd help me. They'd hate me if they knew what I was caught up in, how I'd failed myself, failed Ever, failed everything I believed in. But they'd help me. They'd... they'd know what to do. Gramps would kick my ass.

I dug my phone out of my pocket and called their home phone. It rang eight times, and I was about to hang up when someone answered.

"*Hola?* I mean...I mean, hello? Monroe ranch. How I help you?"

"Miguel?" Why was he answering their phone? "Where's Grams or Gramps?"

He hesitated. "They not here. *Señor* Monroe, he have a stroke. In the hospital, to Cheyenne."

"Gramps had a *stroke?*"

"*Sí, señor.* Very sorry to tell you."

"Is he...is he okay? I mean, will he be okay? Why didn't Grams call me?"

"She have not leave the hospital in many days. Too much upset to call you."

"What about Uncle Gerry?"

"He run the ranch. They not want to worry you. He strong, *señor* Monroe. He be okay. No worry." A voice called in the background. "I tell *señora* you want her call you. I have to go now. Many *potros* this season."

Click.

My stomach churned. Gramps was in the hospital. No one had even called me. What if he died, too? What if I lost Grams and Gramps? They were often afterthoughts, I knew. I'd been too caught up in my own life to think about them, and now they were going to leave me, too.

It felt like a mortal blow.

I had no knowledge of leaving, but somehow I was in my car, and I was driving, driving. I arrived at Eden's dorm, and she was just going down the steps, with a woman who must have been her roommate behind her. Eden saw me, waved at her roommate, and went to the passenger side of my car. She must have seen something on my face, because she didn't hesitate, just got in, closed the door. Sat silent.

"Song for You" by Alexi Murdoch played, although I also had no memory of plugging my phone in.

I drove, and Eden rode beside me silently. I heaved a deep breath, feeling my eyes burn. She reached out and took my hand; she wrapped her fingers around mine, clasping hands rather than twining our fingers together.

"What's wrong?" Her voice was tiny and hesitant.

"Gramps had a stroke."

Eden squeezed my hand. "God, Cade. I—is he okay?"

I shrugged. I felt numb. I knew it would hurt, but right then, I didn't know how to react. "I don't know. They didn't tell me. I called them, to see if they could tell me. One of the hands answered. He told me. Grams hasn't left the hospital. She didn't call me. I don't know how he's doing. I don't...it's too much, Eden. It's too much. I can't lose them, too."

There was nothing Eden could say, so she said nothing, only held my hand as I drove aimlessly.

Eventually, as the sun went down and the playlist on my phone started to repeat, Eden spoke up. "You can't drive away from this, Cade. You can't drive forever. Let's go home." I knew she was as aware as I was of the discrepancy in that phrase. It wasn't her home. There was no us. But I knew what she meant, and I knew she was right. So I drove back to my condo and we went inside. "Have you eaten?"

I shook my head. "No."

"Since when?"

I shrugged. "I don't know. This morning? Yesterday?"

"You need to eat." She went to the kitchen and started rummaging. Evidently she found something to make, because water ran and a pot rattled.

I found myself on the couch, listless, lacking will or motivation for anything. Eden's presence in the kitchen at least meant that I was here. I hadn't floated away, hadn't simply stopped living. I thought I might, somehow. That I'd sit here and if she left, I'd just…go comatose myself. Vegetative. Like Ever. Joining her. But maybe that wouldn't be so bad.

My phone rang. "Hello?" I barely recognized my own voice.

"Caden? God, honey, I'm sorry I didn't tell you." It was Grams. "He's been in the hospital for several days, and I just haven't been able to—to leave him. He's sleeping, and Miguel called to tell me you'd called. I'm so sorry, honey."

"Is—is he okay?"

The hesitation spoke louder than a scream. "He'll require professional care, they think."

"What's that mean?"

"It means he's going to have to go into a—a home. Assisted living. I can't give him the kind of care he needs. Not by myself."

"Grams, I don't—"

"He recognizes me," Grams said, interrupting me for the first time in my entire life. "But that's about it. He can't talk, sweetheart."

My head drooped, and I almost dropped the phone. "Fucking hell, Grams. How could this happen? He's…he's so strong."

"He's old, honey. And he's still fighting. But…"

"What are you going to do?"

She didn't answer for a long, long time. I felt something wet drip down my nose. "I'll go with him,

I think. There's a nice place in Cheyenne. I couldn't stay in that big old ranch house by myself without him. So…I'll go with him."

"What can I do, Grams?" My voice was a rasp.

"Be strong, Caden. You're a Monroe. I know you, sweetheart. I can hear in your voice that you're having a hard time. Don't worry about us. Come see us, if you can. We love you. I love you, Connor, honey."

"Grams, I'm—"

"Caden. I meant…I meant Caden."

I licked away the salty wetness on my lips. "I love you, Grams. He'll be okay. You'll be okay."

"I know." She sighed. "I have to go, sweetie. I have to be there if he wakes up."

"Okay. 'Bye." She didn't even respond, just hung up.

Eden sat on the couch beside me. Put a bowl of something hot into my hands. Macaroni and cheese. I ate without tasting it.

"He's going into a home. A Home." I shoveled the food into my mouth, more for something to do than anything else. "Grams is going with him."

"I'm sorry, Cade."

"Everyone. They all go. They all leave me. Mom left. Dad left. Ever left." I choked, coughed, put the bowl on the coffee table. "Now Gramps. There's no one left. They've all…they're all gone. Gramps barely recognizes Grams. And she…she's—she *is* him.

They've been married for forty years. More? I don't know. If he goes, she goes. And he's going."

"Hey." She set her bowl down and leaned into me. "I'm still here. I know that's not—"

"You're here. I—thank you, Eden. For not…for not abandoning me, too."

She shook her head. "We're all kinds of fucked up, you and I, but we have each other. For as long as it lasts and for what it's worth, we have each other." She reached up and wiped her fingers across my cheek. Wiped away my tears.

She got up, sat on the floor in front of the shelf of DVDs. After perusing for a few minutes, she put in *The Hangover 3.* "Nothing like mindless comedy, right?"

We sat on the couch, and we ended up curled into the corner. Eventually we slid down to a lying position, and neither of us fought the intimacy of the way we cuddled together. I fell asleep before the end of the movie, another first for me. When I woke up, Eden was lying directly on top of me, the TV was off, and starlight shone off the snow out the window, a crescent moon showing in the upper corner. I lay awake then, grateful for a period of sleep free of nightmares but unable to fall back asleep. I watched the moon drift out of sight, watched the black lighten incrementally, eyes burning with the need to sleep, chest aching with the pressure of the storm that was life.

I heard Eden sniff, felt her stir. She turned her face up to look at me. "Hey."

"Hey."

"I'm probably crushing you."

I hadn't noticed until then, but my hands were cradling her ass, familiar and possessive. "You're fine."

I swallowed hard, my eyes on hers. She seemed to sense that I was making some kind of decision, and she stayed as she was, watching me think. I closed my eyes, sighing, knowing I'd come to a point from which I'd never return. I cupped her ass, kneaded it, and then slid my palms up her back. She breathed in, her nostrils flaring. Giving in, surrendering, I unclasped her bra. Pushed her shirt up. She wormed out of the shirt and her bra at the same time, dropped them on the floor beside us. Waited. She was wearing a skirt that came just past her knees, had been wearing knee-high boots with it but had taken those off hours ago. I found the zipper at the side, pulled it down. Tugged the skirt off. She was wearing a yellow thong, and I pulled that down, slid the string out from between the cheeks of her ass. She lifted one knee, pulling her foot free, and then the thong was flying away, kicked off. She was naked on top of me, and I was still fully clothed.

Eden kissed my jaw, my throat. I blinked, held still. She ran her hands up my torso, pushing my T-shirt with it. It stuck on my head, and I ripped it free. She kissed my breastbone. Rolled against the couch back, opened the fly of my jeans with one hand, lowered the zipper. Slowly worked my jeans off, one side at a time, until I kicked them off. They crumpled in a heap on the floor, next to her skirt. Her eyes flicked up to mine and then down, and I waited. She curled her fingers under the elastic of my boxers, pulled it away to reveal the tip of my erection. I waited. She looked up at me, then back down again. Pulled the gray elastic down further, and then more, and then I was bobbing free and I kicked them away.

She rolled back down on top of me. We stayed like that, naked, but not yet joined. "This one is all you," she murmured.

I knew, somewhere in my heart, that if we did this face to face again we'd lose ourselves. I'd surrendered, but I still had to retain that tiniest part of my soul. I didn't have much, but I had that at least. I sat up, and she moved with me. I took her shoulders in my hands, gently but firmly turned her toward the arm of the couch. She knew immediately what I intended, and leaned over it, placing one foot flat on the floor, the other leg spread wide to the crack of the couch. I knelt behind her, my foot beside hers, and she reached down her front, between her thighs, grabbed me, dragged the tip against her folds. Found her entrance, slid me in, and I plunged deep. She gasped, dropped her face to the arm of the couch, arched her back to push into me. I put my hand on the top of her ass, grabbed her hip in the other and began a slow, thorough, pounding rhythm, all the way out, all the way in. She met my rhythmic strokes with arching, rolling thrusts of her own. She turned her head to the side, and her hair fell across her shoulders. She hadn't dyed it in a long time, and her dark roots were showing. I wasn't sure why I noticed that. She watched me over her shoulder, her eyes narrowed and her mouth open.

We didn't slow or speed up, we didn't talk or groan, we only moved. I felt her walls tighten around my cock, and she gripped the arm of the couch with both hands, body lifting up off the cushions as she rocked back into me. She bit down on her lip, face still turned toward me, but her eyes were closed now and her brow was furrowed in concentration, and then I felt the rising of my own climax and we began to rock in earnest.

And then her straightened leg buckled and our rhythm faltered. "Stand—stand up," she gasped.

I knew what she meant. She rotated away from the arm of the couch, and I moved with her, and now she put both feet on the floor, bending over, clutching the back of he couch. I stood up straight behind her and shifted my stance wide. And now…I slid deep, once, slow and soft, and she shook her head, grunting once as she rocked backward, hard, bending at the knees to gain extra force. I picked up speed, and now, having already been close to climax once, felt it burgeon inside me within seconds. She was there with me, judging by the expression on her face and the way she hung her head between her arms and leaned over further, seeking to get me deeper. I pulled her hips back into my thrusts, and then she buried her face in the back cushions of the couch. She was bent nearly double now, and I was slamming into her, her ass shaking with the force of my thrusts, and she was groaning in the back of her throat.

I was there, at the edge, and then I was over, climaxing, coming, slamming hard and fast into her, and she was hanging on to the top of the couch while leaning as far down as she could, thrusting backward into me arrhythmically, trying to match my pace but simply unable to as she was rocked by the force of her own climax. I groaned once as I released inside her. She gasped once, loud, and then she fell forward onto the couch, to her knees, rolling to a sitting position. I flopped down beside her.

Neither of us spoke.

We sat there, panting, sweating, as the sky lightened to gray. I started to doze, and then I felt Eden's hand on my thigh. She leaned against my shoulder, looking down at my cock. I wrapped my arm around her shoulder, and she burrowed into me. She took me in her hand, fondled and stroked me until I felt myself responding. When I was hard enough to stand free, she looked up at me, then slid down my chest, taking me in her hand and into her mouth. She mouthed the head, just the head, and stroked me until I was rock hard again, and then she straightened, stood in front of me, facing away from me. She straddled me, shins on the couch underneath her, and impaled herself on me. She sank me deep, paused there, and then rode me with unrelenting vigor. She set the pace immediately, rising and falling with quick, wet rhythm. I cupped her tits in my hands and played with her nipples as she rode me, and we never spoke a word, never gasped or groaned at all this time. She leaned forward into my hands and I held her weight, and we moved, rocked, fucked.

We came, first me and then her.

After we could move again, we went to my bed and slept until the sun was high in the sky.

Eden

I was sore and tired. I was confused. Cade was… losing his identity. I wasn't sure if sex with me was helping or hurting him, whether I was somehow adding to the crisis of self he was experiencing. Certainly

I understood where he was coming from. He'd lost his mother at a young age, and then his father, and then finally found Ever as his one true love, only to lose her as well. It was simply too many hard blows for any one person to endure. And Cade…he was cracking. How could he not?

I didn't know how to help him. I couldn't love him. He couldn't love me. I couldn't let myself fall in love with him, although I was desperately afraid that was happening despite my efforts. And I feared he would, at some point, if enough time passed, stop caring whether I fell in love with him or he with me.

Couldn't was not the right word in that equation. *Shouldn't*. Had no place. No right. And if I did, or he did, it wouldn't be love built on the right foundation. It wouldn't be based on mutual respect and affection, or a deep soul-bond. It would be about sex, need, lack of anything else as a salve on raw and open wounds. You depended on a life raft in a turbulent sea; you didn't fall in love with it. You didn't develop misguided feelings toward it.

He was still asleep, for once. Usually I woke up and he was already awake, or still awake. And the fact that I could use the word "usually" in that sentence was a kind of scary thing. I watched him sleep. Even at rest he didn't look at peace. He had a slight crease in his brow, lines of worry permanently etched on the bridge of his nose. There was a slight downturn to his mouth, a permanent frown. He shifted in his sleep and a hank of black hair swept across his brow, into his eye. My hand reached out of its own accord and brushed it away. There was no reason for my middle finger to brush again across his forehead, trying to soothe away the lines of deeply carved pain.

I couldn't heal him. I couldn't take his pain. I couldn't replace Ever. All I could do was be there for him, try to ease the agony, try to be a rope to which he could hold as the waves battered him. The way I was doing it was stupid. I knew it was. Sex didn't solve anything. It was only confusing both of us. Yet despite intellectually knowing that, I couldn't seem to stop myself. I couldn't seem to stop wanting him. He'd given me, in a handful of angry, desperate, confused sexual encounters, more pleasure and more meaning than all my previous partners put together. No one had ever made me feel as good as Cade. And he wasn't even really trying. He wasn't attuned to my needs. It wasn't that he didn't care; I knew that. It was that we were both simply taking what we needed from each other. And I couldn't help wondering and wishing I was worthy of knowing how it felt to have his full attention, his affection, his love.

It would be magical.

Glorious.

He very nearly sated me, by the time we were done. But not quite. I was always left wanting…

something. As if, despite the fury and the primal aggression with which Cade fucked me, there was an element missing. I didn't mean love. I wasn't sure that existed for me. But I felt instinctively as if, with the right touch, the just-perfect technique, I could reach a heretofore-unknown sexual peak, a kind of nirvana. I'd sensed it with one or two of my previous partners, but with Cade, I actually got a taste of it. Saw it, could make out its shape in the shadows. But I couldn't grasp it, couldn't reach it.

Maybe someday, with someone.

But probably not.

I slid out of bed, careful to not disturb Cade, and turned on the shower, let it go scalding, steaming up the mirror, fogging the bathroom. I stood under the stream and let the almost too-hot water scorch me, let it soak into my muscles. I didn't wash, didn't shampoo or condition. I just soaked.

And thought.

This thing with Cade, it was a demon. A red-eyed monster clutching both of us by the throat, holding us together, binding us to each other with skeins of unbreakable shadow. I wanted free, but couldn't break loose. I wanted to not need him. I wanted to be able to be comforted by him without it leading to sex. It wasn't normal. People went through situations like this all the time, surely, and they didn't resort to fucking.

It was more than fucking, a voice inside me protested. It might not have been love, but it wasn't empty fucking. I'd gone around in circles on this topic for hours, trying to figure it out as I worked the weight machine circuit, as I cycled and hit the heavy bag and sat through classes. The only time I was free of thoughts of Cade and the nature of our dysfunctional relationship was when I played Apollo. Then, when I drew the bow across his strings and listened to the music resonating from his aged frame, I could float away, and my mind would go blessedly quiet and I would be free, just for those too-brief moments.

I finally got around to washing and condition-ing my hair, scrubbing my body. I was lathered in soap when I heard the bathroom door open. I turned around and saw Cade in the doorway. The shower was glass walled, marble tiled. Room for two. There was a bench in the corner, just the right height. I stood, dripping soap, clutching the poofy orange loofah sponge across my body against one shoulder.

He was naked still, and as gorgeous as ever, despite the rings under his eyes.

I pushed open the door in silent invitation. He sighed, a resigned sound. That hurt. The fact that he was resigned to the time we spent together, resigned to sex with me, that hurt. Deeply. It cut into a dark place in my soul, the kind of pain that you'd never share with another living person. It wasn't fair, I knew, and I did my damnedest to not let it reflect back at Cade. It wasn't his fault. He wasn't trying to hurt me. Maybe I was being naïve or too forgiving, or just a plain slut, but I knew Cade was only using to me cope with the horror show his life had become. I was a coping mechanism. And honestly, he was the same for me. I'd lost my sister, my twin. She'd been my only real friend, the one person I could confide the whole truth to. If this situation with Cade had happened in such a way that Ever wasn't involved, I'd have told her everything. Even that I resented him for making me want him, need him, that I was hurt by his resignation to sleeping with me. But with Ever comatose, I had no one to talk to, no one to confide in. Except Cade, and I couldn't tell him about himself.

Cade stepped into the shower, closed the door, and then simply stood there looking at me. Either lost as to what to do next, or simply too stunned by my beauty to look away.

I was going with the former.

I waited. When he didn't move, I went back to washing my body, but I couldn't help performing a bit. Arching my back as I washed my tits, shoving them forward, leaning over double to wash my calves and feet, which was stupid and unnatural, but effective, since it made his cock twitch. I lathered up, rinsed off, and did it again, all for his benefit.

But still he didn't move.

I wasn't going to make the first pass. Not this time. Just because this was a fucked up and dysfunctional relationship didn't mean I didn't want to feel wanted.

Finally, fed up with his silence and his seeming inability to actually *do* anything, I started to move past him.

"Wait." He stood in front of the door, blocking me. The water rushed past both of us. "All this time, I haven't…done anything. For you. You've given things to me, done things just to make me feel good. But I haven't done the same."

"It's not a *quid pro quo* thing, Cade." Getting cold, I stepped back into the stream of hot water, pulled him with me. "I just want to…help you. Give you something to help you hang on."

"And now it's your turn." He pivoted me so my back was to the water, blocking most of it.

The water ran down my shoulders and back, some of it sluicing down my front. He went to his knees in front of me, and my heart ratcheted to a panicked thumping. He couldn't do that. It would make my job, my one duty in this—keeping my heart my own—that much harder. But yet, I didn't stop him as he kissed beneath my left boob, lifting it and licking away the water running over it, then sucked my nipple into his mouth. I sighed, feeling the tug in my loins. I stood still and told myself to breathe and just feel. Cade's mouth moved across my chest to the other tit, and then his lips brought that nipple to attention and made it hard, and his tongue flicked it and I was already panting. His hands went to my hips as he began alternating boobs, kissing and licking first one and then the other. Palms slid down the outside of my thighs, to my knees, and then arced around to the inside, carved upward. I shifted my feet apart involuntarily. His fingers traced up my inner thighs, and then sliced up and over the mound of my pussy. I gasped, and he seemed to like the noise, because he rewarded me with a single finger sliding down the opening, and then wiggled it into my folds. I had to widen my stance just a little more. He still couldn't even get a whole hand between my thighs yet, because I had thick, muscular thighs with ample flesh padding to boot, and I'd have to spread them apart pretty far before he could do more than finger me. Which he did, and well. His middle finger delved into me, and I bit my lip and whined in my throat as he swiped inside me, searching my walls and finding the perfect spot. Stroking me, curling his finger toward himself. Oh, god, that was good. And then his mouth descended and he sank down so his heels touched his ass, and his mouth kissed my thighs, my hips, and then he used both hands to press my legs apart. I complied, widening my stance until my feet were slightly more than shoulder-width apart. I was embarrassed by my stance for about six seconds. Right up until his lips touched my pussy and his tongue flicked into me.

I held onto his shoulders and tipped my head back, and lost myself in the physical sensation. I forced my brain into the Zen of enjoyment, similar to when I played cello. He licked, tongued, flicked, kissed, sucked. Fingering me all the while.

Holy shit, he was good. He made me weak-kneed and panting, and then he'd alter his technique, slow, almost stop, and I'd lose the edge and he'd start over again, slow and then faster, trying one thing and then another until I moaned or gasped or dipped at the knees or shoved my hips forward, and he'd do that harder and faster until I started to buck into his mouth, and then he'd stop again and do something else.

This was too good. It felt too fucking amazing. I almost expected him to stop and stand up and want to fuck, but he didn't. He brought me to the edge several times, and then when he had me gyrating and gasping and tried to back away again, I shamelessly grabbed his head and held him there.

"No, goddammit!" I said, my voice harsh and demanding. "Don't stop. Fuck…please…don't stop."

He complied, fingers inside me stroking me just right and his mouth attending to my clit, his other hand cupping my ass and holding me against his face. I couldn't stop myself from pinching my own nipples between finger and thumb, and then I felt the lightning gathering, building, and he felt my movements grow desperate and needy and he went with it, faster and faster, until he reached a fervor that couldn't be increased and he held it, licking and sucking and fingering until I was groaning and rocking on the edge of a climax that wouldn't come.

I needed something he wasn't doing. I gripped his wrist to hold it in place, pushed his face away and replaced his mouth with my own hand, pulled him up by his chin and shoved his face against my tits. He obeyed, and I circled myself like I liked it, like I needed it, and he stroked me deep inside like he had been, biting and tweaking my nipples until I hit the peak and felt myself break open, groaning in relief as a climax unequaled in delicious power and overwhelming waves of ecstasy washed over me.

When I couldn't take the orgasm any longer, I pushed Cade's fingers away and tugged him to his feet.

He seemed...troubled. "I'm sorry, I—"

I put my hand over his mouth. "Don't. Thank you. You didn't have to do that. But thank you."

"But I couldn't—"

"It was more than anyone else has ever done for me. So thank you." I smirked at him. "Say, 'You're welcome.'"

"You're welcome." And then…he just walked out of the shower.

Right. Like I was going to let that just slide by. "Cade," I called. He stopped, turned around, his cock at half-mast. "What about you?"

He shrugged. "That was about you."

I shut the water off, stepped out. I didn't bother drying off. "Tell me what you want." His face told me he wanted things I couldn't give, so I clarified. "Tell me what you want me to do to you."

He seemed at a loss. "I don't…I don't know. Just…you." His eyes raked over me. "Just make me come. However you want."

He was thinking too hard, something told me. I sidled up to him, wrapped my fist around his length and pushed him backward, out of the bathroom and into the bedroom until he fell against the bed, sat down. I slid my fingers down his length. He closed his eyes, and I put my mouth around him. His head fell back, and I took him out of my mouth, curled my palm over the top, cupping the broad head and squeezing. With my other hand I cradled his sack, gently massaging, found his taint with my middle finger and pressed in, squeezing my fist down his cock, and then loosened my grip so that I was barely touching him and moved my fingers around him in a swift rhythm. As soon as he began moving in time with my hand, I slowed, gripped him firmly again, and sucked him into my mouth. He was gasping now, and his hips were gyrating, so I bobbed my head for him, taking him deeper and deeper every time I went down. He started moaning. I watched him, watched his face take on an expression of pleasure, and then he opened his eyes and met mine. He watched me take his cock into my mouth, holding the base and working it in short fast strokes.

"I'm gonna…god, I'm coming…" he croaked in warning.

I kept my eyes on his as I took him to the edge of my throat, working the thick base of his cock with my fist, cupping his sack and pressing hard onto his taint. He gripped the blanket on the bed, clearly forcing his hips still as he came. He groaned, cursed, and shot into my mouth, hot and wet and musky. I kept working him, felt another spasm wrack him, and took that, too.

He opened his eyes and stared down at me. When I knew he was done, I backed away and stood up, sat on the edge of the bed beside him.

"Better?" I asked. He nodded, but I sensed an additional weight of troubled guilt in his expression. "What, Cade? What's the point of all this if we're not honest with each other?"

He sighed. "I feel like we're…de-evolving. Devolving."

Ah. Another heavy, searching conversation. Fun. "How about we put this off for just a second. Get dressed. Pour us drinks."

We both put on a minimum of clothing. Just shorts for him, and a T-shirt for me. He uncapped each of us a beer, and we sat down on the couch, close but not touching.

"Now," I said, "explain what that means. How are we devolving? You mean you and me, or humans as a species, or what?"

"Us. You and me. I just mean that this started out as something we couldn't avoid. Couldn't stop. It wasn't about mere attraction. I mean, I'm a guy, okay? And you're hot. Not to put too fine a point on it, you're Ever's twin sister, so obviously I'd be... attracted. But it wasn't just that. Look, you go through life, you see all kinds of hot and attractive people. This is a topic of dissension for most couples, because guys see a hot girl, and they look. Maybe more than look. Maybe they think about what they'd like to do to that girl. Maybe they picture her naked, or wonder what having sex with her would be like. I'd say that's fairly natural. It doesn't mean you have any intention of doing anything about it, right? It's the scumbag cheaters and moral-less sluts who can't control that impulse, who have no filter that tells them, 'No, I shouldn't go around trying to actually fuck that person that I'm attracted to, since I'm in a relationship.'"

"I'm following you, but I'm not seeing the relevance to you and me. What we're doing with each other, I really don't want to think it makes you a scumbag and me a slut—"

He waved his hand to cut me off. "No. No. That's not what I meant. I'm getting to how it relates to you and me. That kind of stuff happens. I have that filter, okay. I could...I could walk down the street with Ever and see a hot chick, and not actually *desire* her, not have any ideas of *doing* anything with her. It would never enter my mind. I'd at most think, 'Hmm, that chick is pretty hot.' It wasn't like that with you. It wasn't like I sat around while I was with Ever—" He cut himself off, choked out a sigh that was almost a sob. "I'm still with her, right? I don't know. That's the real question in my life, isn't it? Anyway. When Ever was—before the accident, I mean, when you and Ever and I hung out, I saw the fact that you were hot, saw the fact that I found you attractive. But that was it. So it wasn't like as soon as I realized Ever was in a coma I thought, 'Well, fuck, here's my chance.'"

"I know that, Cade."

"It started out between you and me, as...just needing *some*thing. Something good, when everything's bad. Something comforting. And somehow it ended up translating into sex. I don't—I don't know why. I really don't. I've tried so hard to figure that out."

"Why is understanding it so important to you?" I asked.

"Because maybe if I understand it, I can stop it."

"Is it that bad?" I couldn't help taking it personally. I knew better. But my ability to think and act rationally was vanishing, or was already gone.

He frowned at me. "Jesus, Eden. Don't pin that shit on me." He got up and got two more beers, handed me one. "It's good, Eden. You need that affirmation? It's always really, *really* good. And that's part of the problem. I don't know what it was that started this between us, why, but now I'm starting to feel like it's something I can't control. More so than ever. I could never control it, I guess, but now I feel like I'm losing myself to it. To you. Like the only thing that makes any sense in my life anymore is...when you and I are having sex. And that's..."

"Fucked up," I supplied.

He slid down on the couch, groaning a long, dispirited sigh. "Yeah. Really, really fucked up." His voice dropped to a whisper so small I had to strain to hear him. "I'm not even sure about Ever anymore. If...if what we had was real. I'm—doubting... everything."

"God, Cade. That's the last thing I ever wanted—"

"I know! I know, Eden. Please know that in no way, no smallest way, do I blame any of this on you. There's no *blame* to be placed. It's just...if I could so

easily forget her, and sink into this with you, then...
did I ever even love her?"

"You did, Cade. You *do*."

"Then how did this happen? How did I get so...
sucked into this?" He groaned again and scrubbed
his face. "God, that came out wrong. Or it didn't, but
I think you have to understand something. You're an
amazing person, Eden. You're gorgeous. You're fucking...*insanely* talented. You've got a rocking body.
You do. I know you doubt it, have issues or whatever, but...look. Yeah, you have curves. But underneath those curves, you're hard as a rock. And that's a
sexy-as-fuck combination." He seemed to be forcing
this out of himself. "I know our relationship hasn't
exactly lent itself to me...I don't know, building you
up, I guess. I should be. I should be making you feel
good about yourself. I haven't been, and I'm sorry."

I had to breathe hard and fast and look away to
keep from breaking down. "Cade, stop. You're not...
we're not—in a relationship. You don't owe me that.
And the fact that you think that, that you're telling me, it means more than you'll ever know." Not
crying. Not crying. "No one's ever—ever said that.
Ever—ever even cared enough to—to—*fuck*. Sorry."
I was crying, and it wasn't the heartbroken kind of
sobbing that can be almost attractive. No, this was
self-pity crying, croaking, snotty, ugly crying.

He pulled me against him. "And that's a fucking crime. You deserve better. You deserve so much
better than what I'm giving you. That's part of my
problem. What this whole conversation is about.
That?" He waved at the bathroom, indicating our
most recent encounter. "That wasn't okay. I meant to
just…make you feel good, because I realized I'd been
selfish. Just—taking what I wanted like—like some
rutting beast. And you deserve better. You deserve
better than going down on me as a returned favor
or something."

I had to think hard about what I wanted to
say. "Are you…feeling like you're…I don't know.
Degrading me somehow?"

He shrugged; it was a small and miserable gesture.
"Yeah. Kind of."

I sat up, pivoted, and sat cross-legged facing him,
pulling a throw pillow onto my lap. "Cade. It wasn't
degrading. I didn't feel that way. You gave me something, and I wanted to give it back."

"Okay, and that makes me feel a bit less shitty,
but it doesn't answer my more central question: Is
that what this has become between us? Sexual favors
given and returned?"

I shrugged. "Maybe. In a way, yeah, I suppose
so. But does that change things? Does it make what
we're doing any better or worse?"

"I don't know. I don't know anything, Eden. I'm a mess. I'm confused, scared, worried. So many things."

"I am, too. I don't mean I'm okay with what we're doing. I feel mixed up about it, too. But it does provide me with some kind of...comfort. Distraction. Pleasure, when being without my sister is...it's fucking hell. Being in this limbo is hell. And when I'm with you, I can forget, if only for a little bit." I swallowed hard, pulling an admission from the buried hole of my heart. "I don't...I don't want to stop, Cade. And yeah, I feel...sometimes I feel like that makes me slutty. But it's the truth. It's just true. I don't want to stop. Not yet. It's selfish. It's horrible. But there it is."

"There's no way to say this without it sounding horrible, so I'm just gonna say it. While you were in the shower, before I went in, I had this thought, this...image. I feel like wanting you, needing this whatever-it-is with you, this odd relationship, the sex, the companionship, everything, but especially the sex, I feel like it's a demon inside me, a hungry demon. And every time I'm with you, I think a part of me hopes that I'll have given the demon what it needs. And then, today, I wondered if I was trying to exhaust the demon, sate him, so he wouldn't... wouldn't need you anymore." He held onto me, talking into my hair, and I felt the exhalation of his breath on my scalp with every word. "I don't want to need this anymore. Not that you're not worth wanting or needing, because you are. But because…who I was with Ever was…a better person. And I want to hold on to him, onto that person. *That* Cade. Not this weak, selfish Cade. You deserve so much fucking better than what I have left, which is what you're getting. You deserve better than sex that's…steeped in guilt, and confusion."

He shifted so I had to look at him, and I sensed the crux of this whole long admission coming.

"You deserve better, Eden," he repeated. "You deserve love, and I—I can't give that to you."

I had no response. I lowered my head to his shoulder and held on to him, onto whatever shred of comfort I could get.

If I deserved better than whatever Cade had left, and if what I was getting from Cade was several orders of magnitude better than what I'd ever known, then…what would love be like? I couldn't fathom it, and I couldn't even begin to wonder where I could possibly find it.

But I wanted it.

final wisdom

Caden

Ever,

My love, my darling. My everything.

Every day, every single day for nearly a year and half now, I've sat in this chair at your bedside and talked to you, read the latest letter. Just sat with you. Sketched. Watched TV beside you. Over 500 consecutive days. I haven't missed one.

That has to mean I still love you, right? It has to mean something.

But I don't know how to do it anymore. I just don't. I want to give up. I'm the most pathetic, shitty, horrible person who's ever lived for saying that, for writing it and thinking it and reading it to you, whether you actually hear anything in that coma or not. But fucking hell, Ever, it's true. It's true. I can't do this anymore.

The worst part? I don't know HOW to give up. Coming to see you, writing letters to you, it's part of me. It's just as automatic as breathing, as eating. Actually, I forget to eat sometimes. If I stopped visiting, would I forget you? Would one day lead to two, and that into a week, a month, a year? Would I just...act like you don't exist anymore?

I wouldn't be able to forget. You are my soul, and even if I never visited you again, I'd still never be able to forget you.

I've forgotten the sound of your voice, though. I've forgotten the way you feel when I hold you. I haven't forgotten the way you smell. That's the weirdest thing. I can't remember the way you'd look at me, and I can't remember how you felt or how you tasted. I have memories of us, but they're vague and fading every day. But the way you smell, that vanilla sugar lotion. I can close my eyes and smell that, clear as day. That smell, it's in me, on me, unforgettable. I was in class the other day, and some girl sitting near me had that lotion on. I couldn't mistake that smell anywhere. I turned around and she had a tube of it, and she was rubbing it on her hands. Right behind me. And I nearly fucking lost it. I had to leave class. I was nauseous. Sick. The smell hit me, and I could see you. Eyes open, awake; I could see you on our bed, in the morning sunlight, naked and just out of the shower, spreading that lotion on your arms and legs. I cried in the bathroom. I sat in a toilet stall and cried.

No matter what, I love you. I'll never stop loving you. I don't know if you'll love me when you wake up. If you'll be able to. But even if you don't, I'll love you. Forever, and after forever. Even if I don't deserve your love back.

Your loving husband,

Cade

I carefully folded the letter and put it in with the rest. I had filled one shoe box, and was well on my way to maxing out a second. I put the box in its place inside the drawer next to the nightstand by her bed. And then, as I did more and more often, I simply sat in silence until I could take it no more. It wasn't truly silence, of course. There were machines beeping, the respirator sighing. Pages over the PA in the hallways, voices passing, shoes squeaking. But I was silent. I didn't know what to say out loud anymore. I could write things to her, but I couldn't form words.

I stared at her, hands curled into fists on my knee, watching the respirator pump and make her breathe. Sometimes, as I stared at her, I'd feel a sense of desperation wash over me. Usually I'd leave then, and try to ignore the feeling until it passed. I'd go home and sketch until the darkness in my skull abated, or I'd text Eden. Some days we'd just hang out, watch movies, have dinner, pretending we were some sick, twisted parody of a normal couple. Sometimes we'd end up fucking, sometimes not.

Today, however, when the desperation struck me with meteoric force, I sat and bore it. I let it rip through me. I let it burn in my gut and churn in my brain. I began to rock in the chair, back and forth. And then I took her cold, frail hand and lifted it, bent over it, pressed my lips to the blue-veined back and hyperventilated until I went dizzy.

I hadn't spoken a word out loud to her that I hadn't written beforehand in four months. The knowledge was a viper in my soul, injecting venom into my bloodstream.

"*Ever…*" It was a hiss, a breathless gasp, barely intelligible as language. "I need you, Ever. I need you to—to live. Or die. I can't *do* this anymore, Ever. Live. Come back to me. Or…let me go."

People said time heals all wounds. But what if… what if this wound couldn't heal, was always being ripped open and kept raw and ragged and bleeding? No matter how much time passed, the wound left by Ever's coma would never heal. As long as she lay trapped between life and death, I'd never heal.

I was trapped, as much as she was. I felt like my entire life was this room, the bed, Ever's unchanging form under the blankets, classes I had no interest in anymore, and Eden. The guilt of Eden, the illicit, stolen comfort of every moment spent with her. It was all a cycle.

I was broken and exhausted.

"I'm gonna go away for a while, Ev," I whispered. "I'm gonna go visit Gramps. I'll be back soon."

I left her, drove to my condo, and began packing. While I was stuffing clothes into my duffel bag, the same black bag I'd taken to Interlochen Arts Academy, I heard a knock on my door, jerked it open to let Eden in.

"Hey," I said, and went back to packing.

"Where are you going?" she asked.

I answered without looking at her. "Visit Gramps."

"For how long?"

"I dunno. Couple of days. Not long." I turned around to glance at her, and wished I hadn't.

She was wearing nothing but yoga shorts and a sports bra, both royal blue, and she was covered in a sheen of sweat. She had her hair pulled back in a tight braid, accentuating her cheekbones and the curve of her neck.

"You're leaving *now?*"

I nodded. "Yeah." She looked…upset. "Look, I know this is sudden, but I just…I have to get away. I can't take it. And I have to see Gramps. I have this feeling that if I don't go see him now, I might not have another chance."

She just nodded. I waited for her to say something, to explain what was eating her, but she didn't.

"What, Eden?"

"I just feel like, why now? What about Ever?"

I jerked the zipper of the duffel closed. "What about her? It's not like she'll miss me." The words dripped vitriolic bitterness.

Eden gasped. "Cade! You don't really believe—"

"I DON'T KNOW WHAT I BELIEVE!" I yelled. "Will she miss me? Won't she? No one knows! I can't stay here anymore, Eden. I just can't. I'm gonna be certifiably committable if I don't deal with the fucked-up mess that is my life. I have to face the reality that Ever may never wake up and I may just be alone for the rest of my life. I can't keep doing this with you, Eden. It's tearing me apart."

Eden closed her eyes, turned away. "I know. I get it."

"But?"

She whirled. "But I don't *have* anywhere to go to get away from this!"

"You think I *want* to be visiting a dying grandfather? He's the closest thing to a parent I've had since Mom died, and now he's—I feel like he's gonna die, too, and I have to see him. I have to."

Her shoulders sagged. "Fuck, Cade. I'm sorry. That was unfair of me."

I sighed, a ragged, defeated exhalation. I stepped toward her, put my arms around her shoulders. She leaned into me, resting her head on my chest, her palms over her face. She radiated heat, smelled not unpleasantly of sweat. Her skin under my hands was damp and hot.

Touching her was never a good idea.

She tilted her head up, and her eyes met mine. "Goodbye, then."

"It'll only be a couple of days."

"I know."

Why did my heart clench when I thought of leaving? Why did this feel more like a true goodbye than it was supposed to be? I stared down into her eyes, not letting go of her. "I'll be back. I swear I'll be back."

"Who are you trying to convince?" she whispered.

"Both of us."

"Am I allowed to say that I'll miss you?" Her hands slid up my chest and snaked around my neck. "'Cause I will."

"Me, too." I chickened out, and forced myself to say it. "I'll miss you, too."

"You will?" She sounded skeptical.

"Yeah, of course I will." My hands were idly tracing the bottom edge of the strap of her sports bra.

"I may be fucked up about you and me, but you're important to me. So of course I'll miss you."

"It's just a couple of days, right? You should just go."

"Yeah, I should."

But neither of us moved. An invisible weight hung between us. Something indefinable yet sharp.

"Why does this feel like more than 'see you in a few days'?" Eden asked.

I shrugged. "I don't know. But you're right, it does. I was just thinking that same thing."

Eden's green gaze wavered, searching me. I watched her expression shift through several emotions I couldn't decipher entirely. Pain? Guilt? Need? All the emotions that seemed to define us, Eden and me, as an entity. I knew what she was going to do as she did it, and I didn't stop it. Her hands threaded through my hair, cupped the back of my head, and her lips met mine. For the second time, we kissed with a slow and passionate tenderness that did not belong to us. It was stolen, and we knew it.

Eden broke the kiss first. She pulled away, stared at me from inches apart, and then peeled my shirt off. Her lips touched my breastbone, delicate touches down my sternum, across my pectorals. Her hands held my back, smoothed and carved and caressed. Kisses over my ribs. Back up to my shoulder. I breathed, and focused on the sensation of her lips on my skin. But not for long. I hooked two fingers under the racer back of her bra and rolled it up to her shoulder blades, followed the twisted line to where the bra cupped her breasts, and rolled it up. Her tits fell free with a luxurious bounce. She paused in her kissing of my torso long enough to let me tug the bra off her arms and over her head, and then resumed planting soft kisses across my shoulder and to my neck. She unzipped my pants, pushed her fingers through the gap of the zipper, and touched my erection through my boxers, then freed the button and shoved my jeans down. She made equally short work of my boxers, and then took my cock in her hand as I worked her skintight workout shorts off.

She pulled away then, and moved backward toward my bed. I followed, and she sank down to her back. I hovered over her, and we slid onto the mattress together. My body was over hers, and my mouth was seeking hers. Her legs came up around my knees, and I slid into her. She gasped against my teeth, and then we were moving together. It was slow, long and languorous, no anger, no desperation, only soft sighs and her hands on my ass, pulling me against her, and a never-ending kiss.

She moaned, and the kiss broke, and now I felt her eyes on mine, and I had to meet her gaze. I didn't look away as I began to stroke into her with ever-increasing speed, and she met me thrust for thrust, her hands clutching my shoulders, her heels locked around my hips.

My mouth fell open and my lungs burned and my eyes felt hot and my chest was expanding, my heart exploding in my ribcage, and I felt her, truly felt her, the essence of Eden, saw her soul fill her eyes with fire and with tears, and I knew my own gaze was the same.

"Cade?" She gasped my name, a jagged plea.

"God, Eden. God..."

I felt her come, felt her body clench and spasm in the grip of climax, felt myself unleashing within her. She clutched me with bruising strength, nails digging into my back, legs pinioning mine. Our hips ground together, and I felt her sobbing against my neck, and I was making broken groans of my own, and my eyes were wet.

Her mouth found mine, frantic. We kissed, clasped together, as if for the first time.

Neither of us spoke for a very long time.

Finally, I rolled off her, but she refused to let go, rolling with me. "Cade? What was that? What—what *was* that?"

"I don't know."

"It was goodbye, wasn't it?"

"I'm coming back, Eden. I swear on my soul."

I was still inside her, our bodies tangled and joined. She rested her forehead against mine. "It's still goodbye. Don't act like you don't feel it."

"I do." The admission dragged out of me. "I don't understand it, but I feel it, too."

She raised her head, placed a palm on my cheek. Her lower lip trembled, and then she pressed her mouth to mine, a sorrowful, quavering kiss. "'Bye, Caden."

"Eden, I—"

"No. Don't say anything else. Please." She moved, and I slipped out of her as she rolled away from me, slid off the bed. Stood facing me, eyes on me. She looked as if she was about to speak, but then she shook her head, scrubbed her palm impatiently across her eyes, and vanished into my bathroom.

I wanted to follow her, but I didn't dare. I wanted to lie in bed and think it through, but I didn't dare. I forced myself out of bed, put my clothes back on. Sat on a kitchen chair and tied my shoes, watching the bedroom door, waiting for her to come out. I shouldered my bag and paused with my hand on the knob of the front door.

She came flying at me, still naked, hair loosed from the braid now and fluttering behind her. She slammed into me, arms around my neck. "I don't *want* it to be goodbye. That was *love*, Caden. You and I both know it."

"Y—yeah." My voice cracked.

She peered up at me. "But it's still not enough, is it? It'll never be enough. I'll never be enough."

I choked. "It's not that you'll never be—that you're not—not enough. It was never that."

"Then *what* is it?" She lost her voice at the end, a hissing, screeching demand.

"You're too much *like* her!" I shut my eyes and turned my face to the ceiling, truth shredding from my lips. "I'll never be able to see you without seeing *her!*"

Eden backed away, barred an arm over her breasts, and crossed one thigh over her core. Her blonde hair, the black roots showing inch-long, cascaded over her shoulders and down her chest. Her eyes were tortured, bleeding pain. "You've…you've been trying to love *her* through *me*."

She was right.

FUCK.

I opened my mouth, but nothing came out. What could I say?

She saved me the need. "You can't apologize. I don't want you to. Don't you dare tell me you're sorry. Don't you dare."

I stared at her, emptied of emotion. I was nothing but a breathing, walking husk.

She straightened her spine and lifted her chin. "Go."

Still I hesitated.

"GO!"

I went. I slipped out the door and closed it behind me. My feet carried me away from my door, but not fast enough; I still heard her sobs.

I called Grams's cell phone on the way to the airport to get the address of the assisted living center they'd moved him into. "He's back in the hospital, sweetie," Grams said. "He's fighting, but he's sick."

"Oh, god, Grams."

"Seeing you will do him a world of good, though, I'm sure." Her voice cracked. "Me, too, for that matter. We'll see you soon, honey."

There weren't any nonstops from Detroit Metro to either Casper or Cheyenne, so I ended up laying over in Denver and flying from there to Cheyenne. I brooded the whole way about what Eden had said. I knew, intellectually, that Eden was her own person. In terms of their personalities, and even their looks, they were completely different people. I mean, they were twins, even with Eden's dyed hair. But...they were different. Ever was quieter, more even-tempered, more reflective and self-contained, in comparison to Eden's voluble hot-temperedness.

I could list their differences one by one. But there was no point. Eden was right. I was trying to put a salve on the wound left by Ever's coma, using Eden. And it wasn't working. It was destroying me. It was slicing Eden's heart into pieces. It would wreck Ever, if or when she woke up and regained some sense of self.

How had I let my life become this…ruin?

I'd barely hung on when Mom died. I'd run away from life when Dad died. Now, with Ever essentially dead, but not enough to let me mourn and grieve and find some way to heal, I was coming apart.

I paid the taxi driver and stepped out into the hot Wyoming sun, and then into the cool lobby of the Cheyenne Regional Medical Center. The receptionist directed me to room 559, and the closer I got to the room, the more my heart pounded. The smell of the hospital, the squeak of my boot soles on the tile, the indecipherable echo of the PA, nurses and orderlies in various colors of scrubs, preoccupied doctors in lab coats…it was all horribly, terribly familiar. Almost second nature now. Waiting rooms, vending machines. The beep of monitors. The whirring of mechanical doors closing behind me. The distant clinking scrape of curtains being drawn.

I'd spent a significant portion of my life in hospitals. With Mom; my own recovery; Ever. Memories inundated me, assaulted me, battering me one after another. Watching Mom waste away. Her weak smile when she said, *Quack*. Dad's fist slamming into the door. Waking up in a bed, broken, alone. Hearing the news about Ever.

I nearly vomited from it all before I made it to Gramps's room. I had to pause outside the door to room 559, catch my breath and focus on pushing away my own problems. Grams and Gramps didn't need to see me struggling. I had to pretend to be strong for them.

When I finally went in, Gramps was awake, holding Grams's hand. Neither of them were speaking. Just sitting together. Gramps…wasn't Gramps. The left side of his face drooped, sagged. He was stick thin. His bones showed through his paper-like skin. His once mighty muscles were gone, just…gone. Evaporated. He heard my step; his eyes found me. His expression…I nearly sobbed…he showed no recognition. He turned his gaze back to Grams, slowly.

"That's Cade. Your grandson. Aidan's boy."

I stood beside Grams, and she clutched at me for dear life. "He'll remember you. Sometimes takes a bit. Didn't recognize Gerry at first." She rested her head against my elbow. "Just talk to him."

Just talk. How many times had I heard that?

"Hey, Gramps. I just wanted you to know I'm… almost done with school. I missed some time with the accident, so I'm behind a bit. I'll graduate in the spring. Bachelor of arts." I blinked hard, swallowed. Took his hand. "You'll be there, right? At the graduation? You wouldn't miss that. After graduation, maybe I can spend a few months on the ranch. Help with foaling season. I don't have any plans yet. Things have been difficult lately. Just lots going on, you know?"

Grams squeezed my arm. She knew I was bluffing.

"I've missed you, Gramps. I've wanted to come see you before now. In fact, some days, I just…some days I wish I'd stayed. Instead of going back for college."

Gramps's eyes focused on me, and I could tell he was listening intently. I could almost see him thinking, fighting to remember. He squeezed my hand. Took a couple of deep breaths. "Cade." His voice was sandpaper, rough and thin.

"That's me, Gramps." I laughed, a thick, teary sound. God, I was about to cry like a baby. Again.

He clutched my hand, adjusting his grip so he was holding my hand as if about to arm-wrestle me. Pulled me close. He was Gramps again, lucid. "Time…to say. Goodbye."

I cracked, my knees faltered. "No, Gramps. You're gonna be fine."

He shook his head. "Tired." He glanced at Grams. "Have a moment. Alone. With…Cade?"

Grams let out a shaky breath. "Sure thing, Con. I'll be just outside. Don't you run away, now, you hear?"

He smiled at her, more with his eyes than anything else. When she was gone, he returned his gaze to mine. "Now. Talk." It was an order, more like the old, strong, stern Gramps than ever.

"About what?"

"You. Hurt." He bumped my chest with our joined hands. "Dyin'. Ain't…blind."

"You're not dyin', Gramps. You ain't allowed to." I smiled at him. "Besides, I'm fine."

He blinked several times. Took several long breaths as if gathering strength. "Bullshit."

I laughed. "All right, Gramps. Never could lie to you for shit." I intended to give him a Cliff's Notes version, heavily edited. "I got married. To that girl I was pen pals with. Ever. We eloped. It was…sudden. Just leave it at that. Only person there was her sister, her twin. Well, the night before Christmas, the one before last…we got in a car accident. Bad. Real bad. I broke my leg so bad I've got all sorts of rods and pins. Tore my arm up good. Concussion. But Ever, she… she's in a coma. Been in a coma for—for—the entire time. A year and a half."

"I remember. Just took me a minute." Gramps blinked at me. "You got…shit luck."

"No kidding," I said, and then laughed bitterly. "Shittiest luck. Everyone…everyone fuckin' dies. Except Ever? She's not dead. Not alive. Not either." This wasn't what I'd meant to say. It just poured out. "And it's…it's tearing me up, Gramps. I don't even know who I am anymore."

He let go of my hand, extended his index finger, and thumped my chest, hard. "Monroe."

"Yeah, I know. I'm a Monroe. But what if that… what if that ain't enough?" I always slipped into talking like Gramps whenever I was with him. "I—I fucked up, Gramps."

"How?"

"I've been…so alone. And it's making me crazy. I can't stand it. I had no one…no one to talk to. No one to tell me what was right or wrong. I've been so lost. And the only person around was…Ever's sister. I messed up, Gramps. And I don't know how to fix it. I don't know if she'll ever wake up. If I'll ever get her back. If I do, how do I tell her what I did? How could she ever forgive me? I can't even forgive myself." I choked on a sob. "Fuck. Listen to me, dumping all this bullshit on you. What the hell is wrong with me? You don't need to hear this. You need to get better."

"You done—what you done. If you…love her, you'll do what's—what's right. In the end. She loves you, she'll forgive you. Won't forget, but she'll… forgive."

"What if she doesn't?" I bowed my head, unable to look at him. "You don't know what I did."

Gramps didn't answer for a long time. He seemed to be thinking, and gathering his strength. "After Korea. Was Reserves. Got…called up. For training… maneuvers. Virginia." He stared up at the ceiling.

"Went out with buddies. Got…got drunk. Met a girl. Susie. Messed up. More than once before I…rotated home. Told your Grams. Six months…she went back to her…her folks. For six months. She came back. Forgave me. Ain't forgot…even now. But forgave."

"How?"

"Women are…stronger. Than men. Ask her how. I couldn't've…done the same. I'm too…selfish."

"Gramps, Jesus. I never knew. You and Grams, you love each other so much. Even back then, you said, when I was talking about staying on with Luisa, that you—you knew how much you loved Grams from the start."

"Being apart. It…fucks with your…your head." He gasped, struggled to get the words out, one by one. "Makes you do…stupid things." He gripped my hand. "You're…better. Than that. Own up. I… believe. In you."

"I don't know how to come back from this. How can I say I love her when I did what I did? It wasn't just once, Gramps."

"Sometimes…in life…the only thing you can do is hope…tomorrow will be…better. Than today. Eventually…it will be."

"I've been hoping for almost two years. Fuck, I've been hoping since Mom died. When I found Ever, when we discovered love…I thought I'd come to a better tomorrow. Things were good. But…then it was taken away. Just like everyone has been taken away from me. Everyone."

Gramps took my hand, put it on his heart. I felt the faint *thumpthump...thumpthump* under my palm. "Keep...believing. Hold on. Just hold on. One—one breath a time."

"I'm trying."

"'Try not. Do...or do not. There is no try.'"

I laughed, genuinely laughed. "Gramps. Did you just quote *Star Wars* at me?"

"That little green guy. Said a lot of true things."

I rested my forehead on the back of the hand holding his. "I love you, Gramps."

"I love you, too, son." He put his other hand on the back of my head. "I want you to go. You've said goodbye...too many times."

"No. *No.*"

He mussed my hair, his hand weak, barely moving now. "Obey me. One last time. Go. I love you. Always."

"No. Fuck. No. I can't...not you, too."

"My time, son." He patted my cheek, and I lifted my head to look at him. My face was wet. "She'll forgive you. Just give her time."

I leaned down onto Gramps, fists clenched against his now-frail chest. He patted my hair, my back. "I love you, Gramps. So much."

"Love you, too, son. Now go. Send in Beth."

I stood up, wiped my face. Straightened my back. Shuffled backward, eyes on Gramps. "'Bye, Gramps. I'll see you later."

He just nodded.

I turned and left. Grams was sagged against the wall, looking as old and frail as Gramps. She took one look at me, wrapped her arms around my middle, and held on. Minutes passed. I couldn't make myself let go. When I did, she wiped at my cheek.

"Don't cry, Cade." She lifted up on her toes and kissed my cheek. "You'll be okay."

"How did you forgive Gramps? When he came back from Virginia?" The question emerged without warning.

She didn't flinch, didn't blink. Just sighed. "It was hard. Took some time. But I did. If you love someone enough, you give them as many chances as they need to get it right. Connor loved me. I knew he did. And I knew I loved him. We made it work, one day at a time. He never went anywhere without me after that, though. Even into Casper, we always went together. You just make it work. Forgiveness is hard, Cade. It doesn't come easy. Feeling love is easy. Living love, *that's* the hard part. She loves you, she'll forgive you, no matter what you did." She looked up at me. Her eyes were sharp and knowing. "But first, you have to forgive yourself."

I blinked hard. There was no end of tears ready to come out of me these days, it seemed.

"He needs me." Grams leaned up and kissed me again. "Goodbye, Cade. I love you. Forever."

She turned away, and I felt the permanence in her goodbye as well. I slumped back against the wall. Listened through the open door. Murmurs. The steady beeping of the heart monitor echoed. I held it together, struggled to breathe. Murmurs. A sob from Grams. The creak of a bed. Soft crying. Flatline.

I listened, unable to walk away.

After a few minutes, the crying stopped.

A nurse flew past me, and I turned to follow her, but she was stopped in the middle of the room, her hand over her mouth. Her eyes were wet.

Grams was on the bed, curled up next to Gramps. Their hands were clasped together. They were both gone.

I turned away, and my steps taking me out of the hospital were slow and measured, beyond empty. I sat on a bench in the lobby for an eternity, unable to think or to move. Eventually Uncle Gerry appeared in front of me.

I wasn't close to Gerry. He was a distant man, closed off and cold. He'd served in the first Desert Storm, and he was divorced. That's all I knew. He'd lived his entire life on the ranch, except for the tours in Iraq. I knew him mainly as a tall, broad-shouldered, dark-haired, hard-eyed man on a horse. He seldom spoke, and sometimes, I would feel his eyes on me as we rode, and they would seem resentful.

"Come on. You can stay with me till the funeral." That was all he said. All the way from Cheyenne to Casper, to the ranch. To his cottage in one of the back fields. I said nothing. There was nothing to say, especially not to someone I knew as little as Uncle Gerry.

I buried my grandparents on June 3rd.

I was sitting in the waiting area of the Denver airport when my phone chirped with a text message.

Call me. Now. It was Eden.

What is it?

Call me.

I called her. The phone rang twice. "You need to get here right now."

"I'm in the airport. I should be there in a few hours. Why? What's going on?"

A long silence.

"She woke up."

ouroboros: a beginning, an end

She was sitting up when I entered her room. Her eyes were open.

She'd woken up, and I'd missed it.

Eden was sitting on the far side of Ever's bed, eyes red. She barely looked at me, barely acknowledged me. She was holding Ever's hand, fingers tangled together.

Ever was staring straight ahead, blinking every once in a while. Her chest rose and fell on its own, the respirator gone. She still had a heart monitor on, but for the first time in a very, very long time, it was muted. The lines rose and fell in the wave-form pattern on the screen, but the steady beeping was silenced. I stood in the doorway, staring at my wife. Awake. Sitting up. Eyes open and blinking.

Eden tried to speak, but her voice gave out. She cleared her throat and tried again. "Look, Ev. It's Cade. He's back. I told you he'd be here soon." Ever blinked twice in a row, and her head pivoted, ever so slowly, toward Eden. She seemed puzzled. Eden lifted their joined hands, gesturing to me. "Over there, sis. In the doorway."

Ever's head twisted again, toward me, and then her eyes followed, stuttering across the room, disoriented. Locked on me. Vivid, arresting jade. I stumbled, lurched, caught myself on the doorway. My throat closed, hot and thick. I forced myself forward. Took her hand.

"Ever." I didn't know what else to say. "I'm here, Ev. I'm here."

She stared up at me. Her mouth was open slightly. Her fingers twitched inside mine, and then, with a visible effort, she threaded her fingers through mine. Her eyes never left me.

"C-Ca…Cade." Her voice, Jesus, her voice. Thin, tiny, weak, fractured…and the sweetest thing I'd ever heard in my life.

Eden slumped forward, sobbing. "She hasn't spoken. That's the first thing she's said since she woke up. Your name." There was faint bitterness in her voice.

I wondered if Ever had noticed it, too. She turned to look at Eden. Her brow furrowed. Her tongue touched her lips, and she sucked in a shallow breath. "Eee—*Ede*n." She clutched both of our hands.

Eden coughed, choked. "Yeah, Ev. God, I missed you."

Ever seemed to want to speak, but couldn't. Her eyes wavered, narrowed with effort, and then went watery with tears of despair. "Eden. Caden." It was all she could manage.

A doctor came in then. Dr. Overton. "Mr. Monroe. Glad you're back." He clapped me on the back. "See? Miracles do happen. And you, my boy, walked right into a miracle. Could you step into my office? There's a few things I'd like to discuss with you."

I turned to follow him, but Ever wouldn't let go of my hand. "I'll be right back, Ever. I promise. I'm just gonna go talk to Dr. Overton. I'll right back."

Her eyes went wide with fear. "Nnnn…" She gripped my hand with shocking strength. "Nnnn."

I closed my eyes, panicked. I couldn't leave her. I couldn't just walk away. Not now. Not even to talk to a doctor. I couldn't miss another moment. I turned to Eden. "Can you go?"

Eden nodded, sucking in a shaky breath. "Sure." She stood up slowly, carefully. She seemed off-balance somehow, holding herself gingerly. I wanted to ask what was wrong, but didn't.

I leaned away from Ever and snagged a chair without letting go of her hand. Sat down as close to her as I could get. "I'm here, babe. I'm here. I'm right beside you." I lifted our hands and kissed her knuckles. "I'll never be anywhere else."

Her eyes were on me. My Ever, her eyes. I didn't look away. I just stared at her, held her hand. Sat with her as time slid by us. Eventually, Ever seemed as if she was trying to speak, but once again she got frustrated, and her eyes teared up. She lifted our hands, touched my chest. Leaned forward toward me slightly. "L... Luh." She blinked hard, green eyes moving back and forth, searching mine. "Y-yuh."

I hiccupped. "I love you. I've always loved you."

She let her head fall back, and her eyes closed. She seemed to be relaxing, falling asleep. My heart clenched. What if she fell back into a coma? But then she jerked awake, her eyes terrified. She looked around, found me, squeezed my hand.

"I'm here. I won't leave. Not for anything."

She blinked, stared at the ceiling. I had the feeling she was afraid to go to sleep, afraid of the same thing I was.

Eden and Dr. Overton returned. I glanced at the doctor. "If she falls asleep, will she..." I couldn't even say it.

"It's unlikely. She has shown remarkable improvement already, and she's only been awake for a few hours. There's no rules that we understand for this kind of thing. Some patients emerge and recover completely, almost immediately. Others can take days just to be able to track you with their eyes. Miss Eliot tells me she said both of your names. That's an incredible improvement. But we'll have to be patient." He focused on Ever. "You can sleep, Ever. You will wake up. But be patient with yourself, okay? This will take time."

He smiled at all of us, and then left.

Eden resumed her seat on the opposite side of the bed from me. Took Ever's hand. "See? You're doing great."

Ever's mouth twitched in an attempt to smile, but she couldn't, quite. One more time she let her eyes close, and this time she fell asleep immediately. I watched her sleep. I was still terrified that, despite the doctor's words, she wouldn't wake up again. After a few minutes, it was obvious she was deeply asleep.

Eden finally met my eyes. "He said it will probably take a long time before she's…'back.'" She made air quotes with her fingers. "And she may never be a hundred percent what she was. He said our support will be the most important thing to her." She peered at me. "How was Wyoming?"

I closed my eyes. "He…he's gone. That was goodbye."

Eden squeezed her eyes shut and then opened them again, and looked at me with concern. "God. I'm so sorry."

"Grams…Grams, too."

Eden seemed at a loss. "I didn't—I didn't know she was sick?"

"She wasn't. But I think she just…she went with him."

"Jesus, Cade. I'm so…so sorry."

"Yeah. Thanks."

"Are you okay?"

I shrugged. "I don't…I don't know. Ever's awake. That's all that matters now. I have to be okay. For her."

Eden glanced past me, at the doorway, then back to me. "I think, for now, that's the only thing that matters. For both of us. Okay?"

I nodded. "Meaning, we don't say anything."

"Not yet. She has to focus on getting better."

I hung my head. "Yeah. I don't see any other way." After a long moment, I looked up at Eden. She was clearly struggling for composure. "She's going to find out. Someday."

"I know."

"I won't lie, when that happens."

Eden nodded. "I know. And neither will I."

She winced, held a hand to her stomach. I frowned at her. "Are you okay?"

She shrugged. "Yeah. I just feel nauseated. No big deal."

"Are you okay…otherwise?"

She tilted her head and rolled one shoulder. "Yes. No. My sister is awake. That's like...I can breathe again. But then again, there's everything that happened, I just don't know how to process it. How to deal. But I will. I'll be fine. I'm always fine."

"Eden—"

"No." She shook her head. "We've talked it in circles, Cade. Enough. No more. Not anymore. As of this moment, we never talk about it again. That's how we deal with it." She met my eyes, demanding an answer.

I let out a long breath. I couldn't think of anything to say, so I just nodded.

And so we sat in silence while Ever slept. We took turns keeping watch. One of us would go to the cafeteria, and then we'd switch. When Ever woke up again, we took turns being alone with her; she seemed to get agitated if I left the room for more than a few minutes at a time.

Night fell, and I slept in an overnight visitor's chair brought up from the maternity ward. Soon I was sleeping in her room more nights than I was at the condo. If I left her for the entire night, when I got there the next day she would be agitated, upset, and find it harder to focus on the recovery therapy. So I stayed. Night after night.

She was awake, and that was all that mattered.

Those words became my mantra in the weeks of recovery that followed.

Eden

My fingers flew across Apollo's strings. The bow sawed in graceful swings. The notes poured out, effortlessly. Endlessly.

In the weeks since Ever's emergence from the coma, I'd spent more time playing the cello than ever. Hours on end. I barely slept, barely ate. I visited Ever, went home, and played. It was my only solace.

Seeing Cade, day in and day out, it was…hell. His devotion to Ever was tenacious, ferocious. He never wavered. But I could see the toll it was taking on him. I could see the toll his grandparents' death had taken on him.

Every time I saw Cade, I saw the way he'd been in the moments before he'd left for Wyoming. The way *we'd* been. How I'd felt. How connected, how cherished.

That was gone now. It had never been mine. He belonged to Ever, and now that she was awake, every molecule of his existence was tuned to her. I didn't exist anymore. It was the best way. I knew that. I was letting him focus on her. He owed me nothing. I owed him nothing.

Except silence.

I felt my stomach lurch and had to quit playing, focusing on keeping my stomach down. I'd been
getting nauseous at odd times for a little over three
weeks now. I'd attributed it to the stress of containing
myself, of keeping my internal struggles to myself. I
missed Cade. He'd given me something, given me a
taste of what it felt like to be cared for. To have someone focus on me, to care solely about my happiness.
It had been a sample, and then it was taken away. That
seemed like the worst sort of cruelty, but I'd brought
it on myself. I knew I had. I'd let my emotions control me. I'd attributed things to Cade that didn't exist,
that *couldn't* exist. And I had to keep all this secret
from everyone. From Cade, from Ever. I'd never
kept a secret from Ever. Not once in all our lives.
Everything I'd done, every heartbreak, every success,
every crush turned to sex turned to rejection, I told
Ever about. Now, with the greatest heartbreak I'd
ever known bearing down upon me, I couldn't tell
her. I couldn't confide in her. She couldn't handle the
stress. Not now. Not for a long time.

So of course I'd feel the physical effects of being
under such intense stress, such pain, such guilt.

But something niggled at the back of my head.
A thought, an errant worry. I pushed it away, took
a deep breath, closed my eyes, and summoned the
notes. Drew the bow across the strings and began
again.

But the longer I played, the more the worry in the back of my head began to take form, began to clarify and gain solidity, until I could think of nothing else.

Finally, I had to do something about it. I put away Apollo, grabbed my keys, and headed out the door. A few minutes later, I was at CVS Pharmacy. I held a box in my hand. It was a small box, but it seemed to weigh a thousand pounds. There were three letters on the front:

EPT.

baby steps

Eden

I sat in my car outside the Home, hands on the wheel, working up the courage to get out. One step. Another step. Stop thinking. Just walk. One foot in front of the other. The elevator carried me up to Ever's floor, where Cade sat, as always, beside her, holding her hand. She was able to focus on him easily now, and could get out a few words at a time. She could move all of her limbs, just a little, when asked. She was lucid. She knew herself, and me, and Cade.

I couldn't speak as I watched Cade kiss each of Ever's knuckles in turn. Four tiny kisses, feather-light. Each one held a universe of tenderness. My heart burned. My eyes burned. I kept my hand at my side, rather than resting it against my belly, as it seemed to want to do now.

I'd claimed I'd had the flu, so I hadn't seen Ever or Cade in almost a week.

My sister saw me, focused all her efforts on lifting her hand, reaching for me. I had to choke back the sniffle as I crossed the room, took her hand in mine. I kissed her palm.

Cade sensed I needed time alone, so he stood to leave. "I'll be right back."

Ever was able to let him go without panicking now. "Eden." She peered up at me.

She was my twin, so of course she would sense my turmoil. I put her palm to my cheek. "I love you, Ev."

"I love you." She'd practiced those words. I'd heard her struggling with them under her breath. Getting each syllable out, one after the other.

"Don't...don't ever doubt that, okay?" I couldn't let on, couldn't let her think this was anything but an average visit.

She contorted her face into an expression of confusion. "Never. Why...would I?"

I shrugged. "I dunno. Just know that I love you. Forever." I thought of a phrase I'd heard Cade say to her in a letter. I'd overheard him once, standing outside the door. "I love you forever, and after forever."

She curled her fingers against my palm. She sensed it. "Eden?"

I shook my head, blinking away the tears gathering. "I have to go. But I'll be back. Later." It was the first lie I'd ever told her.

"Go? Where?"

I leaned in, kissed her forehead, each cheek. "Don't worry. Just get better, okay?"

She clutched at my hand, grasping desperately. "*Eden?*"

I squeezed her hand back. "Cade will take care of you. You know that man, he loves you, more—more than anything, right? He loves you. So much."

A tear trickled down the right side of her face. "I love *you*."

I leaned in again, hugged her, held on until the breaking in my heart was too much to take. "I'll see you later, Ev."

She watched me go, let me go.

I passed Cade in the hallway. "I'm still not feeling great. I just wanted to say hi." I fought to sound normal. I couldn't handle more than five seconds of talking to him without lances piercing my heart.

Now, five seconds was far, far too long.

"You're going already?" I did a weird, awkward nodding shrug, unable to get any actual words out. "Well, feel better, okay?"

I smiled at him, and then, because I couldn't help it, I took his hand in mine, squeezed his fingers briefly. "See you. Take care of her." He narrowed his eyes at me. God, I was being way too obvious. I let go and moved past him. "Don't wanna get you sick. So…yeah. I'll see you." I backed away, waving.

He watched me go, an odd expression on his face. I finally turned around, after looking back for much too long. On the elevator, I allowed myself three tears. I counted them as they fell. One. Two. Three. Then I stopped them, deep breaths, deep breaths.

It was for the best.

I made it to my car. Slid into the driver's seat. Could I do this?

Yes. I had to.

I started my Passat, sat with it in park. Turned around, examined the interior. The trunk was stuffed full of suitcases. I'd had to jump on it to get it to close. Apollo was buckled into the front passenger seat. The back seat was full of everything else I owned: books, sheet music, boxes of knickknacks. The cello solo I was writing was bound in a folder in my purse. I'd left the furniture at the dorm. It didn't matter.

I'd withdrawn from school. I might transfer to Interlochen someday, finish my degree. For now, I had to merely…survive. I had to make it through what was coming.

Nine months. I had to make it nine months. That was the first goal. The only goal.

I put the car in drive, blinked away the tears. I turned on *Thousand Words* by Portland Cello Project. "Taking a Fall" came on as I hit the freeway. I-75 north, toward Traverse City. There was a cabin up there, a family cottage that had been in Mom's estate, willed equally to Ever and me. As children, we'd taken a few family vacations up there, weekends at the cottage on the Old Mission Peninsula. Those were magical memories, for me. When Mom was alive, she'd bring her cello, the very one beside me, and she'd play it on the beach. She'd paint as well. She'd play with us and laugh, dive in the lake surf, swim out with us and dive off the tethered dock.

No one had been up there in years, but there was a caretaker, Mr. Callahan. I remembered Mr. Callahan as a portly middle-aged man with sandy-red hair and a ready smile. I'd contacted him yesterday, and he was going to have the cottage ready for me.

I had enough money from Mom's estate and what I'd saved of Dad's monthly living expenses allowance that I could stay up there for…a while. I'd probably have to find a job at some point. But that was a worry for another day. First, I had to get there.

Baby steps, I told myself. I smiled, thinking about *What About Bob?* Bill Murray, shuffling to the elevator,

chanting, "Baby steps to the elevator." Baby steps to
Traverse City. Baby steps to being okay.

Baby steps.

I choked on the sudden glut of tears and had to
pull onto the shoulder as my vision blurred and my
chest heaved with hyperventilating sobs.

I was pregnant.

the end

a preview from the next book,

saving forever

the third & final book of
the ever trilogy

jumping off the dock

Carter

I dove into the water, slicing neatly into the cold blue. Four long frog-kick strokes under the surface, and then I came up and took a deep breath. My muscles immediately settled into a steady crawl stroke, carrying me toward the peninsula mainland. I had a waterproof scuba diving bag on my back, holding the essentials: wallet, keys, phone, a T-shirt, flip-flops. I kept the steady pace until I felt my feet brush the sandy bottom, and then I stood up, flinging my hair back and smoothing it down. I trudged ashore, breathing hard.

My beach was empty, this early in the morning. It wasn't really *technically* my beach, since I didn't own it, but I thought of it as my beach. Very few people came here, not this far north on the peninsula. It was a secluded spot, away from the bustle of downtown Traverse City, and it was out of the way even for the constant flow of winery traffic on the peninsula itself. It suited me. I could leave my car parked at the post office nearby, stocked with a towel and a change of clothes, lock it, and swim out to the island that was my home. I had a boat, of course, but I preferred to swim when the weather allowed.

I scrubbed my hand over my wet hair, sluicing water down my chest and back, and then stretched, yawning and squeezing my eyes closed, rolling my shoulders. When I came out of the stretch, I saw her.

Five-eight. Long blonde hair with dark roots. A body that made my mouth go dry. Curvy, solid, luxurious expanses of flesh. She wore a pair of cut-off jean shorts and an orange bikini top. God in heaven, who *was* this? I'd never seen her before. There was no way on earth I could ever forget seeing this girl. She was, without a doubt, the most gorgeous creature I'd ever seen.

I stood, frozen, thigh deep in the water. Staring. Blatantly staring. I needed to know her name. I needed to hear the sound of her voice. She'd have a voice like music, to match the symphony that was her body. The need to move closer was an automatic response. My feet carried me through the water, toward the girl.

She was sitting on the beach about thirty feet away from me. A towel was spread beneath her, and she had her nose buried in a book. I couldn't make out the title, but it didn't matter. My attention was on *her*. On the way her hair fell in a loose braid over her bare shoulder. On her arm, the way it flexed as she scratched her knee. She looked up from her book, saw me. Our eyes met for the briefest of instants. In that instant, something inside me shivered and burned. And then she looked back to her book. Almost too quickly. Too intently.

And I? I couldn't make my body stop. I walked straight past the girl. Why? Why couldn't I get myself to talk? It had been almost a year now. I should be over what had happened. But I wasn't. Obviously. I couldn't even get a simple "hello" past my lips.

My feet carried me to my car, and I didn't look back. I wanted to. I *needed* to. Her skin had been fair, flawless, looking satin-smooth and needing touch. My touch. I dug my keys from the dry-bag, unlocked my truck, and toweled myself off. I drove to the winery, thinking about her. About the expression on her face. It had been…tortured. Conflicted. As if the beach itself held as much pain as it did promise. That was a ridiculous, nonsensical thought. I couldn't possibly know that about her. But it was what I'd seen when I looked at her. And it made me want to know her even more. What could have caused her such pain? How could a beach cause such conflicted emotion?

I needed to push her from my thoughts while I tended to the grapes. I couldn't afford thoughts of a girl. Not now. This would be the best harvest yet, and we couldn't afford any distractions. My brothers and I had to get this winery turning a profit if we were going to make it up here.

Yet, as I walked out into the vineyard, pruning and weeding, my thoughts kept returning to the girl. To the heavy weight of her breasts held up by the orange fabric, which almost hadn't been equal to the task. She'd almost spilled out of the top, and that overflow of flesh kept cropping up in my brain. As did her long legs, shining with sunscreen and flexing with thick muscle. Her eyes, god, I'd only gotten a fragmentary glimpse of her eyes, but I thought they might be green. Deep, jade green. Those eyes had held, in that momentary meeting, so many things. Curiosity, intelligence. Vibrancy. Pain. God, such pain.

I wondered if I'd see her again. I hoped I would, feared I would.

Eden

He'd come out of nowhere.

I'd sat down on the empty beach, glad for the solitude. As long as no one was around, I could leave my

cover-up off and let the sun soak me. If I was alone,
I was okay, because there was no one to see when I
remembered what I carried inside me, and the ruin
it represented. At which point I was given to bursting
into tears. So I'd gone to the beach early, right after
breakfast. Not even eight o'clock. It was already a
warm day, promising to be hot. I had my well-worn
copy of my favorite romance novel in hand, and a
bottle of water. The cottage was only a short walk
away, in case I got hot. Or overwhelmed and needing
the solace of four walls and closed blinds.

I'd been deeply immersed in the scene in which
the heroine realizes the hero has been keeping one
significant truth from her and runs away from her
true love, only to have him follow her, explaining
that he was only protecting her. She forgives him, at
which point they clasp together and begin kissing,
and that turns into mad, passionate lovemaking. It
was my favorite scene, and I'd read it at least half a
dozen times, but I never got tired of it.

I'd looked up, surveying the lapping water of
Grand Traverse Bay's east arm, the golden sand, the
sun rising just above the horizon. And him. Thigh-
deep in the water, appearing from nowhere. Six feet
tall, lean and wiry, corded with muscles so defined
they might as well have been cut into his body by a
razor. His hair was black as a crow's wing, dripping
wet, thick. I couldn't help watching as he stretched

his body. Couldn't take my eyes off his long, hard biceps as they flexed, his abs as they hardened and shifted. He wasn't huge, wasn't a burly beast. But he was clearly in incredible shape. He was breathing hard, his chest swelling as he sucked in a deep breath and let it out, rolling his shoulders. He'd swum from somewhere far away, clearly, but where? There were a few sailboats anchored off in the distance, but they'd been there for days, no one coming or going that I'd seen. There was a small island a couple of miles out, but surely he hadn't come from *that* far.

He'd literally just…*appeared*. A mouth-watering vision of male beauty. His face…god, his features were perfection, sculpted into a face that I couldn't look away from.

When our eyes met, I felt a jolt in my soul, an electric shock. I forced my eyes down to my book, but I didn't see the words on the page. They wavered and blurred as I tried to keep from looking up, from meeting his gaze. His eyes, lord, they were a pale blue, so pale they were like sunlit chips of sky-blue ice. They gripped me, even as I kept my attention on my book. Or, pretended to. In reality, I was watching him through my peripheral vision as he strode up out of the water.

He was a work of art from head to toe.

Fucking hell. How could I be thinking that way? What the hell was wrong with me?

I dug my fingernails into my thigh. I desperately wanted to look up, to see if he was watching me. What if he stopped? What if he spoke to me? On the way up here I'd stopped for gas at a Speedway. I'd gone in to buy some Gatorade and snacks, and the clerk had asked me, in a very bored and uninterested tone of voice, how I was doing. The way people do out of habit, as a greeting, rather than actually caring if you respond.

"I'm pregnant," I'd blurted, my credit card held out in front of me.

The clerk stared at me in confusion as he swiped the card. "Oooh…kay. Congratulations." He'd handed me my card back.

I took my card and left, embarrassed. It had just popped out, an admission to a total stranger. The need to tell *some*one had been overwhelming. No, I'd wanted to say. Not "congratulations." "W-T-F, you stupid whore?" That was more like it. That was what I deserved.

What if this model-beautiful angel of a man approached me, and I blurted out the truth to him, too? I'd die. Just…die. So I gripped my thigh and my book, praying he wouldn't stop and try to talk to me, and also wishing, hoping desperately that he would, because *shit*, he was gorgeous.

His step faltered as he passed me, and I thought he might stop, but he didn't. He regained his equilibrium and kept walking, out of range of my peripheral vision.

A few minutes later, I heard—and felt—the stomach-shaking rumble of a throaty engine. Was it his? I wondered what kind of car would make that noise, and almost turned to look. But what if he was watching? He'd see me turning around to look, and then maybe he'd stop, and my wayward tongue would get me in trouble. I pictured a classic car, something low and sleek. Lean and powerful, like him.

He'd moved with easy, predatory grace. He'd drive a car like that, something that would prowl, rumble.

I wondered what his voice was like. Would it be deep? Rough? Smooth? I leaned back on my elbows, staring up at the blue sky. Now that he was gone, I could relax. I'd picked a spot not visible from the road, so I rolled to my stomach, untied the strap of my top, and let the sun bake my back. I'd slathered on a thick layer of sunscreen, of course. Maybe too much sun wasn't good. For me. For…the baby.

I wasn't even sure what I was doing. People talked blithely in books and TV shows and movies about "options." About "keeping it," or "getting rid of it." Those phrases weren't things to toss about so easily. Not for me. Keep it? Be a mother? Single, without a degree, without a family? I wouldn't, couldn't ask Cade for anything. He had Ever to take care of. There was no way to tell how she'd heal, how she'd recover. *If* she recovered. She might not recover completely, Dr. Overton had said. She could progress to a certain point, and then just…stop. Never recover all of her speech, or movement. There was just no way to tell. And if she did recover completely, it would be a long time before she was able to start any kind of life. It wasn't "resume life," really. It was more starting over. She'd have to relearn how to walk. How to use her hands. Fine motor skills. How to write, how to draw, how to paint. Jesus, her painting. That was her life. How would she cope without that? Especially if she found out about Cade and me.

I knew that would happen someday. I'd turned off my cell phone. It was still active, still connected in case I needed it, but I had it off. There was no one I wanted to talk to. I'd been gone for just less than a week. Five days. Cade would probably suspect something by now. I'd never missed a day with Ever. Not in the entire eighteen months of her coma. And now I just…disappeared?

How cruel of me. To him. To Ever, most of all. Just vanishing, no explanation? But I didn't know how else to handle it. Anything else would lead to the truth, and I just couldn't, *wouldn't* lay that on Cade. Not now. Especially not on Ever. And so I was here.

I'd spent the first few days cleaning the cottage. Tom—Mr. Callahan, the caretaker—had pulled the sheets off the furniture and turned on the water and such, but that was it. The whole place was coated in a layer of dust. There were decade-old canned goods in some of the cabinets. I emptied everything, dusted, vacuumed, scrubbed sinks and toilets and mirrors and counters. Mopped floors and cleaned windows. Bought a few cheap pieces of art from downtown Traverse, just to make it homey. Replaced the twenty-year-old couch with something newer. Bought new bed sheets, towels, new dishes, cooking utensils, silverware. Stocked the cabinets with healthy food. No junk—except for a few treats, as a reward for eating healthier than usual—no caffeine. That was hard. No soda, no coffee. Good thing I was alone, because I'd be a raging bitch without caffeine in the morning. No alcohol. That was the worst. Nothing to take the edge off. Nothing to help me forget. Just…my own undiluted thoughts, all the time.

And I ran. There was no gym here, not close at least, so I ran. I started with two miles first thing in the morning. Finished it with pushups and crunches. I couldn't afford to let my weight go, not now. I'd noticed I was hungrier, except midmorning, when the nausea would hit. I usually puked a few times around ten or eleven, and I'd eat some saltines—a tip learned from the Internet. It'd pass, and I'd be fine the rest of the day.

I also played Apollo. Ceaselessly, I played. There was little else to do, now that I wasn't in school anymore. I worked on my solo. I played through the entirety of Bach's suites within the first three days. And then started again. I hadn't dared bring Apollo to the beach yet, but I would. Someday. It was Mom's beach. Mom's cello. I had to play there, for her. For her memory.

I hadn't thought of Mom in a long time. Years. I'd put her out of my mind, my way of healing. I'd bleached my hair to look like hers six months after she'd died, and I'd kept it that color ever since, out of habit. I liked not looking identical to Ever. She was already more beautiful than I was, skinnier, glossy black hair, slimmer hips, svelte waist, delicate shoulders. I'd gotten so obsessed with keeping my weight down that I'd grown to need the gym. Need the rush of a killer workout. It wasn't about Mom, not anymore.

And now, here, at her family's cottage, I found myself thinking of her for the first time in years. Missing her. Needing her. Wondering what she'd say if she knew the mess I'd gotten myself into. Scold me? Yell? Scream? Refuse to talk to me? I didn't have any idea how she would have been as a parent to me in my later years. She'd been fairly even-tempered until she died. I got my temper from her, though, while Ever was more like Dad, inward-focused, quiet, slow to anger. Mom would get irritated with me and Ever. We'd get into trouble, and we'd play the twin-confusion card. She'd get fed up, and she'd yell. We always knew we'd pushed the game far enough when Mom got really mad. We knew we'd crossed the line when she stopped yelling and got scary-quiet. With me as an adult, would she sit me down and lecture? Be a support? She would be disappointed. I knew that much.

After letting the sun roast me for a while, I retied my top, slid off my shorts, got up, and moved toward the water. I walked in, toes, ankles, knees, then up to my thighs. I stayed thigh-depth for several feet. I hit the rope delineating the swim area, and ducked under. Now it was up to my waist, and then my boobs went buoyant. Finally, I had to duck under, swimming submerged in the cold depths. Down, down, following the bottom until the pressure hurt my ears and the cold was too sharp, aching my bones. I let myself float upward, break the surface. I saw in the distance a platform, bobbing gently in the little waves. The dock. It was still there. As a little girl I remembered it being so far out. Swimming out there had seemed so grown-up, so daring and adventurous. Now I realized it was *maybe* twenty feet from the roped-off section. The water was well over my head, though, and I felt an absurd moment of panic as I did a sloppy crawl stroke toward it. I'd been swimming

in pools, of course, but I hadn't been in a lake in…
years. Not since the last time here with Mom, well
over ten years ago. *How long?* I thought, distracting
myself. She'd died when I was thirteen, almost four-
teen. It had been…two years before her death that
we'd come up here. I was twenty-two now. So yeah,
just about ten years.

By the time I'd figured that out, I was at the dock,
rounding it to find the ladder. I held on to the metal
bar, feet kicking in the dark water. Swimming in the
open like this wasn't the same as in a pool. If you
faltered in a pool, you could kick over to the edge
and climb out. In a lake, there was no edge. If you
swam out too far, there was no escape, no easy edge
to save you. It wasn't actual fear of that happening
I felt; rather, it was more the potential, the knowledge of the possibility. I kicked and pulled myself up
onto the dock, lay on my back, staring up at the sky.
The morning air chilled my wet body, but the sun
warmed me.

I had a memory of being here, on this dock, with
Mom. Ever had been on the beach, tanning. She didn't
like swimming as much as I did. So Mom swam out
with me, held the ladder and waited till I climbed up.
Followed me, sat beside me on the rocking platform.
The beach had seemed so far away, miles distant. I
was out of breath from the swim, elated, excited, a
little scared. I was going to jump off. I'd been out

here with Mom the day before, but I'd chickened out of jumping off. That day, Mom and I had lain side by side on the gently bobbing dock, watching the clouds shift overhead. We'd lain until we were hot, and then Mom had climbed to her feet, slicked her hair back, and tugged on the elastic leg band of her swimsuit. I remember thinking, *She's so beautiful*, wishing and hoping I'd grow up to be as beautiful as she was, with her long blonde hair and green eyes and high cheekbones and easy, lovely smile. She'd glanced at me, smiling, winked, and then dove in, slicing perfectly. I'd stood, scared stiff, and watched the deep blue water shift and curl, imagined things lurking in the depths, imagined diving too deep and not being able to make the surface in time. Mom had just treaded water and waited. I shuffled to the edge of the platform, peering over the edge.

"Stop thinking and *jump*, Edie!" Mom had laughed. "You're freaking yourself out. I'm right here, honey."

I was eleven. Way, *way* too old to be scared of jumping off some stupid dock. I'd closed my eyes and jumped. Feet first, arms flailing. I was immediately swallowed by darkness and achingly cold water. I'd fought the panic and kicked to the surface, felt the air on my face and sucked in a deep breath, spluttering, laughing. Mom had laughed with me, given me a high-five, and then we climbed back up and jumped

off together, sending the dock rocking. Again and
again we jumped off, laughing and making a game of
who could jump farther. Finally, drawn by our laughter, Ever had swum out to join us. She'd acted brave
as she climbed up and peered off the edge, the way
I'd done, but I'd seen the fear. I remember admiring
her *so much* for how she just jumped off, no hesitation, despite her fear. That day, watching Ever do
with seeming ease what I'd been scared of, I deter-
mined to never let fear get the best of me. I'd always
been the first after that. The first to try something,
no matter how scared I was. It may have turned into
a slight case of impulsivity, risk simply for the sake of
not letting fear get the better of me.

Now, I lay on the same dock, and I was gripped
by fear. Every moment, I was scared. Terrified. I could
barely breathe, I was so scared. I was scared of life. Of
living. Of what would happen to me. I wasn't a teenager, sure. But I was *way* too young and unprepared
to be a mother. A *mother*. Mommy. Me. Eden Irene
Eliot, a single mother. I didn't know what I wanted
for myself, much less how to be a parent.

I'd never even been in love.

I stood up, clenching my fists and forcing air into
my lungs. Pushed away the rampant terror. Bent my
legs and dove in, the way Mom had, so long ago.

By the time I reached the shore, I was barely
holding it together. I threw my cover-up on, toed my

feet into my flip-flops, gathered my things, and hurried home. It was home, too. It felt like home. What if…what if it was the only home I ever knew? What if I had the baby here and raised him/her alone, here on the peninsula? Just never went back. Could I do that? Cut myself out of Ever's life? She was all that mattered, really. And Cade, of course, but he was a can of worms I couldn't deal with. Not yet. I had to push him out of my thoughts, out of my heart.

I sat on my couch, wet from the swim and sweating from running home, hyperventilating in an attempt to keep the wrenching sobs at bay. I couldn't lose it. Wouldn't. This was life now. Alone, in this cottage.

I hadn't loved Cade. Almost, though. I'd *almost* fallen in love with him. I'd seen it happening, felt my heart curling outward and trying to latch onto him. But he didn't love me and never could and never would, even if Ever hadn't woken up, and anything we'd ever have would've been established on all the wrong foundations, and I refused to let that happen. I wanted better for myself.

His trip to Wyoming had come at the most perfect moment. That last tangle in the sheets had nearly been my undoing. But then he'd left and I pushed him away, knowing it would be the end. It *had* to be the end. We couldn't keep doing it to each other. It wasn't helping him, and it was only confusing me.

I'd teetered on the edge of a cliff, and then had stumbled back at the last moment. Tearing myself away, pushing him away, that had been wrenchingly painful. But far better than spending the rest of my life loving him and never able to have him.

And then…and then I'd found out I was pregnant, and everything had changed. Now I had no idea what was going to happen to me. I had no one. I'd cut Dad out of my life, although being the stubborn asshole he was, he'd continued to pay for my tuition and room and board. Why, I didn't know, and never would. He wouldn't visit us, wouldn't see us, wouldn't make any efforts to repair the damaged relationships, but he'd paid for school. When Ever went into the coma, he'd paid the hospital bills until she'd entered the Home, at which point she'd become a ward of the state. I think he had kick-ass insurance that had covered a huge portion of her bills, but it still must have cost him a staggering amount of money. I think he'd also paid Cade's hospital bills. I don't know if Cade even realized that.

But he wasn't a support system. I wouldn't ask him for money. I wouldn't call him. Wouldn't tell him what was going on.

I couldn't tell Ever or Cade. Mom was long dead, as were her parents and Dad's. So, there was just me.

And I was paralyzed with fear. Had no plan, a limited amount of money, no job, no degree. No friends, no family.

I felt the tears leak out, and I lurched off the couch, pulled Apollo from his case, and sat down in the chair in the middle of the living room. Played, and played, and played. Until I broke through the calluses on my fingers and bled, until my wrist ached from holding the bow, until my teeth hurt from grinding them together. I didn't even know what I was playing, just that it was all that mattered, all I had to keep the fear at bay, to keep the brokenness from escaping.

A thought came to me, as I finally let the bow drop to the floor: Each day, facing my fear and simply moving through the day was akin to jumping off the dock as a little girl. Just waking up was facing my fear. Taking each breath was an act of will. Not breaking down in tears each moment was an effort. All I could do, every single day, was face my fear, jump off the dock, and hope I could swim to shore.

I forced myself to eat, to do mindless time-wasting activities. Cleaning already clean things, watching TV. Reading. Eventually, I went back to playing until the sun went down.

Carter

I took the long way home. I parked in my spot at the post office, locked my truck, shouldered my dry-bag, and circled the block on foot. I wasn't ready to go home. It was quiet, and empty. Lonely. Once I swam home to the island, there'd be nothing to do but kill time until I was tired enough to sleep.

So I walked around the block, hoping for a distraction. I was nearly back to the beach when I heard music. It came from one of the cottages facing the beach. That particular cottage had been empty for years, I knew. I'd thought about buying it, as a matter of fact, when I'd first moved up here and needed somewhere to live that wasn't the winery. It wasn't for sale, I'd been told. I ended up finding the island, which was perfect in so many ways. And now there were lights on in the cottage, windows open. The front door was open, only the screen door in place. I slowed my steps as I passed, and then came to a stop.

It was a cello, being played by a consummate professional. I recognized the skill because Brit had been a classical music freak. She'd dragged me to endless concerts, symphonies at the DSO, in San Francisco and Boston and New York. Her favorite was the London Philharmonic, and she'd brought me half a dozen times. I'd never understood it, really. There were no words, nothing concrete I could grasp. Just the music, and it never quite caught my fascination. The only time I'd really enjoyed a show was when we'd seen Yo-Yo Ma with...I couldn't remember which orchestra. I just remember being captivated by the way he'd played the cello. I'd kept hoping the stupid symphony would shut up so I could hear him play by himself.

What I heard sounded like that. A single cello, low notes wavering in the sunset glow. I edged closer to the screen door and peered in.

It was her. The girl from the beach. Facing me, the cello between her knees, her arm sliding back and forth, the bow shifting angles ever so slightly with each motion. Her fingers moved in a hypnotic rhythm on the strings, flying with dizzy speed and precision.

The music she played was...mournful. Aching. She played the soundtrack of pain and loneliness. Her eyes were closed. I was maybe six feet away from her, but she didn't see me, didn't hear me. I watched through the screen door, captivated. God, this close, she was even lovelier than I'd imagined. But the pain on her face...it was heartbreaking. The way she played, the way her expression shifted with each note, growing more and more twisted and near tears, it made my soul hurt for her. Just watching her play, I wanted to throw the screen door open and wrap her up in my arms, make everything okay. I didn't dare breathe for fear of disrupting her. I knew I was being a creeper, watching her unbeknownst like this, but I couldn't move away. Not while she still played.

Jesus, the music. It was thick, almost liquid. I closed my eyes and listened, and I could almost see each note. The low notes, deep and strong and male, they were golden-brown, ribbons of dark sunlit gold streaming past me. The middle tones were almost amber, like sap sliding down a pine trunk. The high notes were the color of dust motes caught in the rays of an afternoon sun. The notes and the colors twisted together, shifted and coruscated and tangled, and I saw them together, shades of sorrow melding.

She let the music fade, and I opened my eyes, watched her. She hung her head, the bow tip trailing on the carpet at her right foot. Her shoulders shook, and her loose and tangled hair wavered as she cried. God, I wanted to go to her. Comfort her.

But I couldn't. My feet were frozen and my voice was locked. As I watched, she visibly tensed, muscles straining, and she straightened; her shoulders lifted and her head rose and the quiet tears ceased. Her eyes were still closed, but her cheeks were tear-stained. They needed to be kissed clean, the tears wiped away. Such perfect porcelain shouldn't be tear-marred.

The way she pulled herself together, it was awe-inspiring. She was clearly fighting demons, and refused to give in. Refused to let them take hold. I pivoted away from the door as she took a deep breath and clutched her bow. I waited, my back to the wall beside the door, and then, with a falter, the strains of the cello began again, slow and sweet, speaking of better times to come.

I forced my feet to come uprooted, forced them to carry me past her door. To the beach. Into the water. I tugged my shirt off and stuffed it, along with my keys, phone, and wallet into the dry bag, cinched it tight on my shoulders. Strode out into the cool, lapping water, kicking the moon-silvered waves until I was chest deep and then dove in. Set a punishing pace. I'd be exhausted by the time I got to my island, but that was what I wanted. I needed the tiredness, the brain-numbing limpness of exhaustion. It kept the memories from coming back. Let me almost sleep without nightmares. Almost.

I swam the two and a half miles in record time. I could barely drag myself onto the dock by the time I got there, but my mind was still racing a million miles a second. This time, thank god, it was with thoughts of the girl. The cellist. I kept seeing the sadness in her expression, the loneliness. The pain and the fear.

What was it, I wondered, that could cause such sweet and perfect beauty such searing pain? I needed to know. But I might never find out if I couldn't get myself to talk to her.

Or to talk at all.

It had been eleven months since I'd spoken a single word. But for *her*, I might find the courage to simply say hello.

playlist

Note from the author: these songs are not listed in the order in which they appear in the story, but rather are grouped by artist/album.

From *Six Unaccompanied Cello Suites* by Yo-Yo Ma:
"Suite No. 1 in G Major - Prelude"
"Suite No. 2 in D Minor - Menuett"
"Suite No. 6 In D Major - Allemande"

Other pieces from Bach's *Unaccompanied Suites*:
"Suite No. 5 in C Minor - Courante"
"Suite No. 4 in E-flat Major - Sarabande"

From *Songs and Poems for Solo Cello* by Philip Glass and Wendy Sutter:
"Song VI"
"Song IV"

From *Thousand Words* by Portland Cello Project:
"Broken Crowns"
"Taking a Fall"

Unassociated pieces:
"Sonata For Solo Cello" by Zoltán Kodály
"Song For You" by Alexi Murdoch

about the author

New York Times and *USA Today* bestselling author Jasinda Wilder is a Michigan native with a penchant for titillating tales about sexy men and strong women. When she's not writing, she's probably shopping, baking, or reading. She loves to travel, and some of her favorite vacations spots are Las Vegas, New York City, and Toledo, Ohio. You can often find Jasinda drinking sweet red wine with frozen berries.

To find out more about Jasinda and her other titles, visit her website: www.JasindaWilder.com.

CPSIA information can be obtained
at www.ICGtesting.com
Printed in the USA
LVHW092301260721
693778LV00016B/323